Line of Succession

Kristen Grafton

Cottage House Publishing

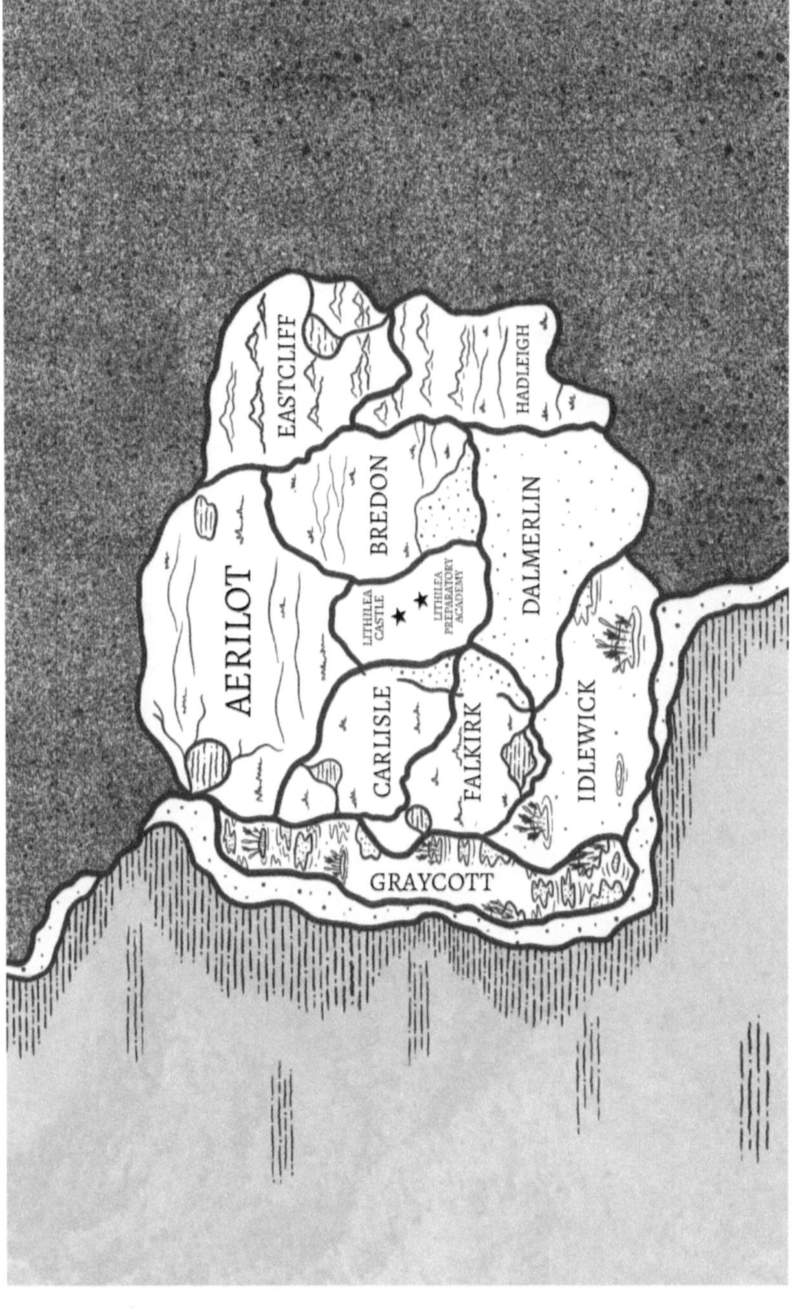
EASTCLIFF
HADLEIGH
BREDON
DALMERLIN
AERILOT
LITHILEA CASTLE
LITHILEA PREPARATORY ACADEMY
CARLISLE
FALKIRK
IDLEWICK
GRAYCOTT

Pronunciation Guide

I hate wondering how fictional places are pronounced in books, and if I find out after establishing my own pronunciations, it's even worse. So, here is a handy pronunciation guide for the places of my fictional kingdom Lithilea!

Lithilea: lith' - ih - lay' - uh

Aerilot: air' - ih - lot

Bredon: bree' - dun

Carlisle: car' - lyle

Dalmerlin: doll' - mur - lin

Eastcliffe: east' - cliff

Graycott: gray' - cot

Hadleigh: had' - lee

Idlewick: eye' - dull - wick

For my professors and classmates at Emerson College:
This was just a scene in my head of a boarding school in a castle.
It became a story thanks to you.

Chapter One

November 30 —

I'm so excited that we're finally going home to Graycott today. Between school and traveling with Mom and Dad, I feel like I haven't been home in forever. Just one more train ride, and I'll get to sleep in my own bed again.

Most of all, I'm excited to see Julia. It's been so long since I've seen her, and texting just isn't the same. We used to be so close when we were kids, but now I'm worried that we're drifting apart. I always feared that would happen one day. We promised each other that we wouldn't lose the special connection we have just because of my position, but I guess promises made between little kids don't matter. Something about my being "Jane Clarke, future Duchess of Graycott" has always stood in the way of our relationship as sisters.

I really think it would've been different if she had come to Lithilea Prep with me, but there was no convincing her. Maybe I should have tried harder to talk her into it. Maybe I should have begged Mom and Dad to force her to go, even if she never would've been duchess, just to keep her close. Maybe it wouldn't have made a difference.

I'm hoping she missed me, too. I'm only home for a few days, but it might be just enough for us to reconnect. Just a few more hours until I see her. I can't wait to—

***

The smell of the exhaust billowing from the train was already giving me a headache. I'd been told that once we transferred train lines at the border that the train quality would be much better, but this was Graycott, so I was out of luck for the next few hours.

The few seats inside the station were taken up, so I had been standing outside, leaning up against the wall of the station, for about an hour. The trains were never off-schedule for important trips like this in Lithilea, and security was minimal, so there was absolutely no reason for me to have arrived so early. I knew that. But I couldn't stand spending any more time at that empty house.

When the all-clear was given to board, I did so immediately, even though Cecily had not yet found me. I was supposed to wait for her, but why should I? Didn't she work for me? At least that's what I was told. That would take some getting used to.

I chose my seat carefully. A window seat so I wouldn't get claustrophobic, the third row to minimize motion sickness and visibility, close to the nicer bathroom. I had been offered a first-class ticket to sit in the restricted car at the front of the train and wanted to turn it down, but Cecily insisted that I not. I wished I'd had the freedom to choose my own class. Sitting in a car with a bunch of people who didn't think I belonged was not my idea of a comfortable train ride. I supposed the only benefit would be that our roomette had a sliding door that could be closed so that the only person I absolutely had to endure during the train ride was Cecily.

With all the doors open for people boarding, the air in the cabin was hot and stale, but I still pulled my sweatshirt as far up my neck as it would go. I didn't want to talk to anyone, and I didn't want anyone thinking they had a right to talk to me. I didn't know which I was more annoyed by: the condolences or the congratulations.

As soon as Cecily spotted me on the train, my chest felt heavy with her disappointment—no, not disappointment really, more like frustration. It must have been frustrating being my handler. I supposed I could have made it easier, but I didn't know how to do that.

"Julia, I told you to wait for me." Cecily flopped into the seat across from me, and I was surprised by how much her small frame rocked the bench.

I shrugged. "You were late."

"I was not." She squinted. "You were early."

"You caught me."

She sighed, but this time not out of frustration—out of pity. That was worse. "Julia, I'm trying to help you. I don't want you to hate me or think that I'm some kind of nuisance you have to put up with. I really do want you to succeed, and I can help you with that."

"Don't think I can succeed on my own?"

"I didn't say that. But there's a lot of schooling and training and experience that you haven't had the benefit of. I'm here to coach you through the rough spots. The world you're about to step into is unlike any other. I'm only here because Jane trusted me to—"

"Don't talk about Jane," I said even harsher than I intended to. But I was tired of people talking about Jane. Like they knew her. Like they *understood* her. Like I was anything like her.

"I'm sorry, I didn't mean—"

"Forget it." I waved my hand dismissively. "I'm gonna take a nap. Wake me up when we reach the province limits."

***

The intensity with which Cecily shook my shoulder gave me the impression that this wasn't her first attempt at waking me up. I forced my eyes open and cringed at how close to me Cecily was sitting. I scooted away from her as subtly as I could and sat up.

The land whizzing past the window was starting to look a little less beachy—bright green grass and large trees replacing brown sand and swampy palm trees—so I figured if we hadn't already crossed the province border, we were about to. Only the very edge of Graycott was grassy like this.

"How long was I out?"

"About an hour," Cecily said, doing her best to suppress the irritation creeping into her voice. That might have been the only good thing about this whole situation: most people had to pretend to respect me now even if they didn't want to, even if they didn't. "We just crossed the border into Falkirk."

I nodded, staring out the window. I wondered how fast we were going, how much it would hurt if we crashed. Would you even feel it if you died in a train crash? Would it be an instant death, or would you suffer? Did they suffer?

"Anything on your mind?" Cecily asked.

I shrugged. "Train crashes."

The way Cecily's mouth hung open in shock gave me a sick sense of satisfaction. No one actually wanted a real, truthful answer to questions like that, which was why I always gave real, truthful answers. Polite conversation was nothing but fake, and I liked exposing it.

Cecily cleared her throat. "I went ahead and ordered lunch. I hope you don't mind. I thought maybe we could go over a few things while we eat."

"Sure."

"As soon as we get to Lithilea Prep, things will move quickly, and I don't want you to be overwhelmed. We've already gone over the representatives from each province, so we should be all good there. Have you been studying their names and faces?"

"Uh-huh." I actually only studied a few. The prince and princess were easy—I'd been able to recognize them most of my life, what with them being on TV all the time. I learned a few names after that but mostly got bored with it. I would just figure it out as I went.

"It's very important that you know them all and use the correct salutations. They are all used to it and will expect it. Even though they are all about your age, you must refer to the men as 'Sir,' and—"

"And the women as 'Lady,'" I finished. "I got it."

"The other students who are not directly in line for a position do not have an official address. I didn't include their names in your information because it is not necessary to know them all as soon as you arrive. You can learn their names as you go."

Of course, because unless you were in direct line for a position, nobody cared who you were. I should have known. That was me my entire life. I still wished it were.

An attendant knocked on the door to our roomette, and when I opened it, she forced a smile to cover the surprised look on her face. I hated that I had become recognizable.

"I have your lunch order ready," she said.

She wheeled her cart a little closer, unloaded two white boxes onto the table Cecily had just let down, and left with another smile. I opened the first white box to some kind of fish with rice. Definitely not me. I slid the box over to Cecily and opened the second to find a turkey sandwich and carrots. Before I could stop it, a small smile crept onto my face. At least Cecily had paid enough attention to get my lunch order right.

"Now," Cecily said in between bites of salmon, "on to the matter of your phone."

"I told you, it's broken," I said around a mouthful of turkey and whole wheat, making Cecily grimace. I had thrown my phone against the wall of my room after they called me and told me that I was now Lady Julia Clarke, future Duchess of Graycott. When Cecily had come to see me the first time at the house, she'd been furious with me because apparently she had been calling for days and I hadn't answered. I pointed to the hole in the wall left by my emotional outburst. She'd never spoken of it again. I'd often wondered what bet she lost or short stick she drew to get stuck being the handler of the ill-prepared surprise heir of gloomy Graycott. She was younger than most handlers are. I couldn't imagine that any thirty-year-old dreamed of managing a teenager who technically ranked above her. She must have been thrilled.

"I'm aware," she said. "I got you a new phone. You're going to need it."

She handed me a phone that looked like it was probably more expensive than all of my earthly possessions combined. Graycott wasn't exactly poor, but people didn't have phones like this. In fact, I only ever saw my father with a phone like this. I tapped the screen, and it lit up with a picture of one of the beaches at Graycott. I was sure Cecily thought she was being considerate setting that picture as the background, but it only reminded me of what had been lost. I would have to change it later when she wasn't looking.

Cecily reached over and tapped an icon of Lithilea's coat of arms. "This program is going to be your lifeline. It's called 'Ledger.' It has information on all of the provinces and their sitting and future representatives, all of Lithilea's allies and enemies, maps, and more. Plus, as Graycott's future representative, you get access to all of Graycott's records and documents."

"All of that is digital now?"

Cecily nodded. "Prince Tristan created it himself. He's quite exceptional with technology. He thought that it would move Lithilea into the twenty-first century and help our representatives at the same time."

I nodded, but I was mostly flipping through the different apps within Ledger. This was detailed. This program would probably be more helpful to me than anything else. Maybe I would actually be able to keep up with this.

"It's also pre-programmed with my number and the numbers of all current and future representatives. You can call or text me anytime. And I know you probably don't want to trouble him, but I'm sure Sir Joseph would be willing—"

"Anything else?"

Cecily sighed. "We won't be at Lithilea Prep until for a while. I suggest you spend some time studying and get some sleep. I'm here if you need me."

I knew Cecily was just trying to be nice, but I had made it my mission not to need her or Joe or anyone. I was going to prove that I was more than just the orphan who got here by accident. I was going to be worthy of the title of Duchess of Graycott.

Chapter Two

August 23 —

Sometimes I just can't wait until I'm Duchess of Graycott. I know I'm still young, and some days I'm glad I won't have that responsibility until after Uncle Joe and Dad both retire, but other days, I'm so anxious to get going. I have so many good ideas for Graycott, but I can't do anything with them for years—decades, even.

I've tried to get Dad and Joe to talk to each other, but they're both so stubborn. Dad hasn't spoken to him in years. Joe hardly even talks to me. I'm still not even sure that I totally understand what happened between them, but it doesn't really matter. As long as they're not talking, I can't get anything productive done between them. Sometimes I think they oppose each other just because.

Hopefully they'll make up. I miss Joe, and at least I could start discussing my ideas with him and Dad if they stopped fighting. Is that too much to ask?

***

The train stop just past the Falkirk border seemed to me like it was bigger than the entire town center back home. For starters, it was an actual building, as opposed to the roof with columns that more or less passed for a train station in Graycott. Tickets were being checked meticulously at this station, and thankfully, most people had gotten off before reaching Central Lithilea. Anyone still remaining on the train was likely headed cross-country to the other provinces, and people didn't do that often. Cecily and I were probably the only ones getting off here and not boarding another train.

We hadn't gotten off in Falkirk at all, so I couldn't have spoken of the weather there, but in Graycott, it was always muggy and hot. The moisture in the air would hit you like a brick wall. Surprisingly, Central Lithilea was just as hot but completely dry. I'd always heard that the center of Lithilea was a desert, but I'd lived my entire life in Graycott; I had nothing to compare it to. Everything seemed dusty, and that was so bizarre to me. In Graycott, the closest thing I had to dust was sand, and was very different. The humidity weighed everything down there, but here, the dust seemed to swirl all around. I certainly didn't look forward to inhaling all of that when we went outside.

Cecily had both of our tickets checked while I tried in vain to scuff the red dirt off of my shoes. Once approved, she grabbed her multitude of bags and my one bag, and we headed inside to wait for the car that would take us to the school. I plopped down on a bench in the corner when Cecily held out one of her suitcases to me.

"Why are you giving me that?"

"It's yours," she said. "I took the liberty of getting you some clothes. I have it on good authority that you don't like shopping, so I thought I would save you the trouble and get you what you need."

Her "good authority" must have been Jane. Somehow she was still doing that bossy older sister thing even from beyond the grave. I didn't like it, but I felt an ache in my heart as I realized I missed even this about her. "What do I need? There's not a uniform."

"No, but there is a kind of unofficial dress code. I didn't want you to stand out. I had to guess a little bit at the sizes, but I think I got it right. Why don't you go try something on? We won't have another break before we get to the school."

I reluctantly took the suitcase and sought out a single-stall bathroom. Once inside, I put down the baby changing table and propped up the suitcase. If I didn't know that Jane and I had had completely different body types, I might have wondered if Cecily had just brought me her old clothes. Everything in the suitcase looked like her style, which I guessed was the style of Lithilea Prep. She had always fit in. She had always belonged. I'd never been able to relate.

I couldn't bear the idea of wearing one of the navy plaid skirts—Cecily claimed there wasn't a uniform, but what screamed uniform more than a pleated plaid skirt?—so I opted instead for a red pencil skirt. It was a little more form-fitting that I would have liked, but looking in the mirror, I had to admit that it looked good on me. If the whole handler thing didn't work out, Cecily could have a promising career as a stylist. I paired it with one of many white button-down shirts, a matching red blazer, and kept my brown lace-up booties. The red was a bold choice, but I wanted to make a statement. She had included jewelry, scarves, and headbands, which was kind of funny, but I decided to humor her, so I rummaged through the bracelets. Most of them were way too gaudy for me, but when I spotted the dainty rose gold chain with a single charm on it, I immediately clipped it onto my wrist. The image of the hibiscus on the charm made me smile. I spotted a rose gold necklace that matched Jane's bracelet perfectly, though I knew Jane hated necklaces—they would always get tangled in her thick, curly hair—so I could only assume Cecily had bought it to match. I was at least grateful to her for this small gesture and the fact that it was done quietly without a big show of gift-giving and an expectation of a profound display of gratitude. If nothing else, that was more than anyone else had done for me since Jane.

I straightened the skirt, touched up the makeup I had attempted to apply on the train, matching my lipstick to my outfit, ran a brush through my perpetually tangled hair, and rolled my shoulders back, trying to convince myself that I looked like the future Duchess of Graycott. Maybe now that I looked the part, everyone else would buy it even if I didn't.

When I came out of the bathroom, Cecily smiled the most genuine smile I'd seen the entire trip. She took the suitcase back from me and held out my arms to get a better look at the outfit.

"You look fantastic," she said, admiring her handiwork. "The red was a good choice. It compliments your light hair."

I shrugged. "I just tried to pick something that looked halfway competent and not so schoolgirl uniform."

Cecily suppressed a chuckle. "You'll get used to the plaid. It's very popular with the other girls." She glanced down at my shoes and frowned. "Oh no, I forgot to give you the bag with the shoes."

I waved my hand dismissively. "Don't worry about it. I like mine just fine. They're comfortable."

Cecily took note of the bracelet and smiled but still didn't say anything about it, thank goodness. Instead, she pointed at the suitcase she'd just given me and one other one. "Those are both yours."

"Both? Seems like a lot."

"I included plenty of clothes options, notebooks, pens, bags, those sorts of things. If you find there is anything else you need, just text me, and I'll get it there within the day."

That would take some getting used to. "I'm not sure I could possibly need more than this." Graycott was not exactly affluent. My family had been decently well off, but nothing compared to this. I wasn't sure that I even knew how to be wealthy, but I supposed that I had better figure it out.

Cecily put a hand on my shoulder and smiled. "You'll get used to this, I promise."

***

The ride to the school wasn't quick, but it sure felt like a flash. I wasn't ready to get there, wasn't ready to meet everyone. I had tried in vain to distract myself by flipping through the profiles on everybody on Ledger, but I couldn't focus. Cecily even tried to go over a few things because she knew I needed the distraction, but it didn't work. I wasn't sure what I was in for, but I had the distinct feeling that it wouldn't be good.

"The Yore siblings will be there to greet you upon arrival," Cecily said as if that was supposed to be a selling point. I couldn't say I was exactly eager to meet the future king and his sister, but I supposed there was no getting out of it. "Remember, you'll be expected to curtsy."

I nodded. "After that?"

"Since you don't officially start classes until tomorrow, I'll show you to your suite so you can get settled."

"Suite?"

Cecily's eyes sparkled. "It's beautiful. You're going to love it."

I was sure the suite would be quite the display of opulence. I probably wasn't going to find it as appealing as Cecily did.

After passing through a large wrought-iron gate, we drove a little further down the same dusty red road we'd been on for the last half hour until we approached what could only be described as a castle. No, multiple castles. I'd always heard that Lithilea Preparatory School was actually some medieval castles repurposed, but I guessed I expected more repurposing than they had clearly done. The beige stonework of the castles was increasingly indistinguishable from the desert clay the closer to the bottom I looked. There seemed to be one main building in the center that was the largest, with rounded turrets at each corner and one in the center. It was surrounded at a distance by multiple smaller buildings so similar I could hardly tell them apart. I knew I could look forward to getting lost a lot in the coming weeks. I suddenly found myself wishing I had accepted one of Jane's many offers to come visit her when she was here. Maybe I wouldn't have felt so overwhelmed if I had.

The driver pulled the car down the center road, stopping quite a distance from the main castle. When he put the car in park, neither he nor Cecily moved to get out, and when I tried, Cecily stopped me.

"Let the dust settle first," she said. "You don't want to ruin your white shirt and be coughing when you meet Prince Tristan."

I huffed and flopped back into my seat. I couldn't care less what Prince Tristan thought of me, but I didn't like the idea of inhaling the ominous reddish brown cloud around our car, so I waited.

As it settled, more details became visible. The center castle was very, very tall—I wasn't even sure how many stories it was. The others were all about two, three, or four as far as I could tell. There was a small structure off to the side, and even though I couldn't be sure of what it was, I could tell it wasn't built during Medieval times and was definitely newer. I wondered what they had decided either didn't fit in one of a billion castles or wasn't worthy to be housed in one.

Two figures became visible, and I recognized them as the Yore siblings. They looked exactly as they always had on TV. Prince Tristan stood tall, hands folded behind his back, with a smile. His brown curls had been thrown a little askew by the heat and dust, but I almost liked him better that way. He looked more human than the carefully manicured TV prince. He carried himself in a way that made him appear to tower over others.

It was his sister that looked different from her TV image. Princess Talia always appeared perfectly coifed, perfectly poised, and perfectly sweet. Looking at her now with her somehow perfectly styled ombre curls, crisply ironed dress, and side-eyed scowl, I was certain that only two of those perceptions were true.

The driver nodded, so Cecily reached for her door. "Stay here," she said to me. "I'll get your door for you."

I took a deep breath, checked to make sure my shirt was still tucked in to my skirt, and tried to force something resembling a pleasant expression onto my face. Cecily opened the door, the driver offered me his hand, and I took it, stepping out of the car as gracefully as one can manage in a pencil skirt. I slung my personal canvas bag over my shoulder—the one Cecily tried desperately to get me to replace—and let Cecily get the rest of my luggage.

Prince Tristan immediately walked over and smiled wide. "Welcome to Lithilea Preparatory School, Lady Julia. My sister and I are so glad to finally meet you."

He kissed my hand, I curtsied to him, and Cecily didn't seem like her head was exploding, so I guessed I must have been doing okay.

"I hope your travels went well?"

"Very well, Your Highness."

He flitted his hand. "Oh please, we're all colleagues here. Sir Tristan is more than enough. Allow me to introduce my sister." He gestured for her to step forward, and she did. "This is Lady Talia."

She offered me her hand, and I took it, but she avoided eye contact and let go as soon as the appropriate politeness window had closed.

Tristan started walking, and when I didn't follow, he beckoned me with a finger, so I followed. I guessed that was how it was as a future king: you could have complete command of people with just a finger. "I realize this must all be very overwhelming, so I want you to know that you have a friend in me. If you need anything, I'm here. Even if it's just to talk."

"I'd think the future king would have more pressing matters than just chatting with the new girl," I said.

"He does," Talia said from behind us.

Tristan shot her a glare. "My duty is to my kingdom and my people, and you are a very important part of that. My door is always open, so to speak. Has Miss Dunn set you up on Ledger?"

It took a moment for me to remember that Cecily's last name was Dunn. "Yes, she has."

"Excellent. You can find everything you need right there. Allow me to give you a brief tour of the layout of our campus."

As Tristan talked through what was in each building, I couldn't help but wonder how real all of this was. Was he really this genuine, or was he just a better actor than his sister? Perhaps this was part of the act, the image to maintain as benevolent prince. But something about the way he smiled at me and the way his facade broke occasionally to condemn his sister's frequent snide remarks made me want to believe that he was being authentic.

"The classrooms, dining hall, and most assembly rooms are in this main building here, Yore Hall. That building east of it has a library and some other resources, though most of what can be found there is now accessible on Ledger. There's a small museum over in that direction. This building is where all of our suites are. My sister and I are on the third floor. Almost everyone else is on the second, including you. Miss Dunn will take you there."

"What is that building?" I said, pointing to the small, newly constructed building I had noticed earlier.

"The post office."

"But you don't need to bother with it," Talia said. "If you need to mail anything, just give it to a servant."

"Housekeeper," Tristan corrected. "Any other questions come to mind?" I shook my head. "Well, I hate to cut things short, but I'm afraid I must be going. I have several meetings to attend to today. Remember, do not hesitate to let me know if you need anything."

With that, the Yore siblings turned on a dime at the same time as if they were in sync and left. I was only sorry to see one of them go.

I looked around where I was, and Cecily didn't rush me. I was trying to cement everything Tristan had told me about the buildings. Yore Hall: classrooms and dining hall. Lithilea Hall: library. Camden Hall: resident suites. Small building: post office. I could do this.

Most people that had been walking by hadn't paid much notice to us other than to stare briefly at me, bow or curtsy to the Yores, and move on, but now that it was just Cecily and me, people were getting bolder with their staring. Two girls in particular who were sitting on a bench nearby seemed to have taken quite an interest. They looked so much alike that I wondered if they were twins. Other than the fact that one was blonde and the other was a redhead, they were both short, thin, over-accessorized, and clearly unhappy with my arrival. I was vaguely aware that Cecily was babbling something about my classes, but I nodded just enough to keep her from noticing that I wasn't paying attention.

It hit me suddenly looking at them that the blonde was Olivia Arete from Aerilot. Her profile was one of the few I had bothered to learn because Aerilot was the province closest to the kingdom and therefore considered upper class and about as close to royalty as you could get. I couldn't be sure of who the redhead was, but I figured she either had to be from Aerilot as well or Bredon or Carlisle based on rank.

A third girl noticed them staring, and sat down next to them and pressed her lips together in what looked to be an attempted smile. "What's going on?" she asked.

The redhead jutted her head out in my direction. "New girl."

"From Graycott?"

"I assume."

The third girl looked at me only briefly, attempting the same smile toward me. "Have you met her yet? I don't really know anything about her."

"What is there to know?" Olivia said. "She's the orphan. Poor man's Jane Clarke."

"Going straight for the new girl, are we?" the third girl said.

Olivia flitted her eyes toward me and then back to her. "We'd be better off if it had been her in the train accident instead of Jane."

The other girl laughed, and my eyes burned from more than the desert dust, and my nails were stinging my palms as I clenched my fists. I wasn't sure if I was going to scream, cry, or throw a punch when Cecily gently touched my arm.

"I think we should go see your suite now."

She led me toward Camden Hall, and I focused on the feeling of my pulse in my temples. Ten minutes. I'd only been here maybe ten minutes and already I'd been judged according to my sister and circumstances. Was this how it was going to be here every day? Should I have insisted that Cecily take me home immediately? Could I have even called my house in Graycott home anymore?

Cecily practically pulled me by the arm up the stairs to the second floor. We walked past six rooms, stopping at number 7. The plate on the door read, "Lady Julia Clarke of Graycott," but the piece that said "Julia Clarke" was newer than the others. Cecily unlocked the door, pushed me inside, and locked the door behind her.

I sat down on the first chair I saw and waited for the pounding in my temple to settle. I was aware that Cecily was talking, but I didn't put in the effort to focus on what she was saying. I just let the sound of her voice, the indistinguishable words she was saying fill my ears in a desperate attempt to drown out Olivia's voice and words. It sort of worked, like sticking your ears under the water when you're floating in the ocean: you're aware of the sound around you, but it's all just a vague blur, the meaning completely lost on you. If only it were that easy now, just to stick my head under the water and Olivia would be wiped from existence.

Orphan. Poor man's Jane Clarke. *What is there to know?*

We'd be better off if it had been her in the accident.

Cecily thrust a glass of water at me, so I took it and drank. When she was satisfied that I had drunk enough, she then offered me a tissue, and I didn't know why until I realized that my face was wet. How long had I been crying? Avoiding eye contact, I took the tissue and rubbed it indiscriminately all over my face.

"Julia?"

"Yes?"

"Are you okay now?"

I couldn't be sure how many similar questions I had already ignored, so I tried to nod convincingly, if nodding convincingly was a thing, and thanked her for her quick thinking.

"Just doing my job," she said. "Well that wasn't exactly how I wanted to walk you into your new suite for the first time, but this is it." She spread her arms wide, gesturing around the room.

I hadn't really looked at it when we walked in except to find a place to sit. It was large and not nearly as gaudy as I had expected it to be. On the contrary, it was actually very beautiful, especially once Cecily opened the curtains. The hardwood floors were a warm cherry tone, and the molding on the all-white walls brought an airiness to the room. The main room where I was sitting had a fireplace with beautiful turquoise sofas and matching white chairs. The blue oriental rug was not exactly my taste, but it matched the room. I'd been told that each suite was decorated with the tenant's home province in mind, which explained all of the sea blue accents. It definitely had a feel for Graycott's seaside atmosphere.

In the back of the suite where the large windows were that Cecily had just revealed was a small half-hexagonal room with a stunning black grand piano with gold trim. I was almost afraid to touch it—it was the most beautiful piano I'd ever seen, and I couldn't even fathom how much a piano that looked like that must cost. Cecily noticed my hand hovering over the keys and smiled.

"From what I understand, you play," she said. "I thought you might like to have a piano to play in your spare time."

"How did you know?"

She smiled, and I had my answer. Jane.

I sat down on the bench and let my fingers hover over the keys before touching them. What does one even play on a piano this beautiful? I decided the answer was obvious, so I started to play Beethoven's *The Tempest* because it was Jane's favorite. I only played the third movement because that was my favorite part to play, and I could have cried at how beautiful it sounded on this piano instead of the slightly off-key piano at the Graycott town hall. The last time I'd played any piano of any quality was at Joe's house as a child, and that couldn't compare to this one.

I played for longer than I had originally intended because it just felt so good to play again. The tonal quality of the piano was so rich that it filled the room, my ears, and my mind so fully that nothing else could penetrate. Beethoven's was the only voice allowed in my thoughts as long as I played, and I was grateful for that.

When I stopped, Cecily sighed. "That was beautiful. I had no idea you could play so well."

I shrugged. "I'm a little rusty. I haven't played in a couple of months."

"I never would have guessed. I should tell you, that piano is yours. I mean, when you leave this school, you can take it with you."

I whipped my head around. "What?"

"Most of the furniture here stays here, but every student is gifted with an item of significant value that is strictly for pleasure. King Tybalt strongly believes that people can only be good leaders if they first take care of themselves. Usually everyone picks for themselves when they arrive, but I wanted to surprise you. I hope you're happy with my decision."

I nodded. "Very."

It seemed a shame to get up from a piano so beautiful—a piano that I *owned*—but I drifted around the corner, around a large white column into what appeared to be a study. The back wall was lined with bookshelves in the same cherry wood as the floors, and in the center was a cherry desk with a cushioned chair the same color as the sofa. The floor was painted with a gold fleur de lis pattern that glistened in the light. In the corner was a chess table, and I had to laugh. I could have counted the number of times I'd played chess on one hand.

I opened the double doors on the adjacent wall and found the bedroom. I realized when I saw it that I had seen pictures of this room before. Jane had occasionally sent pictures to me, and she'd always loved this room. The bed, which sat angled in the corner, had a rounded canopy at the headboard, and the entire frame was trimmed with gold. The bedspread was navy, but the pillows and sheets were the same sea blue. There was a black makeup vanity in the corner, and the wardrobe matched the bed. The same fleur de lis pattern was on the floor here. I glanced in the floor-length mirror by the door and saw that somewhere along the line my shirt had become untucked, so I stuffed it back in. The double doors across from the bedroom opened into the bathroom where all the plumbing was trimmed in gold, but the floors in here were white marble, so somehow the gold seemed to stand out more. I eyed the clawfoot tub on the back wall and looked forward to a long bath later today.

When I came out of the bathroom, Cecily was poking around in the fireplace, which wasn't lit.

"You're not lighting a fire, are you?" I asked.

"No, but I'm going to request that they bring you some extra wood. The wood here is pretty spent, and you're going to want a fire tonight. The weather in the desert is pretty extreme, so the nights can get chilly."

I looked around the suite once more. This suite was massive, beautiful, clean, and mine, though I did feel like at any moment Jane would turn the corner and smile. I could picture her here even though I knew her room was probably next door sitting vacant. This place looked like her, and even though I never visited her, I knew without a doubt that she would have fit right in. I didn't know if I could picture me here. Looking at that piano was the only thing that made me feel like I belonged.

Chapter Three

May 13 —

Border classes are my favorite! I love the classes with everyone in them, but there's something special about the border classes. In the other classes, Graycott is not an elite province—it's one of the provinces that no one else cares about, that no one takes seriously. But in border classes, there's a mix. Sure there's Aerilot and Dalmerlin, but Graycott, Eastcliff, Hadleigh, and Idlewick are just as important in border class. It's like we all become elite provinces, at least for a little while. I think the others really underestimate how important the border provinces really are. Who would defend Lithilea's coastlines if not Graycott and Idlewick?

It's a pretty fun group of people, too. Of course, I miss having Rose in that class, but Stephen and Nicole are pretty cool, too. Wade always has a wise comment to share which makes class so much more fun! Olivia usually rolls her eyes at that, but oh well! I hope Paige and Peter will be there next week for the exam. They've missed so much school lately.

It's crazy to think that this semester is almost over. I'm going home for a few days, then it's back here for summer semester. I'm looking forward to the break, but I can't wait to be back!

***

When Cecily left for the afternoon, she had encouraged me to get outside and get to know the campus and the people, but I hadn't done anything except play the piano. I tried briefly to do some research on Ledger, but I couldn't focus. I wondered if I'd ever be able to focus on that kind of research. What if I just wasn't cut out for this?

I lay down on the couch for a little while and might have dozed off for a little while until I heard a knock on the door. Cecily wasn't supposed to be back until late tonight or even tomorrow, so I could only imagine the delightful encounter that surely awaited me outside the door.

I forced myself off the couch by sort of rolling over the side and stumbled over to the door. On the other side, an extremely perky girl jutted her hand out for a handshake. I accepted hesitantly and then wished I hadn't when she shook so hard I thought she'd detach my arm from my shoulder.

"I'm so excited to meet you finally," she said, finally releasing my arm. "I'm Lady Rose of Falkirk. Welcome to Lithilea Prep."

As soon as she said her name, I realized I had heard of her before. Rose was the name I most heard Jane say when she was here. They were close, best friends even, and she had always talked about how I would get the chance to meet her if I ever visited. I never did, and now here I was face-to-face, no way to avoid her now. Maybe it was a good thing. Maybe Rose could help me. I had to at least give her a chance.

"Julia—uh, Lady Julia."

Rose smiled. "It takes some getting used to. How long have you been here? I was hoping to see you when you got here, but you must have arrived while I was in class."

"Just about an hour ago or so."

"What have you seen?"

I shrugged. "Not much. Prince Tristan gave me a brief tour. I've been here ever since."

She looked genuinely shocked. "Oh no, you have to take a walk around campus. I'm done with classes for today, so I can show you around, but first let me fix your hair."

She pushed past me, and I let her—mostly because it seemed I didn't really have a choice—and followed her to the bedroom.

"All right," she said brightly. "Where is your stuff?"

I pointed at the bag sitting on the counter that had all of my toiletries. "I haven't unpacked yet."

She flitted a hand at my bag and grabbed a brush. "I'll help you unpack later."

"Oh, you don't have to—"

"It's no trouble," she said and started brushing my hair.

Apparently there was no convincing her that I wasn't being polite and actually didn't want the company at all. I'd have to find a way to dodge her later.

"You're going to love Lithilea Prep once you get the hang of things," she babbled on, seemingly unconcerned with whether or not I was listening. "I love it here. It's really a cool idea if you think about it. What other place has a school like this that helps us prepare to rule? I'm so glad the royal family instituted it. Oh, you've met them, right? Aren't they the greatest?

I almost didn't expect her to wait for an answer the way she had been prattling on, but when an uncomfortable silence settled between us, I straightened up. "Who?"

"The Yore siblings," she said as if it were the most obvious thing in the world. I nodded. "I love that they go to school here."

Suddenly, I could picture her sitting with Jane gossiping about the royal family. It was exactly the kind of thing that Jane enjoyed, and I had never really cared. They were just people, right? I never understood why people obsessed over them. But Jane, she had always pored over every little detail of their lives. She even used to write me letters about them. I got more letters about Prince Tristan than I ever cared to.

She brushed my hair with more force than it really required, and I wondered if it was because she was so energetic or because her own hair was thick and voluminous. I actually wondered if that was what initially connected her and Jane—except for the fact that Jane's was blonde like mine and Rose's was black, it was exactly the same texture. Jane used to brush my hair with the same vigor despite my complaints that she was ripping my hair out of my head.

Suddenly, the room felt a little too hot and claustrophobic, and I just wanted out of it. I didn't like picturing Jane with Rose or thinking about how she used to brush my hair or the letters she used to write me. None of that would happen anymore: she wouldn't sit in this room and gossip with Rose, she wouldn't brush my hair, she wouldn't send me letters from Lithilea Prep. Now I was the one at Lithilea Prep in Jane's place, and everything about that felt wrong. I couldn't just step into Jane's life and replace her like she never existed. Olivia had made that very clear, but I wasn't avoiding that because I was "poor man's Jane Clarke." I refused to erase my sister like that.

I stood up so suddenly that I knocked the brush out of Rose's hand, and she jumped when it clattered on the floor. "I have to get going."

"Oh, of course," Rose said, only momentarily confused. She quickly readopted her cheeriness, and I had to turn around so she wouldn't see my eye roll. I grabbed my bag and the key Cecily had left behind and stormed out of the room with Rose trailing behind me.

"My room is right here, so if you ever need anything, I'm only right next door, and my sister is there, too." She pointed at the door right after hers. "That's Lady Nicole of Eastcliffe. She's really sweet, too. She and I don't talk much outside of class, but I know she's really nice. We go way back. We started here the same year."

"When was that?"

She looked up and scrunched her mouth. "Hmm, about eight years ago, I think."

I had to suppress the involuntary urge to shudder. I couldn't imagine going away to a boarding school at age nine to learn how to run an entire province.

"Anyway, it doesn't really look like anyone else is here right now, so let's head out. Do you have your class schedule yet?"

I pulled out the crumpled piece of paper and handed it over to Rose, who celebrated the fact that we shared all but one class together. It made me wonder if Cecily had just plugged me into all of Jane's classes. Surely she and Rose would have coordinated.

"I'll walk you to class tomorrow so you don't get lost," she said, handing me my schedule back. The only class I don't have there is Border Security, Falkirk not being a border province and all."

"So only the coastal provinces are in that class?" I asked. "Must be a small class." Graycott and Idlewick were the only coastal provinces, unless you counted Aerilot which had a tiny strip of land touching the sea.

Rose shook her head. "All the border provinces take it, not just coastal ones."

"Border provinces have all the fun." A guy with a smirk and blue eyes that almost looked white shrugged at Rose but maintained eye contact with me. "No offense, Rose."

"This is Lady Julia from Graycott," Rose said. "Julia, this is Sir Wade of Dalmerlin."

Wade made a retching noise. "Can't stand all that 'sir' and 'lady' nonsense. It's Wade or nothing."

I couldn't help but smile at that. Finally someone who was on the same wavelength as me. "Dalmerlin, huh? Any chance you're in Border Security tomorrow?"

Wade stretched his arm behind his neck, and weirdly, I felt my cheeks blushing. "You bet, love."

Rose lit up. "Ooh, that's right. Would you mind showing Julia where that class is? It's the only class we don't have together."

"Sure thing." He winked, and again, my head felt a little heavy. "I'll meet you outside your room at 8:30."

Before I could answer, he smiled, spun on his heel, and walked away. Handsome, charming—maybe a little too charming—but so far the only person I could have even seen myself talking to for more than five minutes. Rose's energy was starting to wear me down, and who else was I going to talk to? Olivia?

"That was a lucky break running into him. Wade is always so sweet and helpful."

I nodded. "Seems like it."

"He only started here last year, but he sure acts like a natural." Another thing we had in common—we hadn't grown up here like everyone else. "Come to think of it, I think he and Jane used to study together for that class, so you're definitely in good hands."

At the too casual mention of Jane's name, the relative optimism I was feeling after meeting Wade came crashing down. I knew Rose didn't mean it, and I was glad to know that she and Wade were relatively close, but I was tired of hearing Jane's name. It always felt like a weapon being pointed at me.

"I don't want to talk about Jane," I said.

"Oh Julia, I didn't mean to—"

I held up my hand, and Rose stopped immediately. A couple of months ago, I might have felt bad seeing how embarrassed and anxious Rose looked after I silenced her, but this wasn't a couple of months ago, and I was done putting up with it.

"Prince Tristan mentioned the dining hall is in Yore Hall. Care to show me where it is? I'm kind of hungry." The truth was that I wasn't at all hungry, but Rose readily accepted the offer to continue her tour, and it got her off the topic of Jane, at least for now. If I had any chance of surviving here, I'd have to control the narrative concerning Jane.

***

The next morning, I forced myself out of bed by 7:30 in spite of my strong need for sleep after only sleeping a few hours. I wanted my first impression in my first class to be good—not just good, but powerful. I wanted everyone to take me seriously. I was no longer going to be everything they thought I was: the orphan, the accident, the outsider. *Poor man's Jane Clarke.* I was going to be everything they thought I couldn't be, and that started with appearance.

The best decision I had made yesterday had been wardrobe. The red skirt suit had done exactly what I wanted: I had stood out, in a good way, then a bad way. Now I wanted to fit in. I forced myself to pick one of the plaid skirts, though luckily I found that a few of them were pencil skirts instead of pleated. The skirt was navy, high-waisted, and a little shorter than the red one I had worn the day before, but that would be fine. I wore a white shirt, navy cropped blazer, Jane's bracelet, my matching necklace, and curled my hair just enough to give it body, just enough to look like I had put effort into my appearance. *Just enough to look like Jane,* I thought before pushing the thought out of my head. I tried on a pair of heels that Cecily picked out for me, but when I felt a blister forming just walking across the suite, I hobbled back to my old faithful boots. My new image would have to include them, at least for now. I did my makeup with more mascara and eyeshadow than I had used before, the same red lipstick, and smiled when I looked in the mirror and saw someone who looked like a student at Lithilea Prep. This was going to work.

I opened my door when I heard a knock and was greeted with a charming-yet-borderline-sleazy smile from Wade. "Hey love," he said with a wink, "ready to roll?"

I nodded and walked out, Wade following closely behind me. I was aware that I was walking kind of fast, and maybe leaving behind the person who offered to walk me to class wasn't the kindest thing I could do, but it was hard to fight the nervous energy in my body. I didn't want to go to class, but I wanted to get it over with already. I was starting to think that the anticipation of starting classes at Lithilea Prep was worse than the classes would actually be. Of course, one flash of a memory of Olivia—*we'd be better off if it had been her in the accident*—and I doubted whether that would prove to be true.

Behind me, Wade laughed and then caught up to me, matching my speed. "In a hurry to get to learning, are we?"

I couldn't stop the smile that crept across my face. "Not exactly."

"Then trying to set a record for speed walking or something?"

"No, sorry, I just don't really want to think about class. I guess the faster I walk, the less time my brain has to spin its nervous thoughts."

He shrugged. "I get it. I felt the same way when I started at Lithilea Prep last year. It's such a weird dynamic, isn't it? 'Oh, let's just throw a bunch of teenagers together in a weird government-high school hybrid and hope they come out the other side capable of ruling a nation.' It's kind of dumb if you think about it."

I snorted before I could stop it. He wasn't wrong. I understood the logic behind Lithilea Prep, but I'd never understood it. Not really. Jane loved it here, but I knew that I wouldn't. I wasn't the social butterfly, the one who got along with everyone. Jane was Miss Congeniality, not me. But by some cruel twist of fate, I, Miss Sullen and Pessimism, was taking the place of Miss Congeniality, and everyone here knew that was a mistake, including me.

"It is what it is, though," Wade said, continuing. "I guess it'll help in some way. I don't really care. I'll learn what I can and bide time until I can get back to Dalmerlin. The new national taxes are crippling us. They're supposed to be proportionate to each province's status, but Dalmerlin isn't as affluent as everyone thinks. If someone could sign me up for a tax reform class, that would be great," he said with a laugh.

"That sounds so boring," I said.

He laughed again. He was handsome when he laughed. "Maybe, but it would probably be more helpful than 'Border Security.'"

"Isn't that where we're headed?"

He nodded. "You'll see. It's mostly a lot of bickering."

As we walked, Wade talked seemingly without end on the way to class, and while I didn't really pay attention to most of it, I was grateful for his self-indulgent nature because it meant he wasn't quizzing me. Mostly, I watched everyone else as we walked. Most people took what they thought was a subtle look at me, some were a little more obvious, and those who whispered were the most conspicuous. What seemed most interesting is that most seemed to be avoiding any kind of acknowledgment of Wade. He smiled at most, hello'd a few, but no one answered him. I found it a little surprising that he wasn't more popular. Sure, he didn't exactly fit the image of this place, what with his messy hair, fingerless gloves that hid hands that were not manicured, and swagger, but didn't he seem like the kind of guy everyone would like? I guessed this was why I had felt a connection to him. We were two outsiders here, and as far as I could tell, I would take Wade over all of them.

We reached the building faster than I expected—probably due to my speed walking that now came back to bite me in the form of leg cramps and heavy breathing—and I was surprised by the room. The class was bigger than I expected. I kind of always forgot that most provinces sent more than one representative at a time. I wasn't supposed to have a chance at the title, so I was never sent here, but many attended with their siblings or cousins. Unfortunately, I had only barely taken enough time to memorize those directly in line for a title. There was Wade, of course, who was now chatting with one of the other guys, and Olivia, whom I was studiously avoiding. I saw the girl who had spoken to Olivia yesterday, the one who had asked who I was, but I didn't feel much like talking to her either. Anyone in the company of Olivia was not for me.

I spotted the Eastcliffe representative—Nicole?—sitting by herself in the back corner. No one seemed to want to approach her, and she seemed pretty okay with it. Olivia looked at Nicole, rolled her eyes, and started giggling with the girl sitting beside her. Sister, maybe? Or cousin? I couldn't tell, and I didn't want to.

"Kind of intimidating, isn't it?" I turned around with a start to see a surprisingly friendly smile. "Sorry, didn't mean to startle you."

"It's fine." His smile sank into me in a way that settled the storm in my mind just for a moment. I forced a half-curtsy. "I'm Julia Clarke."

He matched my half-curtsy with a half-bow and smirked. "Stephen Sanor of Idlewick. You're from Graycott." He said it as a statement, not a question.

I nodded. "First day. Can you tell?"

He suppressed a chuckle, but laughter danced across his brown eyes. "You're already doing better than I did on my first day. I was late."

I let myself smile. "How long have you been here?"

He looked up and twisted his mouth before saying, "Nine years."

"You started here when you were eight?"

"Nine. I'm eighteen."

"I hardly think you could be blamed for being late at nine years old."

He smirked, and my cheeks felt hot. "You'd think, wouldn't you?"

The instructor standing in the front of the room said, "Okay, everyone, we're nearly ready to begin. Take your seats."

"You're welcome to sit here if you like," Stephen said. "I know it can be kind of awkward when you don't know anyone."

Before I could answer—and I wasn't sure if I would have accepted or not—Wade said with a nod, "Got your seat saved."

"Thanks," I said to Stephen, "but Wade already offered, and since he's the reason I didn't get lost this morning, I figure I should return the favor."

He smiled, but it had lost the spark it had before. "Of course."

"Thanks for making things a little less uncomfortable. I really appreciate it."

This time, he smiled for real. "Any time."

Chapter Four

September 3 —

I miss Julia.

It seems like most people here have a sibling also attending Lithilea Prep. Sometimes I feel like I'm the only one. I know I'm not—Stephen and Wade are only children, and Nicole's brother is the current Duke of Eastcliffe—but seeing just about everyone else here with their siblings makes me homesick.

Sometimes, I like to imagine what life would be like if Julia had been born first. Would I have joined her at school? I think I would have. Would she be better at this than I am? I think so. Julia's always been an outside-the-box kind of thinker, and I've never been good at that. Am I really the best person to lead Graycott?

***

My schedule left an uncomfortably sized gap of time for lunch. It was too long just to eat lunch and go to my next class but not quite long enough to go back to my suite and do anything. I had tried to stall and eat up some time by talking to the instructor, Mr. Porter Something-or-other, but he had just handed me a stack of books, offered a kind smile, and that was that. I wasn't sure how he thought this would help me catch up, but he seemed to mean well.

Just as I dropped the oddly-shaped book on top for the third time, Stephen rounded the corner and smiled. "Need a hand?"

I huffed, but my lips cracked a smile. "I don't know what would make you say that. Obviously everything is going perfectly."

Stephen laughed, and, as if it were nothing, hoisted the stack of books that I had gotten winded just carrying out of the classroom. We walked down the hallway and out of the building in silence. It wasn't until we were about halfway across the quad that he spoke.

"So, have you eaten yet?"

It was a silly question. It was barely noon. Of course I hadn't eaten yet. Still, I didn't call him on it because, for reasons I didn't completely understand just yet, I was hoping he would ask me to join him. I shook my head in response.

"Well, unless someone has already claimed your company, perhaps you'd like to join me? It'd be much less awkward for me to continue to carry your books if you're actually still with me." I laughed but didn't answer. "Has someone claimed your company?"

I shook my head again. "Other than Rose, I'd be surprised if someone did."

"Why do you say that?"

I lowered my voice even though there really wasn't anyone near us. "I'm not sure anyone really wants my company."

He shifted the books from one arm to the other and shrugged with his newly free arm. "Comes with the territory."

"What do you mean?"

He looked at me like he didn't know why I didn't understand. "Well, you're from Graycott. The only thing worse than that in some people's minds is being from Hadleigh or Idlewick."

I didn't respond, mostly because I wasn't sure what I would say if I did. Sure, Graycott has never been considered one of the more "upscale, elite" provinces, but I didn't think that led to the ostracizing of students from those provinces.

"Hey," Stephen said, and I realized that I wasn't sure how long I had remained silent. "Didn't mean to be a downer. Just speaking from personal experience, I guess."

"I kind of assumed it's because I'm new. Obviously I have no idea what I'm doing, and it shows."

"You're doing fine."

We picked up our meals from the dining hall, and since it was still early and the heat of the day hadn't set in just yet, we sat at a small table outside under a beautiful oak. The delicious scent that wafted from our containers made me realize just how hungry I really was. In the dining hall, I'd had trouble deciding between the lemon roasted chicken and the mango glazed pork, so when Stephen shyly offered to divvy up our meals so we could each have some of both, I readily accepted. I'd chosen the pork originally since we ate so much chicken at home, but this chicken was not like any other I'd had. I ate alternating bites, unable to decide which I liked better. Between the two and the side dishes of roasted potatoes and flame-grilled corn, I frequently had to remind myself not to scarf it all down in a completely unladylike manner that would have certainly caused indigestion. Luckily Stephen didn't seem to notice. He was eating in a similarly veiled rushed manner, occasionally pausing to people watch or look up into the glints of sun dancing on the tree branches above us. I had thought his hair and eyes were brown, but when the sun hit them just right, little glints of gold appeared in both. He looked better in the sun—almost as if he were his true self in the sunlight. I could only imagine how much more handsome he'd look not dressed in red and on a beach in Idlewick.

Idlewick was the only province I'd been to besides my own. Joe had taken my entire family on a trip there once when I was young. I had liked it. It had everything I liked about Graycott but had avoided the gloomy gray weather. That was the last trip Jane and I ever took with our parents. I thought that they would have liked Stephen.

I became aware of the fact that I had likely been staring at Stephen this entire time, but, thankfully, he didn't notice. Instead, he smiled brightly and waved at someone walking by who returned the bright smile. I didn't recognize her, and yet she seemed familiar somehow. I must have stared at her picture on Ledger or something. She immediately adjusted her course toward us when Stephen beckoned her. She was beautiful, that kind of classic beauty that persists through different eras and fashions. Her bouncy black hair fell just right, her smile was bright, and she seemed to glide when she walked. I could understand why Stephen liked her. I could picture her on TV one day as the face of her province. She was a natural.

"Hey, Sanor," she said as she sat down across from me. "Why do you insist on eating outside when it's so hot?"

Stephen crinkled his nose. "This is not hot. Just because you're from up north and can't handle a little heat—"

"Oh, I can handle it just fine." She flipped her hair for dramatic flair, then smiled at me. "I see Stephen here has already set out to corrupt you on your first day. Don't believe a word he says." At that, Stephen scoffed. "You're Lady Julia Clarke, right? I'm Lady Valerie Court. You know, we're technically neighbors. I'm from Carlisle."

Court. Court. That's right. I couldn't place her because she was not first in line. Her older brother was, though I couldn't remember his name. I remembered their profiles now. They were the picture perfect sibling representatives.

Stephen asked, "Where's Vaughn?" Vaughn, that was it. Her brother was Vaughn.

Valerie nodded behind her. "He's sitting with his friends. For some reason, he didn't want his perfectly sweet, innocent, and quiet little sister around." She took a big bite of potatoes. "Can't understand why."

"Oh, please."

Valerie laughed. "So Julia, how are you liking Lithilea Prep so far?"

I shrugged. "It's all right, I guess. I'm still alive, so there's that."

She laughed again, and her laughter felt so genuine. "Hey, don't discount that. That's a pretty big feat. It gets easier, I promise."

"I'm sure it will," I said, even though I didn't fully believe it, but I was not about to let anyone else know that.

"I hear you had kind of a run-in with Olivia."

"You did?" Stephen asked, surprised.

I tried to will my cheeks from turning red. "How do you know that?"

Valerie shrugged. "Vaughn is popular with pretty much everyone. You'd be surprised at the things he knows."

"It's not a big deal. She just said something kind of nasty. I'll live."

Valerie threw her arms up dramatically. "Well, that's Olivia Arete for you. A big old wishes-she-were-royal pain." She pressed her lips together sympathetically. "Sorry."

Stephen asked, "What did she say?"

"It's not a big deal," I said.

"It is to me." I smiled, but didn't answer. "So?"

I focused my eyes on my potatoes that I was furiously stabbing with a fork. "It was nothing. She didn't even say it directly to me. She just said something kind of snarky about how I got here. How I don't belong."

Valerie sat up straighter. "Are you next in line to be Duchess of Graycott?"

"Yes."

"Then you belong. Luckilyy for you, and for all of us really, Olivia doesn't decide these things."

"She has no business saying anything like that about you or to you," Stephen said, his grip on his fork tightening.

"Who has no business saying what?" As if he had just walked out of the tree trunk, Prince Tristan suddenly materialized behind Valerie. He looked more like his TV-self today without the wind and the dust roughing him up. More people stopped to say hello to Valerie, Stephen, and I once Prince Tristan was there, and the "coincidence" wasn't lost on me.

"Nothing," I said.

"Sir Tristan," Valerie said, "do you tolerate name-calling and ridicule among your future provincial representatives?"

I reached for Valerie's arm. "Valerie, no."

Prince Tristan looked outraged. "Certainly not."

"Then you might want to look into some matters related to Lady Julia's arrival. It seems that some of our colleagues are not being very welcoming."

Prince Tristan locked eyes with me. "That's unacceptable. Who is giving you trouble?"

"Really, Sir Tristan, I'm not trying to make waves here. It wasn't anything serious." The words started echoing through my head—*poor man's Jane Clarke—We'd be better off if it had been her in the acci-dent*—before I realized the echo was not in my head but on Valerie's lips. Before I could stop her, the words were out, Stephen's mouth was hanging open, and Prince Tristan's face was as red as his jacket. He all but slammed his messenger bag on the table and sat down next to me, his posture as straight as ever.

"Who said that? I demand to know who would say such a thing." When I didn't answer, Valerie cheerily offered Olivia's name, and Prince Tristan took my hand in his. "Lady Julia, I want you to know that this will not stand. I have no tolerance for such cruelty. In the future, please do not hesitate to inform me of something like this. Agreed?" I nodded, and he did, too. "Good. Rest assured I will deal with this matter promptly and discreetly." He lowered his voice then and said, "I did not get a chance to say so earlier, but I was very sorry to hear of Jane's passing. She was a dear friend to us all."

"Thanks," I managed to force out.

I noticed his hand shaking, and it seemed to me that he was clearing his throat more than necessary. "Well, I wish I could join you all for lunch, but, unfortunately, I have a very important phone call I must make before class. I'll see you all in class later."

As soon as he was out of earshot, I whipped around to Valerie. "Why would you tell him that?"

"Because it's not right. She can't just go around making threatening comments about you and get away with it."

"But you can't just tell the prince of Lithilea that."

"Why not? He's in charge, not Olivia, and look, he wanted to know. Now he can fix it."

I covered my face with my hands. "He can't fix anything. Valerie, you shouldn't have said anything."

"Why not?"

"You might as well have put a target on her back," Stephen said without looking up.

I sighed. "Exactly."

"Face it, Val," he said, "things are different when you're from Carlisle as opposed to Graycott. Olivia can't retaliate against you."

"She shouldn't be able to retaliate against anyone," Valerie said a little quieter.

"Sure, but you know I'm right. You know things are different for me than they are for you. It's the same with Julia."

"I was only trying to help."

"I don't need it," I said, picking up my stuff, waving to Stephen, and walking away.

***

On my way to my next class, Wade ran up alongside me.

"Hey, stranger," he said with a smirk. "I tried to track you down at lunch, but I couldn't find you."

"Oh, that's okay, Stephen offered, so I joined him and Valerie."

Wade slowed down, but not enough to be totally out of pace with me. "Stephen?" I nodded. "Well, you have a standing lunch offer with me if you ever need it."

"I appreciate it, but I don't want to be that annoying girl following you around. Besides, Stephen is good company."

Wade winked at me. "Don't be too sure about that," he said, and then walked off.

I couldn't be sure what Wade meant by that, and of course I couldn't help but think about the visible displeasure Stephen had expressed when I mentioned Wade, but I wasn't going to let either of them tell me what to think.

The next class was a large seminar that included everyone in the school, including the Yore siblings. It was titled something like "Good Leaders," which I felt very sure would not give me an accurate sense of what that class would be like. The benefit to this class was that we were seated according to province, so I would not have to decide who to sit by.

I found my seat easily in the third row under a gold sign that read "Graycott." At my desk was a nameplate with my name. There was a metal nameplate in front of the empty chair next to me, but it was blank. It hurt to see that my sister's name had already been removed from something this small. Somewhere in the back corner of my mind, the thought occurred to me that someone likely removed it to avoid upsetting me, but they had guessed wrong. What was more upsetting was to see my sister stricken from history. She was never going to be the Duchess of Graycott now, but she was supposed to be. Didn't that count for anything?

My eyes stung, so to distract myself, I took the opportunity to scan the mostly empty room. The Yore siblings were seated in the front row by themselves. In the first row behind the Yores were the representatives from Aerilot, Bredon, and Carlisle. I avoided eye contact with Olivia, her sister, and the redhead I'd seen Olivia talking to when I first arrived—Matilda, that was her name, from Bredon—and did not return Valerie's attempt at a wave. Her brother Vaughn gave me an odd look when he registered Valerie's disappointment but otherwise did not acknowledge me. Wade winked but made no effort to speak to me again after making vague accusations against Stephen.

The third row seated Dalmerlin, Eastcliffe, and Falkirk, and the fourth row Graycott, Hadleigh, and Idlewick. Stephen smiled at me as he passed on to his seat and seemed to want to say something but was denied the opportunity by Rose's incessant chattering to me that I was not absorbing as she sat on the corner of my desk. I noticed Nicole of Eastcliffe by herself again. Against better judgment, I wanted to say something to her, but it was impossible to silence Rose and get around her to say anything. She still seemed so aloof. I wondered again if it was by choice.

I glanced at the nameplates next to me from Hadleigh which read "Paige Brooker" and "Peter Brooker." I twisted the corner of my mouth. I could have sworn there was only one representative from Hadleigh in the border class, but I supposed I could have miscounted. Just as I was starting to wonder where my miscalculation could have been, I saw her. The girl who had asked Olivia who I was. *Poor man's Jane Clarke. It should have been her.* I hadn't waited then to hear her reaction to Olivia's words. I wasn't eager to hear the laughter. She now held the arm of someone I could only assume was her brother because they had the same dark hair and skin, brown eyes, and small frames, though I suspected that her brother was more slight than she. She held his arm with both arms and whispered in his ear. He smiled sweetly at her and patted her hand on his arm. Jane and I were close, but we were never that affectionate. Were some siblings like that?

She smiled at me as they walked by and tried to say hello, but I made a point of ignoring her and pretending to focus on Rose. From the corner of my eye, I thought I saw her look a little disappointed. Good. I didn't need her trying to act all friendly now.

She pulled out her brother's chair, he sat, and she sat to his left, right next to me. Just fantastic.

"Lady Paige," Rose said with a big smile, leaning around me. "How's it going? I feel like it's been forever since we talked last."

Paige pressed her lips together firmly. "Fine." She gestured vaguely toward her brother. "Just been busy."

Rose nodded knowingly. "Of course. Sir Peter, good to see you as well."

Peter's face broke into an enormous smile, and he nodded. "You, too, Lady Rose. We should get together later. Catch up."

Rose started to nod, but Paige gripped his arm and forced a smile. "Maybe. If we can make it."

Yikes. I certainly wasn't the biggest fan of Rose, but even I thought that was a little harsh.

Prince Tristan stood up at the front of the classroom, and I started to wonder if he taught this class. It would make sense, I supposed. He was going to be king one day. Why shouldn't he teach one of the classes? But when I asked Rose as much, she denied my theory.

"Sometimes he just has a few words to say before classes start," she said. "Especially in classes everyone is in." She then went to her seat in the third row.

"Colleagues," he began. Were we colleagues? That sounded like a term middle-aged businessmen used with each other, not teenagers in school together. "It has come to my attention that our tight-knit community has suffered some division and conflict as of late."

Oh. No.

"Generations ago, my great-grandfather King Terrence established Lithilea Prep not only as a way for the future dukes and duchesses to prepare for their duties but as a way to build community. No matter which province we are from, we are all Lithileans, and it is of the utmost importance that we all remember that. Infighting, prejudice, and antagonism will simply not be tolerated."

Practically everyone in the room turned and looked at me as suddenly as if I had just screamed in the middle of Tristan's words. He hadn't said my name, hadn't called me out in any way, and yet, he might as well have. Any hope I had of assimilation had been completely dashed by Valerie and Tristan's good intentions. And I'd had enough good intentions for a lifetime.

I noted that the only people who hadn't been staring were Stephen, Wade, Nicole, and Paige, which seemed odd—they didn't seem to have anything in common.

Prince Tristan cleared his throat until everyone faced him again. "I expect this to be the end of these types of problems. I'd prefer not to have to address these problems again, but I will if need be. Understood?"

Everyone rang out a chorused "Yes sir," which was creepy in its authoritarianism. Seemingly satisfied, Tristan unbuttoned his suit jacket and sat back in his seat just as the instructor walked in, completely unaware of the horror that had just occurred. My eyes landed on Olivia, who was staring an absolute hole through my head. So much for Tristan dealing with this discreetly.

Chapter Five

September 13 —

Am I too nice?

Sometimes I think that maybe I don't have enough gumption. It feels like I just go with the flow most of the time. I used to think that was a good thing because I never had any conflict with anyone, but maybe I was wrong. Maybe nothing productive happens without conflict.

I just hate confrontation. I hate when anyone is mad at me. I just let other people tell me what to do because it's easier and less awkward than arguing. Is that wrong? Am I doing the right thing? Am I cut out for this?

***

Leadership class dragged on after Prince Tristan's ultimatum. In fact, I didn't think two hours could possibly go that slowly. Stephen had texted me through Ledger to check in, but what was I going to say? How could I possibly put into words what I felt about all of that, in the length of a text, no less?

On the way out of class, despite my best efforts, Olivia found her way to me as everyone else seemed to part in front of her to allow her to pass. I made note of the fact that most of them didn't walk away after that—I presumed that they wanted to see the fireworks.

"Lady Julia," she said with a cloying, sugary tone, "I don't think we've properly met yet. I'm Lady Olivia of Aerilot. Graycott, right?" I only nodded. "I've only ever seen the north part of Graycott since it borders Aerilot. Is that where you're from?"

I shook my head. "I live in the capital city in the center." What was the point of this particular line of inquiry?

"Oh, that's nice. The part of Graycott I visited was just so gloomy and depressing. How nice that you don't live there. Who could stand living in such a humid, rainy place?"

"That's really all of Graycott, actually." I matched her saccharine smile. "Builds character to live some place where everything isn't so easy."

The slight twitch of her mouth gave me a weird sense of strength knowing that I was getting to her. "Well, I just wanted to say welcome to Lithilea Prep. You know, we were all really sad to hear about what happened to Lady Jane." I felt my fingers curling into a fist, and everyone around us hushed suddenly. "She was definitely one of the best. I don't think anyone could ever be as great as she was. I mean she was pretty, kind, intelligent, diplomatic—who could possibly top Jane? It seems she'll always be remembered as the best Graycott had to offer, I suppose."

I started to lift my balled up fist, but before I could say or do anything, Wade looped his arm through mine and smiled. "Lady Julia, now how dare you keep me waiting? You can't just promise a man that you'll accompany him to the post office and then dodge your responsibilities."

I desperately wanted to snap back at Olivia or connect my hand to her face, but Wade threw me off. "What?"

Wade rolled his eyes dramatically and tugged my arm gently. "How easily I'm forgotten. Come on now, before you damage my tender ego once more."

I didn't really have much say in the matter as Wade ever so gently dragged me away from what was about to turn into a full-on brawl, so I let him. I heard a lot of whispering as we walked away, and I couldn't decipher if it was because of Olivia's cattiness, my temper, or my association with Wade, who still seemed to draw ire from many.

"You're welcome," he said once we were out of earshot of the others.

"I didn't ask for your help."

He chuckled. "But you needed it. What were you going to do, punch her out? Right after Prince Tristan's speech about unity and cooperation?"

I yanked my arm from his. "You heard what she said."

He nodded. "And I also know that if you had hit her, you'd be the villain right now."

"I'm already the villain."

"You are not. You're just the new kid in school."

"The worst part is that she didn't even say anything outright mean. Really, all she did was compliment Jane. I probably look like the crazy one now for getting angry, and over what? Her praising my sister to the high heavens? How is it possible for someone to be that manipulative?"

"Those elite provinces have a knack for it."

I rolled my eyes. "Whatever, Dalmerlin. *You're* from an elite province."

"That's a technicality."

We walked into the post office, and based on the exterior, I'd been expecting a very different interior. From the outside the building seemed small, tiny even, and not likely to have very many services, but inside it was quite spacious. There were mailboxes along the side, a worker or two behind a counter, and endless packaging and mailing supplies. Wade picked up some basic stationery and stamps. Who was he writing to? Parents? As far as I knew, he was the only representative from Dalmerlin here, so I didn't think he had any siblings.

"Julia, do you need anything while we're here?" Wade asked.

"No." I certainly didn't have anyone to write to.

"Lady Julia?" the girl behind the counter asked, so I nodded. "From Graycott? Excellent. I have some letters here for you. I wasn't sure if you'd been shown your mailbox yet, and I wanted to make sure you got them."

Letters? "From whom?"

She glanced at the return addresses. "Most of them are from Sir Joseph Clarke of Graycott."

I shook my head. "Keep them."

"What?"

"Keep them. I don't need them."

Wade looked up at me but didn't say anything. The girl at the counter, however, looked utterly confused. "Uh, I'm sorry, Lady Julia, but I don't understand. I have to turn these over to you. It's my job."

I rolled my eyes, snatched the stack of letters from her, and shoved them in my bag. I'd throw them away when I got back to the suite. I gestured toward the door, and Wade nodded, paying for his stationery and following me out the door.

"Everything okay?" he asked, walking briskly to keep up with me. I wasn't sure where I was going exactly, but it was in the direction of a part of campus I hadn't seen yet. No one else seemed to be going this way, and that seemed as good of a reason as any to walk this direction.

"Fine."

"Obviously."

I stopped and faced him. "Just not a good day, okay. Not a good month, really."

"Do you want to talk about it?"

I wanted to say no, wanted to walk right past him to my suite, but something in me compelled me to sit down on a bench under a big tree. We were a ways away from the main part of campus now, and it actually felt nice to have a little breeze over here in the shade. I wasn't sure why I wanted to talk to Wade—I hadn't wanted to talk to anyone about anything since Jane—but I found him strangely reassuring.

"I'm just so tired of hearing people talk about Jane. Everyone here thinks they knew her, but they didn't. No one really knew her but me. Everyone either tries to offer some condolences or weaponizes her either to be my friend or my enemy. No one really misses her, I think. They just miss her being here instead of me."

Wade was silent a few moments before he said, barely above a whisper, "I miss her."

"What?"

He shrugged. "We didn't know each other that well. Sometimes we studied together, but that was it. I'm not sure if she would have even called us friends, but she was so different from everyone else."

"Different?" I asked. Most people thought Jane was the epitome of "like everyone else." She was popular. No one thought of her as different.

"She was just so real. Not everyone, but a lot of the people here are fake. They're either fake like Olivia, or they're faking with the best intentions, to try to fit in or be accepted. She wasn't fake. She was just Jane. I always liked her for that."

I nodded slowly. That was probably the most accurate assessment I'd heard of Jane in weeks. She wasn't pretending to be good at this. She just was.

Seeming to know my thoughts, Wade added, "Other than maybe Prince Tristan, I think she was the only one of us who actually knew what she was doing."

I couldn't help but laugh a little. "That's probably true. I hate to give Olivia any credit, but she might be right. I'll probably never measure up to her, especially now that I'm so behind where she was."

"Why didn't you already go to school here? It seems weird that Jane had a sibling who didn't attend."

"Short answer? I was never supposed to be Duchess of Graycott."

"What do you mean?"

"My family wasn't the direct lineage. My dad's older brother Joseph is the current Duke of Graycott, but since he never had kids, the lineage went to my dad, then my mom, then Jane. My parents were quite a bit younger than my uncle, so it seemed like Jane wouldn't be Duchess until she was much older, and at that point, she'd probably have kids of her own. I would only get further away from the title with time. No one plans for a massive train accident that kills three people, you know?"

It occurred to me that that was the first time I'd ever said those words out loud. The accident just happened, and everyone knew about it. People could reference it without directly saying it, and I'd certainly never had to say it. Until now, I'd never really acknowledged their deaths out loud. Even though it had been a couple of months, I had a strange urge to cry, but I bit the side of my mouth and suppressed it.

Wade leaned around in front of me to make eye contact. "It's okay to be upset, you know. It doesn't make you any less worthy of your rightful title."

"I just don't need to give the Olivias of Lithilea any more ammunition than they already have."

He scoffed. "Olivia doesn't have any actual ammunition. She's just making it up as she goes along."

"If you say so."

"I do, in fact," he said with a gentle smile. "And thank you for telling me all of that. I know it couldn't have been easy."

Strangely, I accepted his offer of a hug and felt myself exhale for the first time in months.

Chapter Six

January 4 —

Getting to work alongside the future king of Lithilea is so exciting. In some ways, it's like I'm living some kind of fairytale. You mean I actually get to call Prince Tristan a friend? But in other ways, it's kind of intimidating. Does he like me? Does he think I'm good enough? Is he looking forward to having me as a representative of one of his provinces one day?

I hope I'll get a chance to get closer to him. I feel like I never really get a chance to talk to him, and since it will be some time before I'm actually duchess, I feel like it's important to build a relationship with him now while I can, while I see him every single day.

I think that's the best part of Lithilea Prep: getting to know everyone and be friends with them. It's so much fun. I love getting to know everyone and learning about their provinces. Maybe one day I'll visit all of them and get to see the rest of Lithilea. That would be really fun.

***

I might have been committing social and political suicide with what I was doing, but when had I ever been a rule follower?

When I checked the Ledger for Prince Tristan's phone number, I hadn't actually expected it to come up. Cecily had told me that all of the representatives' numbers were preloaded in there, but for some reason, my mind had made Prince Tristan and his sister exceptions. Why would the heir of Lithilea hand out his phone number?

I had told myself that if, by chance, his number *was* in there, that I would text him and ask to speak with him. If his number wasn't there, I would wait and see what happened, maybe talk to him in person. But when my phone lit up with a number below his profile picture, I suddenly didn't want to hit send on that text.

I had to talk to him. I had to explain to him why the absolute worst thing he could've done was what he did yesterday, but was that how things were done? And even if one was allowed to make demands of the future king, what would that change? Olivia wouldn't magically stop hating me. I wouldn't magically fit in. Jane wouldn't magically come back to life and reclaim this position that never should have been mine. Tomorrow, everything would still be the same.

But I had never taken a handout or a favor, and I wasn't about to start now.

When he agreed to meet with me, I had offered to meet him at his suite or somewhere else on campus, but he insisted on coming to me. I felt weirdly self-conscious about him seeing my suite, which was ridiculous. It wasn't even really mine. I certainly hadn't decorated it, and the only things in there that I owned were my clothes, my bag, and the piano. It was still strange to think about that.

At the sound of knocking, I straightened my skirt and answered the door. I'd forced myself to wear a pleated plaid skirt to try to look as Lithilea-duchess-to-be as possible, but when I saw Prince Tristan wearing jeans and a polo, I felt pretty ridiculous. Was the heir of Lithilea even allowed to wear jeans? Apparently so.

He smiled wide. "Good morning, Lady Julia. How are you doing today?"

I curtsied fast. Was I supposed to curtsy every time I saw him? I couldn't remember. Cecily would have been furious to know I hadn't listened to her etiquette instructions. "All right, Sir Tristan."

"Wonderful."

"Please come in."

He wandered slowly into the main sitting room, seeming to survey the entire space. I was grateful that I had closed the bathroom door before he arrived; I definitely didn't need him to see the makeup and towel catastrophe in there. Thank goodness the maid would come tomorrow.

"You know," he began, facing away from me toward the unlit fireplace, "Graycott is one of my favorite provinces to visit."

I raised an eyebrow. "You're kidding."

He chuckled. "I assure you I'm not."

"Really?"

"Mm-hmm. I like the coastline. Sometimes I feel so landlocked. I'm always either at the castle or here surrounded by nothing but desert. It's nice to see water sometimes."

I laughed before I could stop myself, and he leaned back just enough to look at me. "I'm sorry," I said, "but that seems a little dramatic."

He smiled and turned back toward the fireplace. "That's another thing I like about Graycott: the representatives are never shy about saying exactly what's on their minds."

I started to smile, but the implication hit me hard: Jane must have talked with him like this.

I couldn't see his face, so I couldn't decipher his expression. Was he trying to be light-hearted? Did he not realize what he said until he said it? There was no way to know as I stared at his back, hands folded behind his waist.

He nodded in a gesture toward the back of the room where the piano sat. "You play?"

"Yes, but not for other people."

He chuckled. "I wasn't asking."

"I didn't want to say no to the Prince of Lithilea."

He spun on his heel sharply, his brow furrowed. "That's not a rule, you know. You shouldn't feel forced into anything by me."

"It isn't really you, exactly. It's just my position."

He sat on the couch and gestured for me to sit as well, so I purposely chose the sofa opposite him. It felt weird to sit on the same sofa as Prince Tristan. "Would you explain?"

I nodded. "That's why I asked to see you. You said you would handle the whole Olivia thing discreetly."

"Yes?"

"That was anything but discreet."

He looked genuinely confused. "I didn't say your name or hers."

"But everyone knew it was me."

"Intolerance is not tolerable, Lady Julia."

"That sounds like a slogan."

He suppressed a grin. "That may be, but it is true. I don't have any patience for that kind of thing."

"Yeah, I get that, but now I'm the inferior new girl who whined to the prince at the first minor confrontation."

"That was not minor."

"Not the point."

He huffed. "Then I don't understand."

"Look, maybe my sister used to fit in here. Maybe she was accepted, but I'm not right now. Can I be frank?"

"Aren't you always?"

"You made things a million times worse. Most people here already hated me without reason, and now you gave them a reason. I wasn't even going to tell you what happened for that reason. Plus, I didn't want to complain on the first day, but Valerie blurted it out, and I wasn't going to lie to you. I need a chance to prove myself, and that's already hard enough, following Jane and all."

He didn't speak for a while, just staring at his folded hands in his laps. I started to worry that I had offended him, that he was contemplating my consequences, but I forced myself to remain calm, or at least look calm.

After a few agonizingly silent moments, he said softly, "I haven't told many people this, but initially, I wasn't excited about coming to Lithilea Prep."

"Really?"

"I was very young, and I didn't like the idea of leaving home. Plus, I had been told that I needed to prepare to be king. I felt like coming here would detract from valuable educational time. I was wrong. Being here has taught me some of the most valuable lessons. There are certain things that I'll simply never be able to learn because of my position. The only way I can learn those things is from the other future representatives. I'm grateful for your frankness, Lady Julia. Hopefully I will be better next time."

"The next time someone insults me using my dead sister?"

His eyes widened, and I knew I had made him feel awkward. I kind of liked the power trip I felt from having that effect on him. "Well, ideally there won't be a next time, but if there is, I will consult you on how best to handle it. Deal?"

He stuck out his hand for a handshake, and I accepted. "Deal."

"We haven't really had a chance to discuss Jane since you arrived."

"And we're not about to start now."

He held up his hands in surrender. "Your choice. But you should know that she was one of the kindest people I've ever known, and she spoke very highly of you. She told me about you on multiple occasions. She was very sorry that you hadn't attended Lithilea Prep with her. I think she thought you perfectly capable of your new title."

My eyes stung, so I blinked repeatedly to force the impending tears back. I had never wanted to be here even though she had begged me to come with her. Now I wished I had if for no other reason than to be with her.

"Also," he added, "that was the most diplomatic way anyone has ever told me off, so it seems to me that you fit right in."

I rolled my eyes. "That's probably because no one has ever told you off at all."

"Not the point," he said, mocking my voice, then clearing his throat. "So, tell me something. Why are you here?"

"Seriously? I just—"

"No, no. I don't mean the literal reason. Whether or not you wanted to be here or were supposed to be here, you are here nonetheless. So what is your goal for Graycott? What does Graycott need most that you can work to fix?"

I thought for a moment. No one had ever asked me that. Not Cecily, not any of my instructors, especially not Joe. What did I want for Graycott? Graycott had several problems—poor economy, incomplete education, crumbling transportation, not the best health care—but what would I choose to focus on when I became Duchess of Graycott?

"I'm honestly not sure," I said. "I can think of several things that Graycott could improve, but I wouldn't even know where to start."

"You never thought about it?"

I shrugged and shook my head. "I was never supposed to be here, so it seemed like a waste of time to think about what I would do in some alternate life where my parents and sister didn't exist."

My voice caught a bit at the end. I hadn't expected to get choked up over that, but I'd hit on something. This *was* an alternate reality, one that I had hoped would never have become reality. I didn't want to be the Duchess of Graycott, and I especially didn't want it if it meant not having my family. No amount of *But now you can make a difference for all of Graycott* would have changed my mind. I didn't tell Tristan, but I would run straight to the train station and leave this campus immediately and forever if it meant having my parents and Jane back. It wasn't even a question.

"What had you planned to do, then, if not this?" he asked.

I nodded my head toward the piano. "Concert pianist."

He cocked one eyebrow. "Really? But I thought you didn't play for other people."

"Not here in my room. That's awkward. Concerts are different. They don't require words, just notes."

He stood, so I did, too. "Well, you should think about what you'd like to do for Graycott, and when you decide, let me know. I'd love to be involved. I have a meeting in about fifteen minutes, so would you mind if I took my leave now?"

"No, go ahead. And thank you. Really."

He smiled on his way out, and while I still found him so hard to read and unpredictable, I felt that maybe Tristan and I could be friends.

Chapter Seven

July 18 —

Maybe I should have taken the summer off.

I just feel so exhausted all the time. Maybe I needed the break. Maybe it was foolish to try to get ahead. I thought it would be a good idea to try to graduate early since Dad and Joe are still not speaking, but I'm really missing home, and I'm feeling a little burned out. Does that mean I'm not good at this? What if I get burned out as duchess? It's not like I can quit or go on hiatus or something.

It's also so hot. Graycott is always hot, but it isn't as sunny as it is here. I feel like the heat is sapping all of my energy.

I'm not going home until November, and that seems so far away. How will I make it until then? No one else seems homesick, so I just keep acting like I'm not either. Maybe if I fake it long enough, eventually it'll be true.

***

Saturday morning, some fool decided that it was a good idea to knock on my door at 8 AM. I tried to ignore it, and while their persistence did not make me want to get out of that ridiculously comfortable bed, it did make me want to give them a piece of my mind. It was likely Rose trying to hang out or something, which was simply not an option for the day. I had made plans with myself to spend the day sleeping, playing the piano, and generally just loafing.

At the fourth knock, I shoved aside the turquoise comforter and forced myself out of bed. I couldn't be sure if it was actually Rose outside, so I changed quickly into white yoga pants and a wine-colored sweater. It looked presentable enough.

I swung the door open with a litany of curses waiting on my tongue, but when I saw Stephen Sanor smiling, I was more than a little thrown off.

"What are you doing here?" I asked.

"Good morning to you, too." He gestured past me. "May I?"

I nodded, and he walked just into the entry way and smiled. He seemed to want to look around without being obvious, but he wasn't nearly as subtle as he likely thought he was. He folded his arms behind his back the same way Prince Tristan had. I wondered if that was intentional, like he was mimicking him. Maybe Lithilea Prep taught you how to stand.

"So," he began, "have I told you about my first weekend here?" I shook my head. "I was an awkward, shy little nine-year-old boy, and I didn't know how to make friends. Plus, you know, everyone hates the kid from Idlewick."

He'd said it in a light-hearted way, but my stomach knotted up a little at the cavalier way he had mentioned his ostracization.

"But there was an instructor back then—he's retired now—named Dr. Golden. He picked me up the first Saturday I was here and took me out for the day. We rode bikes, we got ice cream, we wandered through the hiking trails, and he let me talk about anything and everything I wanted. No one had ever really wanted to listen to me before then. It was nice. That night, he took me back to his house and introduced me to his kids. They were older than me, but they were still really nice and played games with me. I had been afraid that going to Lithilea Prep meant never playing games again. I stayed there that night, and then he brought me back the next day. It was the nicest anyone had been since I arrived, maybe the nicest anyone had been in a while."

"That's really sweet," I said.

He nodded and smiled. "So I'm returning the favor."

"What?"

"I'm taking you out for the day."

"For ice cream?"

He laughed. "If that's what you want, yeah. I don't know a lot about you, and I'm really only an expert at planning the perfect day for a nine-year-old boy, so you'll have to help me out a little, but I've got some ideas."

"Why?"

"It's not like I know what girls like to do—"

"No, I mean why are you doing this?"

"Look, you and I both know that we're the odd ones out here. The lower provinces don't get much respect despite Prince Tristan's efforts. We might as well stick together. Plus, I don't think it'll kill you to have some fun."

I couldn't stop the smirk. "You never know."

"I'm willing to take that risk." He looked down at my sweater. "But you might want to change. It's hot outside."

***

Because I refused to pick the first activity of the day, Stephen took me to the hiking trails nestled behind campus. It was weird to think how close we were to the kingdom capitol. The tips of the castle in the capitol were visible over the trees on the hiking trail. I knew that there was likely some kind of defense in the forest, but in theory, we could've walked there, walked right up to the front door. I'd never been there before. Jane had gone just before the accident and I think once as a little kid. I didn't think I'd ever see it.

The hiking trails were really more like walking paths in this flat desert, which suited me just fine. I wasn't in the mood to hike. It was really hot since there was little shade, but I liked not feeling muggy and gross like I would in Graycott. I could get used to this lack of humidity. Plus, I liked wearing normal clothes for a day. Cecily could swear all she wanted that Lithilea Prep didn't have a uniform, but it might as well have. It was so nice to wear shorts and not care what anyone would think about me.

We stopped for a moment to sit on a bench in between a few cacti. It looked like the perfect photo spot. I suddenly pictured Olivia and Matilda taking obnoxious selfies and felt the inappropriate urge to laugh. I pulled my water bottle from my bag, using the need to disguise my giggling as an excuse to hydrate, and Stephen pulled a small foil pouch from his bag and handed it to me, pulling out a second one for himself.

"What's this?" I asked.

"Snacks."

"You really came prepared." I uncrinkled the foil and spotted dried mango slices. "How did you know?"

"Know what?"

"That I liked dried mango."

"Doesn't everybody?"

"Apparently not," I said, pointing at his pouch of chips.

"Lucky guess," he said, shoving some chips into his mouth.

I squinted at him. "Pretty lucky."

"Not really. You're from the province that exports tropical fruits."

"Doesn't mean I like them. Maybe I hate them, sick of eating them for seventeen years."

He looked me in the eyes. "Are you?"

"No." I took a big bite of mango and tried not to look outwardly satisfied.

"Well then."

I chomped a few slices, thinking it was the best mango I'd had in a while, and thought that there was no way Stephen was just that perceptive and intuitive. Someone definitely told him, and since I could be pretty sure that neither Cecily nor Joe were casually chatting with Stephen, I knew where he'd gotten the intel.

"Did Jane tell you I liked dried mango?"

His eyes widened quickly before he regained control of them, and he avoided eye contact. "She did, yeah."

"That just randomly came up in conversation? 'Hey, fun fact, my sister that you've never met loves dried mango'?"

"No, she, uh, she used to buy it in bulk and mail it back to Graycott. One day I was kind of giving her a hard time for buying absurd amounts of mango, so she told me."

I nodded. I remembered those mango shipments. I ate them, and I certainly appreciated her sending them, but I always thought it was a little weird. I could buy mango at home. Why had she sent it? Was it just her way of communicating with me?

"I'm sorry," he said after a few moments.

"For what?"

"I told myself I wasn't going to mention Jane."

"I mean, you didn't. I did."

"I just didn't want to bring her up. Wasn't sure how you felt about talking about her."

How did I feel about talking about her? No one had ever asked. "You didn't do anything wrong." I waited a moment. "Were you two close? When she was here, I mean."

He shrugged awkwardly. "We weren't best friends or anything, but she was probably the nicest person here. She always went out of her way to hang out with me when I needed a friend, especially before Valerie started here."

Nicest person here. That had been a common refrain lately. "Prince Tristan said basically the same thing."

"Tristan is a good judge of character."

"On a first name basis with the future king?"

He laughed. "Yeah, actually. We've known each other since we were tiny. Our mothers were childhood best friends."

"Really?"

He nodded. "We practically grew up together. He didn't get to come to Idlewick too often, but we used to go to visit his parents."

"And you became best buds with Tristan and not Talia?"

He laughed, genuinely this time. "Definitely not. She's really not as bad as she sometimes seems. She's just not as good at letting down the front as Tristan is."

"I don't know how they do it. I feel like I'm always putting on a front."

"Then don't."

"What?"

"Don't put on a front. I don't."

"No offense, but you also don't have many allies either."

He smirked. "Maybe not, but I don't have anyone else's expectations weighing me down. I know Idlewick better than anyone else here, so why should I let them tell me how to run my province? My real friends like Tristan and Valerie know who I am. That's all that matters. You know Graycott better than anyone else."

"Not better than Jane."

He forced me to make eye contact by tilting my chin toward him. "Do you think Jane was better at this than you?"

"Doesn't everybody?"

"Not me."

"Why?" I asked, but he seemed to hesitate. He shifted a little and tried to mumble something about not wanting to say. The best part of Stephen was that he never held back, so I wasn't about to let him do it now. "Just tell me."

"Honestly? I think she was one of the nicest people I've ever known. She was so good at getting along with everyone, but maybe that's not what Lithilea needs. Maybe Lithilea needs someone who will shake things up and make the upper provinces uncomfortable and expose the not-so-hidden hierarchy."

"Then why aren't you doing that?"

"I do in my own way, but I'm not nearly as aggressive as you are."

"Gee, thanks."

He smiled. "I mean aggressive in the best possible way."

"Making waves wasn't exactly part of my plan for laying low."

"Laying low is overrated."

I laughed. "That is the most cliche thing I've ever heard."

He shrugged. "That's my hidden talent: saying cliche things that sound like they're straight out of a teen movie."

I waved the bag of mango slices. "I thought your specialty was getting date tips from deceased siblings." I wasn't totally sure that this was even a date, but it had crossed my mind, and based on how Stephen reacted, it had crossed his, too.

"Wow," he said, turning bright red. "You just love dropping stuff like that and making people uncomfortable, don't you?"

I laughed and shrugged. "Easier than being sad all the time. Or worse, enduring those insufferable looks of fake pity and hearing contrived condolences."

"Ever occur to you that maybe some of the condolences are not contrived? Maybe people genuinely feel bad?"

"Not in my experience."

"Well, you might slap me for this, but I am genuinely sorry. Jane was one-of-a-kind. It's a loss for all of Lithilea."

I thought that was the first time I'd ever believed that someone was being genuine. I'd thought Prince Tristan might have really meant it, but it was so hard to separate Tristan from the title. Maybe Stephen was right, and I was underestimating Tristan. But Stephen—Stephen was different. So far, he and Wade were the only people I felt like I could really talk to since Jane.

"Thank you," I said when I was sure that my voice wouldn't shake.

"But *you* are Lithilea Prep's gain," he added with a smirk. "I haven't seen Olivia that mad in a while. I was kind of rooting for you to knock her out the other day."

I mimicked Stephen's smirk. "Okay, that would've been funny. Probably not what Tristan wanted though."

He shrugged. "Tristan would get over it."

"Olivia, however."

"That might have made you instantly popular."

"Or instantly expelled."

He laughed, and I found myself admiring how Stephen looked when he laughed. I mean, I'd noticed that he was good looking pretty much immediately, but there was something special about him when he laughed. Most adults—honestly, most teenagers, too—never truly laugh freely. Children laugh so freely until they're taught to restrain their outward expressions of joy to fit in with society, to avoid disrupting others, to fit in. Stephen still laughed like a child, with freedom and shamelessness. It was beautiful to watch.

I decided to go for it.

"All right, we're taking a picture," I said.

"What? We've been walking for hours. We're red and sweaty."

I laughed. "You didn't strike me as the vain type, Sanor."

He turned a little redder than the heat permitted. "I'm not vain."

I held out my arm. "Then come here and smile."

He rolled his eyes, but he did move to stand next to me, looping his arm behind my back. Everything since I'd gotten to Lithilea Prep had been so formal, so forced, so inauthentic. I was glad for this moment. It was normal, just two teenagers having fun and taking a selfie. In this moment standing next to some cacti, wearing shorts, and laughing together, I felt the most normal I had felt since the day I got the phone call that my life was forever changed.

***

When Stephen and I got back from our adventure, he walked me to my suite, and even though it wasn't that much of a grand gesture since his room was two doors down, it was still nice. I didn't think I was likely to forget this day for some time.

I was anxious for a shower, but the stack of letters on the table by the door caught my attention as I made a beeline for the bathroom. It was the stack of letters from Joe. I should have thrown them away right there at the post office. What was a letter from Joe going to do for me? I didn't need the current Duke of Graycott to tell me anything. Wasn't that the whole point of Lithilea Prep? Besides, if he couldn't be bothered to show up to his brother's funeral or even call his niece after her parents and sister died, then maybe I couldn't be bothered to reply to his letters. Why was he sending so many anyway? I'd only been here a few days and there were already ten letters. Seemed excessive.

They probably weren't even really from him. They were probably form letters or something written by his secretary that he signed. They didn't matter.

I swiped my hand across them to push them over the edge into the garbage can, but they didn't all fall, and I noticed that a couple of the envelopes were not Joe's stationery, so I picked those up. One was a letter from the dean of Lithilea Prep welcoming me to the school. Seemed odd that the dean should send a letter instead of personally meeting me like the freaking heir to the Lithilean throne did, but whatever. The second was from Lithilea Transit Authority, which seemed out of place, so I opened it. It was a letter from the investigative team assigned to look into the train accident. It was customary—whenever there was a significant accident or an accident involving heirs, they had to conduct an investigation by law—so I half-skimmed the page. I didn't really need to read it. I knew what it said. Really, this letter was just a quasi-insensitive reminder of what had happened. But when I caught sight of the word "explosives," my eyes locked onto the page.

Low-grade explosives were found in three critical areas: the engine, the car connectors, and the hull of car #10, the car connected to car #11 in which Sir and Lady Clarke and Lady Jane Clarke were occupying. Though the investigation is still ongoing, it is the belief of the investigative team that these explosives were placed deliberately and triggered either with a remote device or set on a timer. The exact motive has not yet been determined, nor are there any suspects.

I dropped the letter and fell to my knees, my hands shaking.

It wasn't an accident.

In moments of intense fury or despair, I often imagined that it must have been intentional. I couldn't comprehend that something so cruel could happen by chance. But everyone told me that sometimes the world wasn't fair, that sometimes the good people in the world fell victim to the cruelty of randomness. Something tiny but nagging within me felt that it was too much to be random, but despite that feeling, I never thought that I'd be right.

I forced my hands to stop shaking and picked up the letter again. I read the rest of it, but it offered little other information that I didn't already know. I did notice that the letterhead addressed Joe as well as myself, so he must have received a copy of this letter. I quickly flipped through the envelopes from him, but none were postmarked after this letter. He had received this letter and not even contacted me about it.

I sniffed and rubbed my nose, resolving to do something instead of feeling sorry for myself. I didn't need Joe's help. I didn't need the approval of anyone here. I needed to know what happened to my family.

I grabbed my phone and texted Tristan: *I know what I want to do for Graycott. Can you meet me later today?*

And immediately upon sending it, I texted Cecily as well, who, unsurprisingly, answered immediately.

Chapter Eight

September 20 —

If there's one thing I've learned in my time at Lithilea Prep, it's how to ask for help. It's not something I'm naturally good at, and if I'm being honest, I think it's because of my dad and Uncle Joe. They don't always see eye to eye on how to rule Graycott, and I think Dad kind of resents Uncle Joe for not abdicating and letting him rule. I'm sure Uncle Joe has his reasons, but he's obviously so busy, and it probably wouldn't hurt him to ask Dad for help once in a while. It also probably wouldn't kill Dad to do the same.

I've seen this play out with my peers. One day, we'll all be ruling either our provinces or the country, and we'll have to work together. We'll have to ask for help. I hope I didn't inherit that stubbornness that they have. But then I wonder: have I asked Julia for help? Like directly asked her for it? I've hinted, but maybe that's the problem. Maybe if I just asked her point blank for help, then she would.

Maybe it is a Clarke family curse to try to go it alone.

***

I paced around my suite endlessly because I couldn't really find myself capable of doing anything else. I had tried to play the piano, study, even browse Ledger, but I just couldn't do anything except spiral. Someone had killed my family. Someone had *meant* to kill my family.

It still didn't seem possible. No matter how much I knew deep down inside that this couldn't have just happened, strangely, it still seemed completely inconceivable. In the midst of all of the noise in my head, the buzzing of questions, doubts, and emotions, one word dominated, rising to the top of my thoughts like the crash of a cymbal in an orchestral piece: *why.*

Why my family? Why *all* of them? Why a train accident? Why now? Why not Joe? Why Graycott?

That last question seemed to reverberate in my head. Graycott was not an elite province. It wasn't even considered one of the average provinces. It wasn't responsible for something crucial to the Lithilean government. If someone had wanted to take out a powerful duke or duchess, I would have thought they'd target one of the elite provinces. We weren't exactly facing threats from the ocean. And if some kind of political assassination was the goal, why was Joe spared? Did the bombers just not know that he wasn't with them?

The knock on my door startled me disproportionately, and I worried that I would be permanently on edge until I figured out everything. For now, I opened the door to Cecily who held two cups of coffee, one jutted in my direction.

I took the coffee. "You're a genius," I said.

She smiled. "I figured you would want it."

When she waited in the hall, I gestured for her to come in, remembering that we had that weird employer-employee relationship that still didn't really make sense to me. She walked slowly to the sofa, seeming to take in everything as she walked. I imagined that she was cringing at the mess I'd already made, but she said nothing. When she finally sat on the sofa, she didn't look relaxed.

"I assume you contacted me because you heard about the investigation." It was a question, but Cecily said it as a statement, almost an accusation.

I nodded. "So it's true?"

Cecily pressed her lips together and sighed. "Unfortunately."

I sat opposite her on the other sofa. "So what's happening?"

"A thorough and complicated investigation. They know very little at this point, so it's really just a process of gathering information and evidence. The discovery of the attached explosive has sent everyone involved into a kind of frenzy."

"Are you involved?"

"In the investigation? Only loosely, mostly to keep you informed."

I wanted to say more, but another knock on the door startled us both. Cecily looked somewhat concerned, though I could tell she was trying to hide it by the way she reclined slowly and rested an arm on the back of the sofa. I assumed it was Tristan because he was the only other person I had contacted since finding out, so I wasn't surprised to see his concerned face when I opened the door.

"May I come in?" he asked, and it seemed silly to me that a prince should have to ask such a thing. Did anyone ever say no?

"Miss Dunn," he said with a hint of surprise.

Cecily immediately shot to her feet. "Your Highness. I wasn't expecting to see you."

"I'm sorry," Tristan said to me, "I hope I'm not interrupting. I came over as soon as I saw your message."

"You're not," I said. "I'm glad you're here."

I gestured to the couch, and he sat down opposite of Cecily, so I took one of the chairs because I didn't feel like Cecily and I were close enough for same-sofa-sitting, as ridiculous as that thought seemed at this particular moment.

Tristan inhaled slowly. "Lady Julia—"

"Just Julia," I interrupted. "If we're going to have this conversation, I think you can just call me Julia."

"Julia," he began again, "I am incredibly sorry to hear the latest from the investigative team. This was not what any of us expected to hear, and I am so sorry for this unsettling news."

"Do you know anything? Anything we don't already know, obviously."

He shook his head. "We likely won't for a little while. These teams are very careful to examine crime scenes meticulously so that no detail is missed. They don't typically like to release any information without backing, but this one was different, of course."

Crime scene. Those weren't words I had heard associated with the deaths of my family as of yet. I found that I intensely disliked hearing Tristan say those words aloud, and I hoped I would never hear them again, despite the reality that crime scene conversations were inevitable at this point.

"Once they have news, who gets it first?" I asked.

"Excuse me?"

"I mean, do you find out these things first? Does Joe? Do I? I don't have any idea how any of this works."

"Frankly, I'm not sure I know how it works either," Tristan said, and I was shocked by his vulnerability. "I haven't been involved in an investigation of this sort, but I imagine that early reports will come to me first and then to your family."

I bristled at the term "family." Though Joe was biologically and genetically my uncle, it was nearly impossible to think of him as family right now.

"Will you please tell me anything you find out?" I asked. "The not-knowing is killing me."

Tristan stood and buttoned his jacket. "I will, but try not to worry too much. The Lithilean government takes this very seriously, and they will use all available resources to find out everything they can."

It felt weird to talk to him while still seated, so I stood, too. "Isn't there anything I can do? To help, I mean. I don't feel like I can just sit back and wait."

Unexpectedly, Tristan wrapped a hand around my upper arm. "No, Julia, unfortunately there's nothing you can do right now. Just try to focus on your work here, and I will keep you as up-to-date as I can. We will find out who is responsible and bring them to justice. Can you trust me on that?" I nodded, and Tristan cleared his throat somewhat loudly. "Excuse me, I'm sorry, I just realized I have a meeting I must attend. I'll see myself out." With that, Tristan abruptly headed toward the door and left.

The problem was that I wasn't sure I could trust him. Not yet, anyway. Tristan hadn't really done anything to make me believe that he couldn't be trusted, but I also knew that Graycott was never really at the top of anyone's list ever. What if Aerilot had a more pressing concern come up? What if the bomber turned out to be someone powerful and untouchable? What if resources were needed elsewhere? I just didn't feel like I could sit by and trust the government to prioritize a province that hadn't been prioritized in its history, if my facts were right. I had very few people in my life that I trusted, and I wasn't totally sure that Tristan was in that circle yet.

I looked over at Cecily who had sat back down on the sofa and was sipping her coffee. I hadn't really wanted to, but I found that I did trust Cecily. She was paid to take care of me, and I knew that she was simply good at her job, but I also knew that she had gone above and beyond her compensated responsibilities. She hadn't been required to have a necklace made for me that matched Jane's favorite bracelet, and she hadn't been required to pull me away in the midst of a breakdown when I first got here and was confronted by prejudice, and she didn't have to come when I called, but she did and she had. Cecily had proven that she cared about me beyond her job requirements, and she was from Graycott—right now, that was good enough for me.

This time, I did sit on the sofa next to her, and she raised an eyebrow at me when I did so. "Cecily, can you do something for me?"

"Anything," she said, though the shakiness in her voice seemed to suggest that she was a little concerned about what I might ask.

"I want to know that someone from Graycott is going to be involved in this investigation." When Cecily raised her eyebrows again, I quickly added, "Of course I know that Prince Tristan is right, and they're doing everything they can, but I would feel better knowing that someone a little more personal was involved. If I didn't have to be here, I would go myself, but obviously that isn't an option. Would you check in from time to time on what's going on? Just to give me updates and maybe contribute anything you might know about my family or anything I can tell you? This is just such a personal issue for all of Graycott, and I think it can only prove valuable to have someone from our province around."

Cecily smiled sweetly and said, "Of course, Julia, I can check in from time to time. I don't want to go too far in case you need me, but I'll pop back and forth."

I felt a tiny bit of the weight I was carrying lift from my shoulders. "Thank you. I just don't feel like I have very many people in my life that I trust right now, and, well, you're pretty much it," I said with a laugh.

I could see Cecily's face brighten as she smiled. "You can always trust me. But can I make a suggestion?"

"Sure."

"You might want to consider contacting your uncle—"

"No."

"I know there's a lot of tension there, but he's going to be involved, and it might make you feel better to—"

I don't need his help," I said. Then, to soften it a little, I added, "Not right now, anyway. You're good enough for me."

She smiled and patted my arm. "I'll do whatever you need me to do. Anything I should take care of before I leave?"

I shook my head, and Cecily stood, snapping her fingers. "Oh, I meant to tell you. Jane's possessions that had been here have been shipped back to Graycott. I believe your uncle has them. I just thought I should let you know in case you look for them in her room."

"Thanks," I choked out.

I hadn't gone into Jane's room despite it being right next door to me. I was too afraid of what I would find or not find in there. It seemed somewhat pointless to go in there if Jane wouldn't be there herself.

"Well," Cecily said as she walked toward the door, "I will contact you as soon as I have an update."

As I watched Cecily leave, I found myself oddly grateful for her for the first time. Cecily wasn't family, and I wasn't even sure if I would call her a friend yet, but I considered her trustworthy and reliable, and right now, that was about all I could really ask for.

***

With Cecily gone to keep an eye on the investigation, I found myself unable to stay in my suite. It felt like the walls were closing in, and I needed to be anywhere else, so I shoved my feet into my boots, grabbed my bag, and headed out the door. I wasn't sure exactly where I was going to go, but honestly, despite being at this school for a little while now, I still didn't know where everything was. It seemed as good a time as any to explore a little. I didn't have any classes today, so I had nothing but time to kill.

I walked out of Camden Hall and wandered aimlessly in the direction of, well, everything else. I hadn't been to the library yet, so I thought maybe that would be a good place to go, but something about the idea of silence and studying and wary, annoyed glances from my classmates turned me off to the idea. Instead, I drifted over to a slightly smaller building but no less grand near the library. I didn't know what it was, and despite desperate attempts to remember anything from Tristan's tour when I first got here, I couldn't remember anything about it. Once I was close enough, I could see the word "museum" in gold lettering above the door.

I hesitantly pushed the door open, pleasantly cooled by a blast of air conditioning, and looked around. There didn't seem to be anyone in front in charge, so I decided it was okay just to walk around. I peeked around some corners and found that no one was in here. Perfect.

I didn't exactly love looking at art or anything, but I was alone, and there were enough things to look at, read, and research to keep my mind occupied well enough. I studied some suits of armor that were apparently from centuries ago, I saw some busts of former Yore monarchs, and I even saw some tapestries and pottery that had been gifted to Lithilea by its allies. It was all very grand and beautiful, but it all felt a little too historic for my taste. I had never loved history because I struggled to find any way to connect with anything in the past unless it was music.

I turned a corner to a room of paintings that seemed to have no uniting theme whatsoever. Every other room in the museum seemed to be from a certain time period or revolving around a specific theme in history, but this room, as far as I could tell, was just random paintings.

Honestly, it was the room I had liked best so far. It felt more real, less artificial and forced.

I was never much for art myself, but I could admit that all of the paintings in here were beautiful. They were all different artistic styles, but they all portrayed the skill of the artist. I stopped a while in front of a painting of the Yore family. They all looked so serious, just like in real life most of the time. Tristan didn't smile at all, looking solemn and lofty. Talia betrayed a hint of a smile, but she remained demure and composed. Their parents looked up, as if to signify their royal status. I almost had to remind myself that I actually knew these people in real life.

Unsettled by the idea of Tristan's painted eyes boring into mine, I moved on to the landscape portrait at the end of the hall. It was beautiful. It reminded me so much of Graycott. Everything here was all desert and sand and heat, but this watercolor had ocean waves, and I felt like I could imagine that the cool air of the room was actually the ocean breeze. I glanced at the museum placard that gave the information on each piece of art, but what I read made my jaw drop:

"*Graycott*. Medium: watercolor. Artist: Jane Clarke."

I dropped to a squat, then down to my knees, and despite my best efforts, tears streamed down my face. They seemed to come faster than I could wipe them off my face, and I started to cry audibly. I had come to the museum for a distraction from everything that was happening, and instead, I had come face to face with a reminder of everything I had lost.

I held my face in my hands, but when I heard a scuff on the floor, I whipped my head around and attempted to wipe my face as dry as possible with the hem of my shirt.

"Sorry," Wade said from the end of the hall. "I didn't know anyone else was here."

I tried to laugh, but it came out more like a weird cough. "Neither did I."

"Are you okay?" After a short pause, he added, "I'm sorry, that's such a dumb question to ask right now."

Wade walked over and knelt down on the marble tile right next to me, and when I finally worked up the courage to look over at him, he was looking up at the painting.

"Is it accurate?" he asked.

"What?"

"The painting. Is it an accurate depiction of Graycott? I've never been there."

I nodded and sniffed. "It's perfect. I didn't know it was here."

Wade nodded, too. "Last year, there was an art competition. Anyone at Lithilea Prep could enter. The winner got their art displayed here in the museum. Jane won, obviously."

"She never told me."

"Probably didn't want to make a big deal about it."

"No," I said, shaking my head, "she didn't tell me because we fought so much. Sometimes we were inseparable, and other times, we barely spoke while she was here and I was in Graycott."

"Did you know she was an artist?"

"Yeah." I laughed. "She used to get paint everywhere. It made my mom furious."

I remembered her yelling at my sister for getting paint on the table, the carpet, the chairs, really anything. My dad was usually reading something in the background, clueless to what was happening, but he would always back my mom with some kind of supportive statement. I would give anything to hear all of that right now.

He chuckled. "You Clarke girls, always making a mess of things."

I felt my eyes starting to burn again. "Yeah, except Jane's messes were always beautiful. Mine are just messes."

"There always has to be a mess before something is beautiful. That's what my dad always says, at least."

I nodded, but I didn't trust my voice enough to say anything, so we both just sat in silence for a few minutes, staring at Jane's art. If I focused hard enough, I could imagine her actually painting it, blending the blues and greens to make the water, and using more yellow than I thought sand had until it looked perfect. It didn't seem like anything she created ever went through a "messy" phase.

Wade stood and seemed like he was going to leave, and before I could stop myself, I blurted out, "They were murdered."

Wade froze in his steps. "What?"

"I just got a message from the investigative team. There were explosives. It wasn't an accident."

Wade ran a hand through his hair and fidgeted. "Oh my gosh, Julia."

"I was just barely holding it together, you know? I mean, all at once, I get news that my entire family has died in a train crash, that I'm the new heir to the Graycott duchy title, and I have to leave home to come here so that everyone can compare me to Jane and find me wanting. But fine, I was handling it. How am I supposed to just go on now? I never wanted this. Any of it. I don't want to be the duchess of Graycott, I don't want to be at this stupid school, I don't want to study international relations or budgets or history. I want to be at home in Graycott playing the piano while my mother sings, smelling my father's pot roast, and watching Jane paint beautiful things like this."

I hated the way my voice sounded, all hoarse and blubbery. I hated being this person who sat on the floor and cried. I desperately wanted to turn back time, before Lithilea Prep, before the accident, before all of it. I just wanted to go back to the way everything was before.

Wade knelt next to me, brushed the hair out of my face, and then took my hand in his and gave it a squeeze. "I really wish this hadn't happened."

I snorted. "Yeah. Me, too."

"Jane was beautiful. Not just—you know—I mean she was pretty and all, but she was—"

I was surprised that I was capable of laughing. "I know what you mean."

I pushed myself up off of the floor, grabbed my bag from where it had fallen off of my shoulder, and pushed past Wade. "I'm sorry," I said, stopping only for a moment. "I didn't mean to unload that all on you."

"You have nothing to be sorry about."

"I just hate everything about being here. Everything is so hard, and everything is just a reminder of how I shouldn't be here because Jane should be here. Everyone here knows it as well as I do."

"If you ask pretty much anyone here, I'm not supposed to be here either. But I am. And so are you. That's all that really matters."

I thought about how everyone here reacted to Wade when he was around. No one wanted to associate with him. He was such an outsider, a black sheep. He obviously had a reputation for being a loner. But honestly, I probably had the same reputation. Maybe I had judged a little too harshly based on the opinions of others. I could only imagine what people said about me when I wasn't around considering what had already been said practically to my face.

"I'm sorry you had to witness this meltdown."

"Eh, I've seen worse."

I looked up at Jane's art again and felt the tears welling up, so I blinked them away as best I could and said, "Sorry."

With that, I practically ran out of the museum, leaving Wade, the painting, and everything else in that museum behind me, something I couldn't seem to do with anything else in my life.

Chapter Nine

Some people are just so hard to get along with. Does it make me a bad person to think that? I wish I could get along with everyone, but some people just make it so hard. I'm really frustrated right now because I feel like I'm trying so hard to work with people for the betterment of Lithilea, but not everyone cooperates. It makes it hard to work out any kind of realistic plan.

Sometimes the small part of me that is cynical wonders if they do it on purpose. I hate that there's a divide between the "elite" provinces and all the others, but it's the truth, and sometimes the elite representatives don't want to cooperate with us.

How are we ever going to work together one day as dukes and duchesses if we can't do it now for an assignment? I'm trying my hardest, but maybe it'll never work. Some days, it feels like everyone hates me, like everyone is out to get me. Would any of them miss me if I were gone?

***

My mind was still hung up on everything I had learned in the last twenty-four hours. Adjusting to Lithilea Prep on the heels of the deaths of my family had been hard enough, but now, I felt that I didn't have any kind of peace, no chance of moving on, until I knew exactly what had happened.

None of it made sense, and I was determined to make sense of it myself. Did the investigative team know that my father and Joe had been barely speaking before the accident? Did they know Joe hadn't gone with them? Did they even have any suspects? I knew that they didn't; the letter had said so.

I had promised Tristan that I wouldn't get in the way of the investigative team, and I had promised to share everything I knew with them, but I hadn't promised to stay out of it or to quit looking for an explanation. No one knew my family better than I did, and I was determined to get to the bottom of whatever had happened one way or another.

Unfortunately, it would have to wait until later. Right now, I had to get through another new class. It seemed like a neverending list of classes kept getting added onto my schedule. Also, unfortunately, this was another class that had everyone in it. I found my assigned seat and sat down without acknowledging anyone else or even making eye contact with them. I wasn't particularly in the mood. When Stephen waved, I waved, too, but he seemed to recognize that I wanted to be alone.

"Hey," I heard next to me, so I turned and saw Paige smiling at me. "Mind if I slide past you?"

I gestured next to me without really looking her in the eye. "Go ahead. The seat has your name on it."

She furrowed her eyebrows just slightly then slid past me and sat down. "Lady Rose kind of introduced us the other day, but I'm Lady Paige of Hadleigh."

"I know," I said, and then deciding that that was maybe a tad harsh, I held up my phone. "I studied Ledger."

"Of course."

Finally getting the hint, she turned away from me and started writing in a notebook. It was only then that I noticed that her brother Peter wasn't with her again.

"Lady Julia?" the instructor said, walking up to me with a smile. "I'm Professor Tenneton." He was exactly what I pictured a professor at this school to look like other than not being a thousand years old. He had brown hair, thick glasses, and a thicker beard, and he wore one of those jackets with the elbow patches. He was carrying a comical number of books, but he had a kind smile. "I wanted to let you know that you can skip today's class if you like."

"Skip it?"

He nodded. "In this class we discuss lineage succession and processes, and while I really don't want you to miss class since you're already behind, today's class will focus on succession in the event of unexpected retirement or untimely departure."

I nodded slowly, finally understanding. Professor Tenneton had found a kind and discreet way to acknowledge my situation, but I didn't have to take my eyes off of his face to feel the weight of the stares around me. Most of the people in this room probably wanted to see me leave the class right now, unable to discuss hypothetical circumstances that had been my reality for months, but I wasn't going to give them the satisfaction.

I shook my head. "That's fine. I'm ready to start this class."

Professor Tenneton smiled. "Well, then welcome to class. Let me know if you need help catching up."

"Thank you," I said, trying to emanate as much confidence as I possibly could.

Professor Tenneton dropped his stack of books onto the podium at the front of the room, and I wondered if he actually intended to use all of those books for this class. Did he not have an office or something where he could keep those? Did he just walk around reading randomly about lineage succession?

"Good morning, everyone," he said, and everyone echoed his good morning in a creepy cult-like way. "We're going to continue our discussion of how the lineage functions in the event of untimely or unexpected departures of the seated heir. For the royal family, it is much simpler. His Royal Highness King Tybalt is the current king, and as we all know Prince Tristan is the first heir in line followed by Princess Talia. That is actually a relatively new update in the process. The former king His Highness King Trent signed into law that the first heir of either the throne of Lithilea or a duchy can be either male or female, breaking a very old tradition of only men being eligible in succession. However, God forbid something goes wrong in the Yore family, the lineage shifts to the closest relative, though the family is very well-protected to prevent anything going wrong.

"It is similar but a little different in the duchies. As with the royal family, the lineage passes to the first-born, though abdication is far more common in the duchies. In the event of an abdication, it passes to the next oldest sibling. If there is no next sibling, it passes to the closest sibling, cousin, niece, or nephew of the abdicating heir. This is why most duchies have multiple representatives at Lithilea Prep. It is impossible to predict who will abdicate or become unable to perform their duties, so it is better to have multiple people trained for the role."

I knew all of this; it wasn't new. But it did make me wonder why I hadn't attended Lithilea Prep from the beginning. I knew the straightforward answer—I was way too far down the line to ever be in this position—but it still seemed kind of foolish on the part of my family to hear it all laid out like this. What if Jane had decided to abdicate? It was a silly thought, of course. Jane never would have abdicated. No one had ever been so enthusiastic about being a duchess.

I risked a glance at Paige. Peter still wasn't here. It had been a while since I had really looked at Ledger, but if I remembered correctly, he was the heir, not Paige. So why was she the only one that came to class most of the time?

Professor Tenneton continued, "In the event of a severe illness or death, the process is the same, though it often results in additional people attending Lithilea Prep just in case. If someone is severely ill but has the potential to recover, they remain the primary heir regardless of their health until it can be proven that they will never be capable of performing their duties at which time the title passes to the next closest relative.

"This brings us to our discussion today. Most dukes and duchesses retire and do not pass on while still serving their position, allowing for a more natural transfer of power. In the event of an untimely death of the seated heir, whatever the cause, the title immediately transfers to the next in line, and that person becomes the new duke or duchess as soon as they are sworn in. If they are too young, they are still declared the current duke or duchess, but the duchy is run by proxy of the local government until they are of age. If it is the heir who dies, then the seated duke or duchess will continue in their position until the next heir can claim the position."

Olivia's hand shot up, and she didn't wait for Professor Tenneton to call on her before she started speaking. I wondered if that was normal since she technically ranked above him or if she was just arrogant. It really was a toss-up.

"In that case, does the new heir have to complete a certain number of training hours or a certain number of semesters at Lithilea Prep? It seems odd to me to replace a qualified candidate with an unqualified one simply because something happened."

Something happened. What a lovely way to phrase my sister's death.

"Ideally, yes, that person would want to complete as much training as possible," Tenneton said. "Unfortunately, in some circumstances, that just isn't possible, and a duchy has to work with what it's got. A duke or duchess with limited training is still better than a duchy without a leader."

"What if the current duke or duchess has a child after that? Do they usurp the lineage since they are the direct line?"

Oh, I had to answer that one. "My uncle is an unmarried man in his sixties, Lady Olivia. I don't think he's having kids any time soon."

There were snickers and low murmurs around the room, and I didn't care to hide the smile that spread across my face. We all knew she was talking about me, so why shouldn't I answer her? She should have known by now that she wasn't dealing with nice, conflict-avoiding Jane. I wasn't just going to smile when she insulted me. I noticed that Tenneton's face was a little red, and I wondered if he, too, was holding back laughter.

He said, "In a hypothetical scenario, yes, but the significant age difference would mean that the other heir would probably retain control until that heir was of age."

"And if that heir is never able to catch up?" she said with her hand still raised. "If they are simply too far behind to be an effective duke or duchess? What then?"

Tenneton started to speak, but Prince Tristan held up his hand for him to stop. Lithilea Prep was such a weird dynamic. Sometimes it felt like normal school with teachers and authority, but then at any moment Tristan or Talia could completely take over, reminding everyone that the professor had no real authority at all.

Tristan stood and faced the class. "I don't think it's a good use of our time to speculate about our colleagues' abilities, don't you agree, Lady Olivia? Nor is it helpful to our efforts to build community, partnerships, and shared goals. We should all hope for the best from and for our colleagues."

Tristan had dodged my messages after we had spoken yesterday. He had convenient excuses—he was the heir after all—but I felt like I'd interacted with him enough at this point to know that he was avoiding me.

He sat, handing control of the room back to Tenneton with a gesture, and Tenneton smiled. "Prince Tristan is correct. One of the core values of Lithilea Prep is a shared desire for mutual success. Sometimes situations concerning succession are not ideal, but that is why this school was established by King Terrence. It is a way for us to help each other. After all, we are all citizens of Lithilea, and when one province prospers, they all prosper."

Olivia smiled and nodded like a good little student, but her arms were folded, and even from the back of the room, I could see her knuckles whitening from gripping her arms. It made me smile.

Tenneton seemed not to know how to continue from here, and since I had a question I'd been wondering, now seemed like a good a time as any to ask it. It might not make me very popular, but that train had left the station, so what did I have to lose?

"Professor Tenneton," I said, raising my hand. "What happens in the event of assassination?"

The room hushed, and the tension was palpable.

Tenneton said, "Assassination? Of a royal?"

I shook my head. "Of a duke or duchess. Obviously I know the line of succession would continue, but what would the process be if it was discovered that there had been an assassination?"

"That's not really relevant to this class," Olivia snapped.

"No, that's okay," Tenneton said. "Well, if it were a foreign nation attacking Lithilea, it would likely prompt investigations, diplomatic dealings, and possibly war. If it were a domestic attack, there would be an internal investigation. I imagine the consequences would be pretty severe."

Tristan shot me a glare that fully conveyed his dissatisfaction that I had asked this question publicly, but simply said, "An investigation of that magnitude would be lengthy, and *if* it were to be proven beyond a shadow of a doubt, the guilty party would likely be imprisoned and stripped of any titles. But that would be a very weighty accusation to make."

The last sentence was a warning to me. I knew that. But no one else did, and so class continued as normal. Tenneton finished his discussion of extenuating circumstances that could cause an unexpected change in rule—who knew that faking your own death was considered an abdication?—but I thought I had made my point. I had wanted to see how everyone would react to that question in case they knew anything. I knew it was unlikely that anyone in this room was responsible for my family's deaths, but I still had to try. No one seemed to have an unusual reaction, so I didn't push it. Only Tristan and Olivia had reacted with anger, albeit for different reasons, but everyone else had been surprised. I was expecting someone who knew to fake surprise or avoid eye contact, and no one had done that as far as I could tell. It was a dead-end. But I wasn't going to let this go, no matter how much Tristan wished I would.

***

Tristan texted me just before class had ended, requesting to talk afterward. I was tempted to decline—I knew what he'd say, after all—but somehow, even though he had told me that I could turn him down at any point, it still felt wrong, so I accepted. Besides, I wasn't about to turn him down after I'd been pestering him since yesterday afternoon to meet up. As everyone stood, he walked past me, gesturing with his hand for me to follow him to another room. I didn't know if I'd ever get used to being beckoned like that.

Once Tristan had closed the door behind me, he let out an exasperated sigh. "Julia, why would you ask such a provocative question in class?"

I was irritated by his disapproval, but it wasn't lost on me that he hadn't called me "Lady Julia," just *Julia*. Was that because we were finally becoming friends and he no longer felt the need for formalities, or was it more out of frustration with me for being difficult? Had I actually lost favor with Tristan?

"I had to know," I answered.

He huffed. "Had to know what?"

"About the investigation. What else, Tristan?" Somewhere in the back of my mind I was aware that I was likely breaking some kind of royal protocol, but Tristan didn't seem to react. He didn't have the slightest hint of an expression on his face. "I want to know what everyone knows about my family's murder."

"I understand that."

"That's all you have to say?"

Tristan sighed and pinched the bridge of his nose, though it wasn't out of annoyance—more like exhaustion. Or maybe pain? He was so hard to read, and I didn't have Stephen's gift of Yore insight. "Well, when I was informed of the potential attack a couple of days ago, I—"

"*Days* ago? And you didn't say anything?"

"It wasn't my place."

"Not your place? Your constituents and future leaders are murdered, and you don't think you should mention it to me?"

"It has not been confirmed yet that it was murder, and by the time I got further information, you texted me about the investigation," he said, but I let out a strangled scoffing sound in response. "Situations like these need to be handled with discretion."

"Does everyone else here know about the investigation?"

"Talia and myself. No one else. Discretion, Julia. If you keep asking questions like that in class, you're going to create talk, and trust me, it won't be the kind of talk you want."

Something didn't sit right with me about Tristan's attitude toward this whole thing. I would have thought he would have been angry or passionate or *something*. Not lecturing me for finally speaking up for myself.

I folded my arms again. "People are already talking about me. Why shouldn't I use it to my advantage? I have to find out what happened or *if* anything happened."

He leaned against the table behind him in a way that seemed oddly informal, both for this conversation and his status. "That isn't the way to find out. What did you think would happen, that someone would stand up suddenly and claim responsibility?"

"Of course not. I just thought maybe someone here would know more than I do."

"Why would we?"

"Don't you all know more than I do?"

He rolled his eyes, and there was something indescribably humorous about the crown prince of Lithilea rolling his eyes. "Don't be self-deprecating. If anyone here had any information, it would have been brought to light already." Softening a little, he added, "Julia, there's already an active investigation. The best people are on it. I made a call myself to make sure they are using all available resources and manpower."

"You made a call?" Tristan had actually put in a royal order on my behalf? Or was he doing some kind of damage control, trying to keep this whole thing quiet?

He nodded. "Of course I did. I do take this seriously, whether or not you believe it."

"I do believe it, I just—"

"I understand your desperation, but please trust me that it's being handled."

Tristan was doing that thing he didn't do often—at least he hadn't with me in the short time I'd known him—where he was talking down to me, pulling rank, and reminding me that I couldn't question him, not really. "I can't just sit here and do nothing."

He put a hand on my shoulder, and I was shocked by its weight. "You are doing something. You are preparing to be the Duchess of Graycott someday. That is the most important thing you can do right now. Now, will you please promise me that you'll be less reckless in the future?"

This time, I rolled my eyes, but he didn't look away or remove his hand from my shoulder. "Yes, I'll be less reckless." I hadn't promised I'd stop looking into this, though.

"Good." He opened the door and gestured for me to walk out, not seeming to want to follow. "Please try to relax, okay? For me?"

I caught sight of Olivia attempting to bore a hole straight through my head simply with her gaze, so I smiled at Tristan and said, "I'll try, for you."

I walked out of the room without making eye contact with Olivia. If she wanted to cause a scene, I wasn't going to make it easy for her. She'd have to commit. The door closed behind me, and I realized that Tristan had stayed back, and I kind of wondered why, but any thought about Tristan was interrupted by Olivia stepping into my path.

"Getting kind of friendly with Prince Tristan, are we?" Olivia said with a sneer.

"Isn't that the whole point of this school?" I said.

"I know you haven't been here long, but the *point* is to learn how to govern your own duchy, not suck up to the future king."

"Like it or not, Olivia, one day I will be duchess of a province just like you, and we'll have to learn to work together and with Prince Tristan."

"What were you even talking about?"

"It's really none of your business."

Her eyes narrowed. "Well, you should know that Prince Tristan and I are kind of a thing."

"Good for you."

"Which means you and he are not a thing."

I actually laughed out loud. "If you're really that insecure, then I'm not your biggest problem."

She stopped walking, checking around us to see if anyone was listening, and when she decided we were sufficiently out of earshot, she hissed, "Watch it, Graycott. You don't have any idea who you're dealing with. You may have lucked into this position, but—"

"Luck?" I said loudly, now hoping someone would overhear me. "You think I 'lucked into' being duchess? You think my family dying is 'lucky'?"

Flustered, she stuttered, "I-I just mean that—"

"No, I think you said what you meant. I know you don't want me here, and frankly, I don't want to be here either with you shallow, self-obsessed people if it means that my family is gone. But they are, and I am here, so deal with it. You're not going to get rid of me, and you're not going to stop me from doing my job here, whether you like it or not. So *you* watch it."

She huffed and stormed off, and I was proud of the fact that I had silenced Olivia even for a moment. Actually, *she* didn't know who she was dealing with. I may have been conflicted before, but not anymore, not now that I found out that my family had been attacked. Tristan wanted me to calm down, but I wasn't going to stop now until I got the truth, until someone paid for it. And if there were a few social casualties along the way, then so be it.

Chapter Ten

*A*pril 10 —

What is a friend? I don't mean that to sound super philosophical or anything, but seriously, what is a friend? I'm starting to think I don't know. It seems that everyone around me is either faking it or wants something in return. Is all friendship conditional? Is real, genuine friendship a myth?

I consider Tristan a friend, but isn't he here doing a job just like me? Aren't we forced to interact for the sake of the country we'll one day lead?

Rose is my best friend, but would she be if we weren't in school together? Is it a friendship of convenience?

Wade calls himself my friend, but is that just so we'll study together? Is he only passing his classes because of me? Do I care? Does he?

Julia and I always insist we're friends, but are we? If we weren't sisters, would we be friends? We're so different.

There are other people here that I consider myself friendly with. I might even call them friends. But do I really know them, know anything about them beyond their name, province, and position in the line of succession? Does that make me a fake? Or does that mean I'm playing the game just right, just like everyone else?

***

It was hot outside—it was always hot here, it seemed—but today I found that I didn't mind it. I was used to the heat since Graycott was pretty much always hot and humid unless you were on the coastline and could hope for a stray breeze. The dry heat of central Lithilea was something I wasn't really prepared for, but there was something refreshing about it. The humid air in Graycott was so heavy and oppressive. This heat felt clean, dry, purifying. Somehow, the hot air and visible sizzle felt good in the way that a hot shower feels good after a long day or the way baking in the sun on the beach until you almost burn doesn't feel as hot as walking through town. Maybe it was melodramatic, but I liked feeling the heat. I liked feeling anything.

It was quiet here. I was tucked a little ways off from the main trails, and that was intentional. I didn't want to run into anyone, but I knew Stephen would know exactly where to find me. It was where he had shared dried mango with me and offered the first sincere condolence I had ever heard. It wasn't possible, of course, but in a weird way, it felt like Stephen had given me a part of my sister back, and I intended to get more of her back, whatever it took.

I checked my phone for a message from Stephen, but I didn't see one. I scrolled through Ledger for a few moments, but my eyes were glazed over, and I didn't really internalize anything I read. Somehow, it bothered me that the report about my family's not-so-accidental accident wasn't on Ledger at all. I had expected to be—I had braced myself for the fallout when that news became public, but it never did. Tristan assured me that was a security measure while the investigation was active, but somehow I resented it. If it had been Aerilot or Bredon or another elite province, would it have been newsworthy, or did we just not care about Graycott? Well, I was determined to make it everyone's business whether they liked it or not. Didn't they all tell me constantly how much they loved and respected my sister? I was prepared to make them prove it.

I heard the crunching of footsteps coming up the pathway, so I shoved my phone aside and peered around, careful to keep myself inconspicuous if it wasn't Stephen, but happily, I saw his honeyed hair and eyes and caught myself staring at his smile when he saw me. Stephen had a way about him—he always made me feel at ease.

"Hey," he said, sitting next to me, just as we had on Saturday. "Don't think this is your special hangout spot now. I have dibs."

I laughed, but it came out more like a hideously unattractive snort. "Dibs? Are we eight?"

"No." He shrugged. "But we're future political leaders. Isn't that all politics is? Calling dibs on stuff that doesn't belong to you?"

"Careful, don't let the school officials hear you. You'll get yourself kicked out of school."

"Nah, they can't. I'm all Idlewick's got."

He'd meant it as a lighthearted joke, but somehow it sounded sad. His jokes always did. "I never asked. Do you not have any siblings?"

He shook his head. "Only child. My mom had a lot of miscarriages before me, and she had a lot of complications giving birth to me. Too dangerous to produce another heir."

It amazed me how Stephen managed to say such cynical things with a genuine smile on his face and levity in his voice. I'd always considered myself a realist, but Jane would claim that that was just what pessimists call themselves because they don't want to admit that they're negative all the time. Looking at Stephen, I wondered whether he'd consider himself an optimist or a pessimist, and I also wondered which one was actually true.

I said, "So, I guess it's really important you don't flunk out then. What would Idlewick do?"

I didn't expect a real answer to my sarcastic question, but he gave one anyway. "Honestly, I don't know. I don't have any cousins. Not close ones, anyway. I come from a lot of only children. But my grandfather is still the duke right now, so I've still got my dad's whole reign ahead of me."

"Jane used to complain about that. She said she wouldn't get to be a duchess until she was a grandma because our uncle seems like he's eternal."

"I've never heard you mention him. Your uncle, I mean. Do you get to talk to him often?"

It wasn't Stephen's fault, but I didn't like the use of the word "get" like it was a privilege to talk to Joe. I dealt with Joe when I had to, but I didn't really need to talk to him.

Instead of answering him, I pulled out the letter and held it out to Stephen who took it without question. "This is why I asked you to meet me today."

"Oh," he said, and there seemed to be a hesitancy in his voice and the way he took the letter. He skimmed quickly, but I saw the moment his eyes backtracked and reread the critical moment. His eyes lingered there like he expected the words to change, the same way I waited for them to evolve or offer something, *anything* more than what little they provided.

"When did you get this?" he asked.

"A couple of days ago, but I didn't read it right away. I assumed it was a routine communication."

Stephen chewed the inside of his cheek for a moment. "Is this why you were asking questions about assassination in class the other day?"

This time, I shrugged. "I needed to know the answer, and I wanted to see how everyone else would react."

"Well, how did you expect everyone to react? Who else knows?"

"Wade. I kind of melted down in the museum the other day, and he happened to be there."

Stephen clenched his jaw. "Anyone else?"

"Tristan. I think that's it."

He sat back a little. "Tristan?"

"Yeah, well, I didn't know that he knew, but I guess being the prince and all."

He nodded slowly. "Yeah, that makes sense. Have you found anything else out yet?"

I shook my head. "Tristan says the investigation is pretty complex, but I haven't heard anything, and if he has, he isn't telling me."

"He'd tell you if he knew anything."

"I guess so." I still didn't like the way Tristan had reacted to me yesterday, but I knew it was futile to complain about him to Stephen. Stephen would defend him like his own blood.

Stephen lifted his hand before hesitating, then took my hand in both of his and gave it a gentle squeeze. "Julia, I'm so sorry. I don't know what to say."

"I have to know what happened. Will you help me?"

"Help you do what? What are you going to do?"

"I'm not sure. But I can't sit around and wait for the investigation. Who knows how long that will take? I need to do some research, and honestly, I don't even know where to begin. I don't know anything about Lithilea, it seems, and you, well, you've been here for a long time, and I don't really trust anyone else here."

He chuckled. "A ringing endorsement."

"Will you help me?"

He still hadn't let go of my hand, so I placed my free hand on top of his. He stared at them for a moment before sighing and lifting his eyes to mine. "What do you need?"

****

Tristan didn't want me to tell anyone else, but if we were going to figure this thing out, there was no pretending: we needed more people.

If nothing else, I needed people to be around when I wasn't to hear what gets said behind my back. I wasn't sure that I necessarily wanted to hear all of that, but I knew that the conversations going on without me were probably more useful than the ones going on that included me.

So far, the only person who had shown up to my suite was Tristan, and he was none too happy about everyone else being late.

"I'm not even sure why you want to include anyone else," he said.

"People are not going to be honest with you."

"And why not?"

I rolled my eyes. "Seriously?"

He huffed. "Fine, but I still think you're taking this to an extreme level. Do you not trust the investigative team? After all, they are the ones who discovered the explosives and alerted you. They must be doing something right."

"I'm not saying that I don't trust them, but I also know that someone here probably knows more than we think."

"Why, why do you think that? Why would anybody—"

"I don't know, but don't you know when your family is doing something even when you're not with them?" I asked, and he nodded rather reluctantly. "Well, someone else might, too."

"Why are you so sure it's an internal problem?"

"Who's going to attack us? Lithilea isn't at war, and we currently have no antagonistic dealings either. There's no threat of war anywhere. Why would another country attack us? Besides, the real hostility is internal with all of the animosity between the provinces."

He sat back. "You've researched Lithilea's international standings?"

"You really thought I wouldn't make sure if this could've been foreign terrorism?"

"No, it's not that, it's just—you really sounded like a duchess just then."

"Future duchess."

He shook his head. "I said what I meant."

Something about the way he was looking at me—I couldn't be sure of what I thought, but Olivia's words floated back into my head despite my best intentions. It was too much eye contact, too little nervous fidgeting, too intense. I couldn't help but wonder if maybe Olivia saw something that I didn't.

"You once told me that I should always be frank with you," I said.

He looked puzzled. "I did."

"So can I do that now?"

"Be frank?"

"Yes." I said, and he gestured for me to continue. "Okay, in order for what I'm about to say to make sense, I have to tell you something, and I don't want you to freak out or do anything about it. It's just context. Okay?"

"All right."

"Olivia and I had a—a less than pleasant conversation the other day after class, and—"

"What did she say?" he said angrily.

"Context, remember. Context."

He sighed. "Fine. Go on."

"Anyway, she got pretty jealous with me."

"Jealous? Over what?"

"Uh, over you."

At first, he didn't move or say anything, but after a moment, he very suddenly burst out laughing. It was so shocking that I found myself laughing, too, though I didn't know what the joke was. He composed himself after a moment, but he still chuckled slightly.

"You don't have to worry about that."

"Because she's wrong?"

"Because we're not together."

"Oh, I kind of assumed—"

"We dated once," he said. "A few years ago. It seemed like the 'right' thing to do at the time. It would be respectable for me to marry someone from Aerilot, but it never would have worked. It would have been very challenging for her to be duchess and queen. Impossible, even. She could abdicate, I suppose, but she'd never let her brother Owen be duke."

"Oh."

"And I never loved her. I don't think she really loved me either."

"Can I ask why?"

He fidgeted, flicking his thumbs back and forth. "We weren't right for each other. I guess you could say she's not my type?" After a long pause, he added, "And I found that I loved someone else."

Someone else? Who? Was Olivia right? "That's not me, is it? Because Olivia—"

He held up his hands. "No, no, I'm sorry, I didn't mean to give you that impression. Not that you're not wonderful, it's just—"

"No, I get it."

"We've only just gotten to know each other, and—"

"Well, I wouldn't want to—"

"Oh, of course."

We sat in silence for a few moments after that, carefully avoiding eye contact. Well, at least it wasn't me. I was glad for that. I liked Tristan as a friend and ally, but I didn't want him to be more than that, and I definitely didn't want the pressure of having to turn down the crown prince of Lithilea.

He looked up. "You weren't asking because you—"

"No," I said quickly. "I just wanted to make sure that Olivia wasn't right."

"I value our friendship, Julia. That is all."

"Same here."

We both laughed nervously, letting the tension in the room dissipate.

His mouth twitched up into a smirk. "Besides, I'm pretty sure someone else is interested in you, and I wouldn't want to interfere."

"Who?"

"Is it not obvious?"

"Clearly not."

"Julia, I'm not totally out of the loop, you know. I think I know my best friend well enough to know when he has feelings for someone."

It took me a moment to put the pieces together. "Stephen? Did he say something?"

He shook his head. "But I've known since the day I saw you eating lunch together."

"It wasn't exactly a date. Valerie was with us."

"That hardly matters. I've never seen him look at someone quite the way he watched you that day."

Stephen was *watching* me? I wasn't totally sure how I felt about that.

"Don't tell me you never noticed," he said.

"I never noticed."

He chuckled. "You will now."

Before I could come up with a snappy response, there was a knock on my door, and when I saw Stephen's face as I opened the door, I suddenly became paranoid that perhaps he had heard everything. But a smile and a mock bow assured me that he was still in the dark, though apparently I was the one that had been in the dark.

"Hey," he said, offering a truly endearing smile. Then, noticing Tristan: "Oh hey, Tristan. I didn't know you were going to be here also."

He smiled. "Hope it's all right if I crash the party."

I shot him a glare, and I swore that I saw mischief in his eyes. "A few others might also be coming."

"Are you talking about me again?" Wade said, turning the corner and leaning against the door frame.

"Wade?" Stephen said.

"One and only."

Stephen pressed his lips together, turning to face me. "I didn't realize you invited Wade."

"Should we be expecting anyone else?" Tristan asked.

I shrugged. "I asked Valerie, but I don't think she's coming."

"Why not?"

"I think she's still mad at me."

Stephen chuckled. "You're still mad at her."

"Okay fine, but I still asked her."

Tristan furrowed his eyebrows. "Why are you mad at Valerie?"

Stephen, Wade, and I simultaneously shot him a look as I said, "Really?"

He sunk down into the sofa a little. "Oh, yes."

I wasn't sure if I was allowed to sit on the same sofa with Tristan—and I couldn't help but think how silly that thought even sounded to myself—but I decided not to risk it, so I sat on the sofa across from him. When Wade sat down next to me, Stephen seemed unsure where to sit. It looked like he started toward the open seat next to Tristan, but Tristan propped his elbow up on the headrest next to him and seemed to stretch out blocking the seat, so Stephen awkwardly sat on the other side of me. I wondered if Tristan had done it on purpose; was he trying to get Stephen to sit next to me? Of course, I could have just been paranoid after the conversation we'd had, and Tristan did not betray a bit of emotion, so I suppressed the thoughts as much as I could. This was about Jane and my parents, not me. I had to focus.

I could tell that Stephen wasn't happy about Wade being there, but he already knew about the investigation because I had told him in the museum, and I felt like he understood. I was aware that he was not the most popular person at this school, but then again, neither was I, so what did that really matter? Wade had a bit of a reputation for being a loner, and he didn't seem to get along with anyone particularly well except for me and maybe Rose, but if I cared enough to ask someone, I likely had the same reputation: *She's a loner. She only ever talks to Stephen. She's certainly not her sister. Poor man's Jane Clarke.* Reputation was not something that was going to stand in my way, for myself or anybody else.

"Here's the deal. I don't exactly have many allies here."

"Julia, that's not true," Tristan said.

"No, it is. You can say what you want about how we're all supposed to be on the same team, but the fact is that most people here do not see it that way."

Wade stretched his arm out across the sofa back behind me, and his hand nearly brushed Stephen's shoulder. I saw Stephen lean away. Wade said, "Can't give Olivia and her groupies that much power. They're no different than regular mean girls in high school."

"Except they have real power," Stephen said, a hint of irritation touching his words.

"The point is," I continued, "that I don't particularly trust anyone else at this school outside of this room. Well, except maybe Valerie. Somehow I think she'd be painfully honest even if I didn't want her to be."

"You could trust other people, too," Stephen said, a little softer this time. "Lithilea Prep isn't all Olivias and Matildas."

"That may be, but so far, you three are it. So I need your help."

"Anything, beautiful."

I winced when Wade called me "beautiful." It felt like the kind of thing that shouldn't happen at this level—did guys really still refer to female colleagues as "beautiful" that casually? Didn't we have the same ranking? I guess sexism pervaded even this space that seemed to strive for some level of equality.

I noticed that Stephen flinched, too. I couldn't stop the small smirk that crept onto my face. I could certainly respect a man who reacted that way to such so-called endearments.

I said, "There's an active investigation into what happened, but they have not yet figured out whether it was internal or external. Personally, I think internal is the only logical explanation."

"Why is that?" Tristan asked.

"If an enemy of Lithilea wanted to arrange some kind of attack on the country, I just don't think they would pick Graycott and not even target the current duke."

"There are still a lot of unanswered questions about that," Tristan said, and I could tell that he was getting frustrated with me and trying to hide it.

"She makes a good point," Stephen said. "I hate to say it, but if someone really wanted to cause damage to Lithilea, they would target an elite province, a major land border, or—well—you," he said, pointing to Tristan. "It just doesn't make sense that it was an enemy."

"Besides," I added, "Lithilea isn't at war with anyone right now, and neither are the allies."

Tristan seemed to want to add something to that, but he refrained, and I decided not to push it.

I continued: "I don't believe that everyone here is being totally honest, and I'm too new here to know what's going on with everyone. I want to look into anyone that would have had reason to want my sister and my parents dead. Even if someone wasn't involved, they might know more than they are willing to say. I just think that there has to be some kind of clue that someone here has."

Tristan sighed deeply. "Julia, there is an active investigation. They are using every resource available to them, and that is more than you have here. What do you think you're going to find that they won't?"

I wasn't sure exactly, to be honest, and I was tired of Tristan dismissing me by repeating that same old thing about the investigation. I just knew that I couldn't possibly sit around and wait for them to find something. I owed it to Jane to figure out what happened to her, and I only trusted myself to do it.

"The investigators didn't know Jane like I did," I said finally, and I felt it was true. "I know things about her that no one else would know, and I'm sure people here knew and saw things that the investigative team wouldn't find out. I'm not saying everyone here is a killer—"

"It kind of sounds that way," Tristan said abruptly, and it seemed he regretted his words immediately as he pressed his lips together until they turned white.

Stephen finished my thought: "People might not realize that information they have could be meaningful, and unless the investigative team has reason to contact students here, they probably won't."

"Yes, exactly," I said.

"I'll keep my ear to the ground," Wade said, "but I'm not sure what I'd be listening for."

"Anything. Everything. We can decide if it's important later."

"Julia," Tristan said, his tone softer than before. "I'm worried that you don't know what you're getting into. Let's say you're right and someone here did have reason to hurt Jane. Aren't you concerned they could come after you?"

I hadn't allowed myself to consider that possibility, but yes, I was concerned. I didn't like to think about it because it still felt so unreal that my family had been murdered and were not just the victims of a horrible twist of fate. As much as I had wished I didn't exist in the wake of their deaths, I didn't want to die and certainly not at the hands of the very people I wanted to bring to justice as a form of vengeance.

"I can't just sit by and not do anything," I said. "It's my responsibility to find out what happened to my family."

"I'd hate to see anything happen to you," he said, and I believed that he meant it. Tristan and I had had our issues, but I didn't think he'd lie to my face.

"I'll be fine," I said, and I didn't believe myself as strongly as I had believed him.

"We'll make sure you're safe," Wade said, and it was probably the most sincere thing I'd ever heard him say.

Stephen said, "I don't know if anyone would tell me anything."

"They might tell you more than you think," Wade said. "Especially if Prince Tristan is around."

"What do you mean by that?" Stephen said, obviously irritated.

Wade shrugged. "You never know what people will do to get close to the royal family."

Stephen leaned forward to say something, but he glanced over at me and sighed. "I'll tell you if I hear anything," he said to me.

"Thanks,"

"I'm still not sure about this," Tristan said.

"I'm not going to give up," I said. "Nothing is going to stop me until I figure out what happened one way or another."

Tristan seemed about to say something, but his phone rang, and when he checked the caller ID, he furrowed his brow. "I'm sorry, but I have to take this. I'll talk to you later, Julia."

Tristan shook Stephen's hand, and when Wade held his out, he paused only for a moment and then shook his as well. He walked out so briskly that I felt a breeze as he passed me. Stephen lingered, seeming unsure whether or not he wanted to stay.

"I should probably get going," he finally said, his eyes flicking briefly to Wade. "Julia, do you still want to study together tomorrow after class?"

"Yes."

He smiled slightly. "Great. I'll see you then."

He waited as if expecting something more, but neither I nor Wade said anything else, and so he left. When the door clicked behind him, Wade sighed.

"I'm so sorry you're dealing with all of this. Are you doing okay?"

No, obviously not. "I'm fine. As fine as I could be, I guess."

"It's so hard to lose someone suddenly. People really don't get it unless they've lived through it."

"That's true," I said, though I wasn't sure Wade really could understand. No one did. People don't lose family members to intentional train explosions every day.

"Did you ever hear about how I ended up here?" he asked, and I shook my head. "My uncle was the duke of Dalmerlin, and he died, and he didn't have kids. My mother had gone to Lithilea Prep with him when they were young, but she never expected to be the duchess. All of a sudden, I found myself here, too."

I was surprised. I didn't think anyone here was like me. It seemed like everyone had been here forever and was just built for the role. I didn't realize anyone else had wound up here because of a family tragedy.

"How did he die?" I asked.

"Heart attack," he said, but he didn't seem to flinch or react to his own words. I knew the feeling well. At some point, it's self-preservation to go totally numb. "It was pretty unexpected. He was healthy, worked out twice a week. The doctors were as surprised as we were."

I didn't say *I'm sorry* or *that must be really hard* or any of the other idiotic phrases people had said to me. It didn't help, and they didn't really mean it. It was usually pity or attempts at empathy, but it fell flat when the person who was saying it had a life that wasn't totally crumbling into pieces before their eyes.

Instead, I asked, "How do you do it? Be here, I mean. Does it ever get easier?"

He shrugged. "I guess so. Lithilea Prep, it's all about finding your groove."

I snorted. "Your groove?"

"Yeah. Everyone is good at something, as cliche as it sounds. You just have to find what you care about, what you can actually do for your province. Eventually, you figure out where you fit even if others don't think you do."

"Easy to say when you're from an elite province, you know."

His smirk faltered a little. "Look, I know that the in-fighting here is brutal, but we'll all be working together someday."

"You sound like Tristan."

He shifted. "I doubt it. But you have as much of a right to be here as your sister did."

I looked at Wade. Sometimes, he got under my skin. He seemed to be an expert schmoozer, and normally I didn't care for his attitude or his demeanor. But then I had conversations with him like this and like the day at the museum. He was the first person who had even come close to understanding my life. Maybe the side of Wade that I didn't like was just an exterior, a front. Everyone here put up a front, and that included Tristan and his sister. Maybe Wade's front just wasn't curated to be desirable or likable. Something about that was appealing to me: he didn't live his life to earn the favor of others.

"Can I be honest about something?" I asked.

"Of course."

"I just don't know how to do this without Jane. I wasn't supposed to be here at all, and I just don't see any way that this works without her. We were always such a good pair. We balanced each other, you know? We're so different, and we knew how to help each other. I just don't have anyone like her in my life anymore."

He nodded slowly. "It's so hard. My uncle was such a good duke. My mom is good, but my uncle was made for that position. I wish I could have learned from him."

"I wish I could have learned from Jane."

We sat in silence for a few moments. It wasn't that I didn't know what to say, but it felt like there just wasn't anything to say. It wasn't an uneasy silence; it was the silence of understanding and shared experience.

I was glad I had invited Wade even if Tristan didn't trust him and Stephen didn't like him. He understood a part of me that I hoped, for their sakes, Tristan and Stephen never would. I didn't know where

Wade and I would end up, but I felt more comfortable around him than I did most everyone else here.

After a few minutes, Wade stood. "I should get going. I have an appointment. Thanks for trusting me, Julia. I hope we can carve out some kind of friendly partnership for our provinces."

"Me, too."

Wade kissed my hand as he always did—a strange habit, but I didn't feel like rejecting it—and left me to myself.

What I had said to Wade was true: I needed Jane somehow. I missed her, and it felt so wrong to be here at this school that she attended for years without her. I needed something, *anything*, to cling to that was hers.

I stepped into the hallway, checking to see if anyone was around, and when I was sure no one was, I stepped in front of the door that still had Jane's name on it. I had assumed that the door would be locked, so when the handle turned, and I pushed the door open, I was surprised by how sad it made me. I stepped inside without turning on the light. There was enough sunlight coming through to see, and somehow turning on the light felt illegal or like I was going to get caught sneaking into a room—a room no one was occupying. A room I couldn't technically break into because it wasn't anyone's.

The room was identical to mine in layout and style. The bathroom and bedroom were both clean, though the bed linens had been stripped and the bathroom mirror betrayed some dust when the light from the hallway hit it. The little office nook looked the same except the desk was cleaner than mine and no computer sat on it. But when I turned the corner to the back room, the sob that had been choking my throat finally forced its way through. Sitting in front of the window mostly covered with gauzy curtains was a large cherry wood easel. There were no paint supplies in the room, and the easel bore no canvas, but I immediately pictured the floor strewn with rejected canvases, paint-splattered sheets of paper, and half-opened tubes of paint. I could picture a cup of dirty paint water filled with brushes sitting on the pull-out table on the side of the easel. I could picture Jane standing here painting as she always had at home.

The easel had a glass backing, and there were multiple pull-out resources, most of which I didn't understand the purpose for, but I knew Jane must have. I used to sneak into her room at home and watch her paint. I was always amazed by it. She had always said that I was much better at playing the piano than she was at painting, but I couldn't create like she could. I could play music already written by someone else and make it sound beautiful because it already was. I couldn't take a blank canvas and create something beautiful on it out of nothing but colored paints. I never understood how she did that.

But really, that was what Jane did in everything. She always made everything she touched beautiful. She made her room at home beautiful, she made me beautiful when she styled my hair or did my makeup, she made other people beautiful with the way she would make them laugh or smile. She would have made Graycott beautiful if she'd had the chance.

I sat on the floor, clutching the easel and sobbing like a small child. I had so little of her left. Pieces of her were getting erased at every turn, both here at Lithilea Prep and at home. I couldn't lose any more of her—I just couldn't.

I knew that her personal possessions had been shipped back to Joe at the Graycott estate, and I desperately wanted those things. Technically, Jane had left everything she owned to me, but since that was all stuff she'd had with her on the train, it had been temporarily confiscated as evidence, so by the time it was released, I was already here at school. I didn't know what I thought I'd find in her stuff that would help me, but somehow, I felt that anything that was hers would matter. Any post-it that she scribbled a note on, her doodles on her class notes, canvases she had discarded, letters she and I exchanged, anything.

So I did what I swore I would never do: I went back to my suite, grabbed a piece of Lithilea Prep letterhead and wrote a letter to Joe, as short as possible, to ask him to mail Jane's things to me.

Chapter Eleven

*M*ay 28—

By far, without a doubt, unequivocally, my least favorite class is "Domestic Relations." It's so stressful. I feel like I never know what I'm doing in that class. It really scares me how bad I am at it because it's supposed to be the most realistic class I'm taking. Uncle Joe says it functions exactly like parliamentary meetings, and that's why I'm so nervous. What does it matter if I learn all the content and ace all the tests if I can't handle this? I've always been a good student, and that's always been celebrated, but I'm not sure it really matters in the end. It feels like school, both in Graycott and at Lithilea Prep, is kind of a waste if it hasn't really prepared me for the real world.

But maybe school isn't the problem. Maybe I'm really good at memorizing and studying and test-taking, but I'm not good at proposing bills or designing legislation at all.

What if Julia and I had started going to Lithilea Prep at a really young age? Would I feel more confident in my abilities if we had? There are so many students here who started at nine or ten years old. I didn't start until I was twelve. I guess that was the point when my dad and everyone else realized that Uncle Joe really was never going to get married and have kids. I know it was kind of controversial that my parents didn't enroll Julia and I right away, but Dad saw no reason to rush us into something. Besides, I'm glad that I didn't start until later. Julia and I had a chance at a normal childhood.

Some of my classmates have younger siblings that I've never spoken to or rarely get to hear from. It's like they don't matter because they're not the primary heir. Olivia's sister pretty much never speaks in class. Matilda's brother is younger. Nicole's is older. Valerie and Vaughn are close, and so are Paige and Peter, though Valerie and Paige are definitely the more vocal siblings despite being the "spares." Ugh, I hate that term. It seems so insignificant. But is that what younger siblings have to do to avoid being considered insignificant? Be loud and vocal? Is that why Julia is so strong-willed? Does she think she's insignificant compared to me?

***

I'd never taken a class as strange as my "Domestic Relations" class. Aside from the content, all of my other classes felt like normal high school classes. I attended, a professor lectured, sometimes students asked or answered questions, and we were assigned homework. This was the one class that functioned more like a group study session. There was no professor for this class; instead, Tristan led it. It was such a strange format without an actual professor in charge. It felt a little bit like a random group hangout with people who didn't always particularly like each other. The goal of this class was to mimic what future parliamentary meetings would be like with all of us working together. I was told that sometimes current dukes or duchesses attended to facilitate discussions, but that hadn't happened yet since I had started attending.

We sat at several long tables arranged in a massive rectangle around the room. The Yores sat at one table. At each of the other tables were two seats, ideally one for each representative. The chair next to me was painfully vacant. I wondered if Jane used to feel my absence in these meetings.

The only other tables with vacancies were Idlewick, Dalmerlin, and Eastcliffe as Stephen and Wade were only children and Nicole's brother was the ruling duke. Everyone else had two representatives, and I found myself wondering if every current duke or duchess had decided to have exactly two children close together in age to carry on the lineage or if there were forgotten third, fourth, fifth children at home that felt unimportant as I had for many years. I knew that there were some younger siblings here in other classes, but were there more? I wondered if information like that could be found on Ledger. Were those siblings considered significant enough to be put on Ledger?

I actually didn't mind this class. This was the only class that actually felt useful because we were discussing real-world problems that were currently affecting the provinces in Lithilea. Some of the other classes felt kind of forced or pointless, like classes they decided they probably should offer but didn't really teach anything, but this class was the only class that made me feel at least somewhat competent in government.

I'd gotten there early, so I was by myself in the classroom for a while before anyone came in. First it was Paige and Peter from Hadleigh, and they both avoided any interaction, which was perfectly fine with me. Rose and her sister Rachel entered, too, and they chatted mostly with each other, though both stopped by my table to say hello. Rose wasn't getting on my nerves nearly as much anymore. She and I didn't exactly mesh, but she meant well, and considering that I didn't have many allies, I had to take the ones I could get, and Rose had done nothing but try to be nice to me.

Olivia, her brother Owen, Matilda, her brother—even though he was much younger and was only in this class to fill out the room—and

Nicole entered after, and all went to their seats without talking to anyone else. Rose and Rachel had stepped aside to talk to Peter and Paige, so there was no one between me and Nicole. I didn't think that I'd even spoken to Nicole since starting here, and it seemed she didn't talk to anyone herself. She seemed like the kind of person I should get to know. People often didn't notice really quiet people like that. Who knew what she'd overheard lately.

"Lady Nicole," I said, quietly enough that I didn't draw attention but just loudly enough that she turned. "I don't think we've officially met. I'm Lady Julia."

She smiled, and though it was a very small smile, it seemed genuine. "Nice to meet you. How do you like Lithilea Prep so far?"

I looked around and lowered my voice. "Can I be honest?" She nodded in reply, so I got up and sat in the empty chair next to her. "It's so hard."

She chuckled in reply. "Tell me about it. This is all pretty overwhelming."

It was working. She was getting more comfortable with me.

"Have you attended here long?" I asked.

She nodded. "Since I was nine, so about six years, I suppose. Wow, time flies."

I hadn't realized she was only fifteen, but it made sense. She probably isolated herself because she was younger than the rest of us. It seemed like most of the students in our classes were somewhere between sixteen and nineteen. I never interacted with the younger students at the school. "You're the second person who's told me they started here at nine years old. I can't even imagine starting that young."

"It's the normal starting age."

"Still."

She shrugged. "It wasn't so bad back then. My brother Nolan used to attend back then, too, so at least we were together."

"He's the current duke of Eastcliffe, right?"

"Yes. There's a bit of an age gap between us. He left a few years ago."

"And you don't have other siblings?"

She shook her head. "But it's okay. When he goes to Lithilea Castle or the capitol for business, he stops by to see me. Plus, I'm taking extra classes to try to graduate early. I might be able to get back to Eastcliffe by the time I'm seventeen."

"Wow, that's impressive," I said, and I meant it. I hadn't even realized that graduating early was an option. I couldn't blame her for wanting to get out of here faster, but I was impressed by her work ethic. Maybe that was why I never saw her: she must have studied all the time.

"I just want to get back to Eastcliffe, you know?" she said. "Not just because I miss Nolan but because he could use the help. He's kind of on his own in our province, so the sooner I can get back there, the better."

"Is he struggling?"

"Kind of. He became the duke really young, and he's never really had any support. He's not even married. I just think it's too much work for one person, and now he's overwhelmed. I just want us to be a team, you know?"

I nodded, but I found her words deeply unsettling. Was the job too much for one person? I'd only ever known Graycott being governed by Joe. He'd always seemed fine. Was it just easier for him because he was older and Nicole's brother was so young? Maybe my dad used to help out more than I ever realized and eased some of the burden.

Would I be able to handle this on my own one day? I would have to now that the rest of my family was gone. Maybe that was why Jane was so upset with me for not coming here with her. Maybe it had nothing to do with wanting to spend time with me or thinking I was directionless. Maybe she hadn't wanted to do this job alone. And I had left her all alone.

And now I was all alone.

I struggled to find something to say in response to Nicole, but I couldn't think of anything that would feel at once authentic but not like over-sharing. I was saved from having to respond when Tristan stood at his table, and all the others who had entered while Nicole and I had been talking took their seats, so I gave Nicole a small wave and returned to my own table. Stephen smiled at me from his table next to mine.

"Good morning, everyone," Tristan said. "I'm glad to see you all today. Our goal for today's meeting is to cover the primary needs of each of your provinces. While your relatives back home may have current plans to address each of your provinces' concerns, I want you to think beyond that. What could you do to further address the current issue of your province, or what other current issue could you begin to tackle now? I want you to have a forward-thinking mindset. Many of you have very limited time left at Lithilea Prep, and soon you will return to your duchy. You may not take power for many years, but you will begin your work immediately upon graduation. I want you all to be able to go back to your province with something practical."

I smiled a little to myself. Tristan had told me to start thinking about what I wanted to do for Graycott. He was preparing me for this moment so that I wouldn't step into it blind. It was likely that the others here had been working on this for a while, so I was grateful for the heads up. Of course, the thing I most wanted to do for Graycott was to find my family's killer, but that wasn't something I could casually bring up in the middle of class. I was pretty sure that Tristan's head would explode if I did that. Still, I knew that if I was going to learn anything from my classmates—if they knew anything—I would have to be subtle. I had decided on a decoy issue. It was realistic, so it wouldn't be wasted effort, but I would also be able to learn other things in the process. Hopefully Tristan didn't catch on.

Tristan sat down next to Talia and said, "Would anyone like to start?"

No one volunteered right away, but after a moment, Vaughn stood and cleared his throat. "We've been working on some education reforms for Lithilea for some time. Our concern is that we do not have sufficient STEM curricula to train students for the extensive STEM career opportunities we're trying to offer nationwide. There's a significant disparity."

"Agreed," Wade said.

"But those jobs are necessary for Lithilea's success," Matilda from Bredon said.

Vaughn said, "I agree, which is why I am proposing a mandatory STEM program to be implemented in our schools nationwide. It would train students in the necessary skills to support the job programs implemented by Bredon."

Vaughn continued his explanation, and periodically, other students interjected with concerns, questions, or suggestions. It was actually really cool how respectful everyone was. I'd certainly had some rocky encounters with several students here, but a meeting like this made me think there was hope for us all working together like Tristan wanted.

But I also knew that there was a chance that not everyone in this room could be trusted. I had to stay focused. Olivia, Matilda, and Paige had made it clear that they didn't care about my family at all. Stephen, Wade, Rose, and Rachel had all made an effort to reach out to me. Valerie had caused me problems, but if I believed Stephen about her good intentions, I could overlook her for now. I had found Nicole and Vaughn to be likable when I talked to them, but that was about all I had on them.

That was it. Everyone else was an unknown. I'd had to come to terms with the fact that a lot of the people in here might be at least know something about my family's deaths, and I also knew that, more than likely, there were people in here who had specific information that I wanted.

Vaughn's issue was resolved, and it worked together with Matilda's plans: Vaughn's program was simple and wouldn't require too much extra funding. Tristan assured everyone it could be covered by the national budget. Previous sessions of this class hadn't had such easy resolutions, so this was a welcome surprise. Tristan asked for others, and when no one else stood right away, I took my opportunity.

"I would like to discuss transportation adjustments across the nation but particularly in the outer provinces. We have increased security needs that have not been addressed as of yet."

"Wouldn't that be better discussed in our border class?" Olivia asked, not bothering to make an effort to hide her snarky tone. "If it's an issue of national security, then it isn't really a domestic relations problem."

I forced myself to smile. "You're right that it should be discussed elsewhere, Lady Olivia, but I think it merits discussion here as well. Transportation is not consistent across the different provinces, and I think that causes some problems. For example, the quality of the railroad system varies wildly by province. Some provinces have faulty equipment or damaged tracks that have yet to be repaired. Others rely more heavily on water transportation or local transportation, and those need maintenance as well."

"I haven't heard of any problems with the railroad system in other provinces," Olivia said.

"Well, that's why I'm bringing it up, so you can hear about it now." I smiled, but I could tell Tristan was a little annoyed based on the way he kept cracking his knuckles. "I think the safety of Lithilea's citizens needs to be paramount. I think we need some kind of standardization for transportation regulation across the country."

"I agree," Wade said suddenly before Olivia could snark at me. "Right now, regulations are by duchy, and that doesn't seem to be the best way. It often causes problems for trains when they cross provincial borders."

Tristan cracked his knuckles once more. "How do you propose we fix this problem, Lady Julia?"

"We need to assemble the top engineers in our railroad industry and have them put together a standardized set of regulations, and we need some kind of regulation board or verification committee to ensure that standards are met. It's possible that one of the regulation sets in a specific province is already sufficient and just needs to be implemented across the nation. That's for the experts to decide."

"And how would that be implemented?" Tristan asked.

"Excuse me?"

Stephen added, "He means how would it be organized and funded? If we are going to require this kind of regulation, then we would need to pay the engineers involved, pay the members of the compliance board, and find a way to fund the provinces who would need to get their systems up to code."

"Oh," I said. I hadn't thought about that. I knew we needed to fund the committee, but I hadn't considered the costs of fixing the existing problems. Lack of compliance could result in more fees that provinces wouldn't be able to afford, especially if they couldn't afford the fixes in the first place.

"Lithilea's state budget can cover the cost of hiring the engineers," Tristan added. "There is funding set aside for such things annually. The bigger issue is how each province will cover the cost of fixing the existing safety concerns identified."

"Is it not possible for Lithilea to cover those costs as well? Perhaps out of some national transportation budget?"

Tristan shook his head, but it was Olivia who answered. "There isn't a national budget for that."

Talia added with a softer tone, "Transportation varies so wildly by province that each province manages its own. It would be difficult to have a national budget for such things when some provinces rely on railroads, some on water, and some on cars."

It made sense, of course, and I felt stupid for asking. But how was I supposed to know?

Nicole sat upright suddenly. "This isn't a bill Eastcliffe could front on its own. Eastcliffe needs a major overhaul of its railroads. Lady Julia is right about that. But we have way too many other budgetary concerns to devote that much money to that."

"There's always raising taxes," Matilda said.

Stephen suppressed a laugh. "That's not something all the provinces can handle."

"The raise would be proportionate."

Paige said quietly. "A small percentage when you don't have a lot is still a lot."

I didn't like Paige agreeing with me on anything, but I didn't have many allies in this room, so I supposed I had to take any agreement where I could get it.

"Maybe a reallocation of funds?" Rose said. "Surely there are gaps in the budgets that could be reassigned."

Peter said, "There aren't always gaps."

It occurred to me that I didn't think I had ever heard Peter speak. When he was in class—which wasn't often—he never spoke. Paige always spoke for him. I wondered why that was. Most of the sibling sets let the heir speak. The younger siblings never did with the exception of Talia, of course, and Paige. Paige pretty much always spoke for Peter. I imagined it was hard to get a word in edgewise with Paige. She had strong opinions, and Peter seemed like a quiet type. I imagined that this was how they would run their duchy: seemingly side-by-side but with Paige pulling all the strings. I almost felt sorry for Peter.

"What if we increased exports?" I asked. "Each of our provinces has a main export. Would it be very challenging to increase them just a little to cover costs over time? We could even write in a provision that provinces have a certain time frame in which they have to complete the renovations."

Stephen added, "Or maybe we could create some kind of clause in the bill that allows for provinces to prove compliance by developing a long-term plan. That way they could spread the budgeting out over years to avoid strain but still meet the demands of the bill."

Tristan tapped his pen on the desk. "Yes, that's great. That's an excellent solution."

Olivia muttered, "Of course."

"Something to add, Lady Olivia?" I asked.

"I'll repeat my earlier concern. I'm not sure this is the place to discuss this. Transportation is not an immediate domestic concern."

Wade said, "Actually, there have been significantly more train related breakdowns in the last year than in previous years. In light of recent tragedies involving the railroads, Lady Julia's suggestion is not unreasonable."

"One train accident doesn't equate to a transportation problem."

I could feel my face getting hot, and I dug my fingernails into my thighs under the table to avoid visibly reacting to Olivia's comment. A million things ran through my head as I thought about what I could say back, and as I fought the urge to say a lot of them, I simply didn't have the willpower to censor every nasty comment that passed through my brain.

"I wonder, Lady Olivia, if you'd feel differently if it had been your sibling and parents who died in a train accident." I heard gasps around the room. "Perhaps then you'd be more open to the idea."

Olivia placed her palms flat on her desk as if she were about to stand, but a gentle hand on her elbow from her brother kept her down. "Is that a threat, *Lady* Julia?" She made sure the word "lady" dripped with disdain.

"Of course not," I said, my voice miraculously remaining calm. *I should win an award for this performance,* I thought. "But maybe contextualizing the problem will help you understand the severity of the situation. I know people from Aerilot don't die in suspicious train accidents, but other people do, and maybe we should all take it a little more seriously."

Tristan cleared his throat loudly and stood, but not before everyone gasped again, Wade choked until he coughed, Stephen's and Rose's mouths hung open, and I thought I heard Valerie chuckle. Maybe there was still hope to repair that friendship after all.

But what I really relished in was the look on Olivia's face. She didn't have an answer for that, and I loved knowing that I won, even just a little bit.

"Excuse me," Tristan said louder than normal. "I think this is a good time to remind everyone that we need to focus on the issues at hand. Fighting with each other will never result in solutions."

He sat down, and everyone else seemed to relax a little while simultaneously stiffening under his warning. I took the opportunity to look around the room and observe some reactions. Nicole was avoiding eye contact. Not surprising given what I'd learned from her before class started. Stephen mouthed, "What are you doing?" but I couldn't respond to him now. Rose and Rachel looked concerned, as did Vaughn, but Valerie gave me a smile that suggested that I was right about her. Wade gave me a subtle thumbs up and a not-so-subtle wink.

Peter left class suddenly. He looked very pale and he'd seemed pretty frustrated during the entire debate, and he seemed to take Tristan's lecture as an opportunity to depart. I wondered what it must be like to be able to walk out of a class like this so boldly at the first sign of tension. Paige looked as if she wanted to follow him, but she remained seated, and I didn't miss the glare she shot in my direction.

Owen, Matilda, and her brother Mark all looked at me in shock. Owen looked angry, but Matilda and Mark seemed frozen, as if they didn't know how to react. I couldn't help but take in those reactions. I'd caught them off guard, and while I reveled in the fact that "poor man's Jane Clarke" had surprised everyone, I couldn't help but wonder if maybe I'd hit a nerve with someone in the room. Maybe a few someones. I'd made Olivia, Owen, Peter, Paige, and Tristan angry. I knew why Tristan was angry—I'd blatantly defied his order. Olivia and Paige had hated me since day one, so no surprise there. I figured Owen and Peter were just supporting their sisters.

But anger was still surprising. They'd been dismissive at best, cruel at times. Even Tristan had been harsh with me. But none had expressed such rage before. Putting aside my direct approach, I had to wonder why suggesting train safety regulations right after an entire lineage for a duchy was wiped out because of a train accident provoked such strong reactions. Maybe I was closer to the perpetrators than I thought. I'd been assuming that maybe someone here knew something they weren't willing to share. Now I wondered if someone in here was at fault.

No one seemed sure who was supposed to speak now. If we didn't count Tristan's scolding, I was the last to speak. Did that mean I technically still had the floor? Or was I not supposed to speak again? I still didn't understand how all of this was supposed to work, and I was starting to think that maybe no one did. Maybe everyone was making it up as they went along and trying to avoid a lecture from Tristan. That was a scary thought for the future of our government.

Finally, Talia stood, and it was times like these that I could almost picture her as the heir. She seemed to carry herself in a very regal way. "Perhaps there is still more research needed into this issue. Does anyone else have any other concerns they would like to raise today?"

If anyone did, no one volunteered that information now.

"All right then," she said decisively. "Tristan, why don't we end class here? It's nearly time anyway. That will give Lady Julia more time to flesh out her proposal."

Tristan looked at Talia with a classic sense of sibling annoyance—I guessed that was universal even if you were royalty—but sighed in resignation. "I suppose that's a good idea, Talia. Lady Julia, I want a full proposal of exactly how this would work by the next meeting. Sir Stephen, perhaps, you could collaborate with her to implement your compliance clause idea."

"Of course," Stephen said.

"Between the two of you, we should have a reasonable solution to discuss next week." The words were complimentary, but his tone was laced with cautious warning.

He continued: "Everyone else, please bring a proposal of your own within the next two weeks. I want everyone to be prepared to participate. Understood? Lady Paige, could you relay the message to your brother? I see he slipped out."

Paige seemed a bit irritated. "Of course, Sir."

"Meeting adjourned." Tristan's tone was so formal that I half-expected him to slam a gavel. He was obviously making a statement, and no one was anxious to tick him off any further than Olivia and I already had.

Everyone started to trickle out, and I was torn between lingering in the room to let everyone else leave so that I wouldn't have to talk to anyone and staying too long that I would give Tristan an opportunity to scold me. So when Stephen walked up and asked if I wanted to get together now to work on the proposal, I immediately said yes, grabbed my bag, and followed him out the door, ignoring Tristan's stern glance and Olivia's daggered stare.

Chapter Twelve

September 4—

If you really think about it, Lithilea Prep is such an odd concept. Sometimes, I wonder if a school atmosphere is the right setting for us to learn to be governmental leaders. It's kind of odd—we'll never all be together like this again except for the rare meeting.

But maybe it is the best idea. It helps us create relationships, partnerships, and collaborative plans all together before we're actually in power and have too much responsibility to care about each other. I mean, without Lithilea Prep, how would I ever have gotten to know everyone here as well as I do?

Yesterday I wrote that maybe Julia would be better at this than me, but maybe that's the point of siblings attending together. Maybe we could have helped each other. It seems like Talia helps Tristan. I know Rose and Rachel study together all the time, and Vaughn and Valerie seem to have such opposite personalities that it really helps them. One day only one of each of the families will hold the titles, but they'll have their siblings to fall back on. I don't think I'll have anyone to fall back on. Sure, Julia will be there, but she won't be able to help me. Maybe she won't even want to. If I fall, it'll be flat on my back without anyone to break the fall or share the blame. It'll be all on me. And I don't know if I can handle that responsibility.

But a weird part of me deep down (that I'd rather not acknowledge) wonders if I can really trust everyone here. Does us all being school buddies, studying together, and graduating as one actually make us partners who want what's best for all of Lithilea and each of our provinces? It's hard to imagine anyone else wanting what's best for Graycott—it's always the bottom of the barrel. I guess that was the idea when King Terrence created the school. It kind of forces us to care about each other. Part of me wonders how authentic that really is.

***

Stephen suggested working in the nearby courtyard just outside the hall from where our class met, and it seemed as good of a suggestion as any, though I didn't love the idea of the others being able to walk by and see us. Would Olivia interrupt? Would Tristan scold me? Would Wade try to join in?

Did I want to be alone with Stephen?

To my surprise, Valerie was the one who stopped by. We still hadn't spoken except in class since that day at lunch. I wasn't really angry at her anymore. She had only done what she thought was right. Just like me, she was furious at Olivia and had wanted her to have to pay some kind of consequence. She just didn't understand. I had wanted to hate her for it, but I couldn't, not really.

"Hey," she said cautiously. It was so completely contradictory to the air of confidence she had presented when I first met her. I wondered which was the real Valerie: was she naturally confident and felt somewhat apologetic and sheepish now, or was this shyness the norm and she feigned confidence to avoid the piranha at this school?

"Hey," Stephen said, then looked at me.

"Hi," I finally said, and I tried to make it sound as neutral as possible.

"Julia, I just wanted to say that I thought you were really impressive in there just now. 'Domestic Relations' is such an intimidating class structure. I let Vaughn do all the talking for such a long time. I still do sometimes." I guessed that was the answer to my question. "But I'm impressed that you proposed a bill so soon. And that you stood up to Olivia."

I scratched the side of my arm nervously. "I probably shouldn't have lashed out at her like that."

"Oh, I absolutely think you should have. No one ever talks to Olivia like that, and maybe that's the problem. Maybe someone should."

I had to laugh at that. "So you don't think I'm going to get expelled or exiled or something?"

They both laughed, and Valerie said, "I seriously doubt it."

"I guess they can't, really," I said, and with a wink to Stephen, I added, "I'm all Graycott has."

Valerie gave me the same look that I must have given Stephen when he made the same joke. He and I had both meant to be light-hearted, but it was hard to make light of such a heavy situation. Joe was older, and at some point, he was going to die. I really was it for Graycott.

"Well," Valerie said after she had readjusted her smile, "I enjoyed the show. And I would bet you that a lot more people in that room than you think appreciated it, too."

"Thank you."

"And I would back you up on that any time."

I tried not to let my smile waver as I said, "Thanks." She still didn't get it. She still thought I needed back-up. I guessed that that was just part of who she was.

"Well, I'll let you two work. See you later!"

"See you, Valerie," Stephen said with a wave as Valerie walked away. Then he started shuffling through his bag looking for something. "Okay, one second."

A soft breeze blew through the courtyard, which was pretty unusual. It felt like there was never a breeze in this desert. I hadn't realized how used to wind I was until I came here. It seemed like a silly thing to think about—who thought about something as simple as wind?—but I missed the coastal breezes of Graycott. It was so dry and boring and flat here. This artificial breeze caused by a courtyard being between two different buildings made me miss home all the more.

I was never looking forward to coming to Lithilea Prep, but when I first left, I was excited to get away from Graycott for a while. Everything in Graycott screamed the loss of my family back at me in echoes and reverberations that never seemed to lessen in severity. Getting on that train that day with Cecily, I had a lot of mixed feelings about Lithilea Prep, but I wasn't sorry to see the only place I'd ever really known fade away from view. I desperately wanted to be away from everything that reminded me of Jane and my parents and everything that had been lost. I wanted to be away from the friends who didn't know what to say to me anymore. I wanted to be away from government officials who looked at me with strange expressions mixed with pity, confusion, and doubt. And I wanted to be away from Joe who hadn't even come to the funeral.

I knew my father's relationship with his brother had been strained at best for some time. I never thought that it would stop Joe from attending his brother's funeral or from honoring his niece's life. He never even came to see me afterward. Instead, I got official letters of business and endless forms to sign for the funeral, the house, the duchy. I got letters on stationery from his desk with stamped signatures that weren't from his hand that he likely never even saw, never even knew they were sent. I imagined that was what most of the letters sitting on the table in my suite were: impersonal, cold, governmental letters. So if that was what Joe and I were to each other now—nothing more than current duke and future duchess—then I wanted to be far away from him, too.

But as much as I would have liked to deny it, I was still homesick for Graycott and for Joe. We used to sit on the balcony of his house and look out at the ocean. We could only barely see a sliver of water since the house is further inland to be close to the town square, but that sliver was enough for us. We would sit in the breeze and talk about nothing. It was so refreshing. We did that less and less as his rift with my dad got worse. I couldn't even remember the last time I'd been on that balcony. Even so, if I closed my eyes, I could still picture it.

"Julia?" Stephen said, and it snapped me out of my daydream. I wondered how long I had zoned out for, how long he had been waiting for me to notice him. I couldn't be sure how much time I had wasted.

"Sorry, I got distracted for a second."

"Is everything okay?" he asked. But when I nodded, he still didn't say anything and seemed to expect me to say something.

"I was just thinking about Graycott," I said. "The breeze here reminds me of home."

He smiled. "That's why I like it out here. It reminds me of Idlewick. Well, as much as a desert can."

I shrugged. "Sand is sand, right?"

He laughed. "That's one way to look at it, I guess. Do you miss Graycott?"

"I didn't think I would, but yes, I do."

"It's a weird feeling to leave the only place you've ever really known. I always thought I couldn't get away from Idlewick fast enough, even when I was little. But when I'm here, I'm usually counting down the days until the next time I go home."

"When was the last time you were there?"

Stephen thought for a moment, then said, "Not that long. We went home for Christmas."

"Still, that's a few months now."

"I guess. Time flies during the semester. It's the summers that feel long."

"I feel like I've been at Lithilea Prep for ages, and yet some days, it still feels like the first day."

He chuckled. "I'm not sure that feeling ever goes away."

I shook my head, trying to snap my brain back into action. "I'm sorry, you had something to show me or tell me, right?"

"Yes," he said, grabbing hold of the notebook in front of him. "I had a feeling that you'd want to do some investigating into the railway system at some point, so I pulled some notes from the reports."

The notebook was nearly full. This hadn't been a casual attempt. "You didn't have to do that much work. This is my project, not yours."

"I know I didn't have to, but I wanted to help."

There was that feeling again, the same one I had with Valerie. Unsolicited help that was well-intended but still made me uncomfortable. I suppressed my feelings in favor of appreciating the way Stephen's eyes glinted when he smiled.

"Anything significant in there?"

He flipped through the pages carelessly. "Probably nothing you don't already know. But it'll be good research to support whatever claims or guidelines we want to put in our bill."

"We?" I asked with a raised eyebrow. "*Our* bill?"

He smiled again. "Well, sure. I kind of thought we were in on this together. I mean, if you want to be."

"I mean, Tristan kind of ordered us to do a group project."

That laugh again, the laugh that made me want to laugh even when I hadn't felt like laughing in months. "He did not 'order us to do a group project.' It's just that these are hard to write by yourself, and generally bills that are co-written or co-sponsored pass more easily than single-authored bills. They show wider interest."

"I just mean that I wasn't intentionally trying to drag you into something you didn't sign up for."

He shut the notebook and looked me in the eye. "You're not dragging me into anything, Julia. I want to help. I care about this reform, too. It's been a problem for a long time, and it shouldn't have taken a tragedy to force some change, but here we are. I don't want any more harm done. So I'm in this with you if you want me to be."

I glanced down and realized that somewhere in the middle of his speech, he had taken my hand. I couldn't believe that I hadn't noticed because now the warmth of his hand on mine was all I could think about. When I looked back up, I became acutely aware of the fact that he hadn't taken his eyes off of me.

"I want you," I said, then added quickly, "in this with me, I mean."

He chuckled. "Of course."

"I'm not good at asking for help."

"I noticed. That's why I'm offering."

"Then I accept."

"We have to stick together, us lower provinces."

"But why?"

"Well, with people like Olivia around—"

"No," I waved my free hand. "I mean, why are you offering to help me?"

"Because you desperately need it."

I smacked his arm. "Shut up."

He laughed, but he quickly sobered. "Because this job is hard, and while Lithilea Prep prepares you to do the job, nobody prepares you for how hard it is. We're not meant to do this in isolation, but sometimes this environment isn't exactly conducive to cooperation. Nobody really helped me when I first started here except for Tristan and Talia." He paused, seeming unsure of what he wanted to say next, but he finally added, "And Jane."

My eyes stung a little, but this felt like a rare moment in which I didn't want to cry. Stephen hadn't made me sad by mentioning my sister. Instead, he had kindly and quietly acknowledged who I had always known her to be: a kind, selfless person who always thought of others. It was Jane's strength, not mine. It was a part of me that felt like it was missing now that she was gone.

When I didn't say anything, he cleared his throat and said, "And I want to do this for you."

"Why for me?"

He didn't answer, but I realized he was leaning in a little bit. Was that his answer? Was Stephen about to kiss me? I'd been ignoring any signs that Tristan was right about his potential feelings for me, but this was pretty hard to ignore since my hand was still in his, and he was close enough now that I could smell his cologne that smelled like salt air.

But a twig snapped behind him, and he jumped, releasing my hand in the process. He was just startled. It wasn't anything more than that. But it was hard to ignore the way he had dropped my hand so rapidly.

We both turned toward the sound and saw Tristan and Talia a little ways down the path from us. They didn't seem to be heading toward us, though they both waved when they saw us looking. It didn't matter, though. The moment had passed, ruined by the very person who had made me aware of Stephen's feelings. I wouldn't know, now, if he had been leaning in for a kiss. I didn't know if I had wanted to kiss him or not.

I did know that I felt a sense of disappointment when he said, "Ready to get started on this bill?"

***

"Ha!" Valerie shouted, holding up the final spoon. "I win again."

"Why are you so good at this?" Stephen asked.

"Why are you so bad at this?"

I laughed. "I didn't know a game of spoons could get so competitive."

"That's on you, Clarke," Valerie said. "You should know by know that *everything* is competitive at Lithilea Prep."

Stephen had suggested he, Valerie, Vaughn, Tristan, and I have lunch together today and try to have a little bit of a break. When he had asked, I hadn't been sure if I wanted to do that, but I was glad now that I had said yes. I was actually having a little bit of fun. Valerie and I had gotten back on pretty good terms. I didn't think that we were best friends or anything, but with as few friends as I had, I didn't really have the luxury of turning away people like her just because she'd rubbed me the wrong way while trying to help. She was good-intentioned, and that had to be good enough.

Vaughn ran an extra napkin from lunch across his sweaty forehead. "Who's idea was it to sit outside again?"

Stephen laughed. "Can't handle the heat, can you?"

"Carlisle is never this hot, even in the summer. That one summer school session I spent here, I thought I might drop dead."

"That's a tad dramatic, don't you think?"

"There's no air in the desert!"

I laughed. He wasn't wrong, but I guessed since Stephen and I were from the more tropical parts of Lithilea, we were better equipped to deal with it.

Tristan said, "It definitely takes some time to acclimate to the desert climate."

"It's just absurd," Vaughn said. "I don't think some grass and the occasional breeze would hurt anything."

Valerie added, "Carlisle is so picturesque with its rolling hills. Every time we come back here from a break, Vaughn complains like this."

"I've never been to Carlisle," I said. "I've heard it's worth visiting."

"Oh, it is," Valerie said. "Julia, you have to come visit us during a school break. We'd have so much fun."

I hadn't thought about what I would do over a school break. I definitely didn't want to stay here at school, but why would I go home to Graycott? There wasn't really anything for me there other than Uncle Joe with whom I wouldn't spend any time. Carlisle didn't seem like such a bad option.

"Maybe I will," I said, and Valerie seemed to light up at my acceptance. It was a tiny token of friendship, but it was a token nonetheless.

Stephen spread out his arms. "What, I don't get an invitation?"

Valerie flitted her hand at Stephen. "You've seen Carlisle."

"Don't worry, Stephen," Vaughn said with a laugh, "you and Sir Tristan can come hang out with me. We'll have more fun anyway. Valerie only likes the boring stuff."

"Deal," Tristan said.

Valerie shoved Vaughn by the arm, and he flung himself forward so dramatically that it was out of proportion with how hard she had hit him. This was nice, honestly. Every moment since I got to Lithilea Prep has felt so stressful and chaotic, and with the latest investigative reports, it was starting to feel like I hadn't been able to come up for air.

I couldn't say that I was totally distracted, but I was at least enjoying myself for once.

"Well," Tristan said, standing. "I have to go hop on an important call. I'll see you all later."

We all said goodbye, and Tristan walked off, but not long after he had left, Stephen's shoulders slumped.

"Oh, great," Stephen said, rolling his eyes.

I looked in the direction of Stephen's gaze and saw Wade approaching.

"He's not so bad," I said.

He scoffed, but before he had a chance to say anything, Wade said, "Well, hey there, everyone."

"Hi, Wade," I said.

"Hey," Valerie and Vaughn said simultaneously.

Wade sat in between me and Vaughn. "So, I did a little digging, and I found out that a couple of people left the state dinner early."

"Is that even allowed?" I asked.

Valerie said, "The state dinner itself is required for all dukes and duchesses and those immediately in line, but there are a host of other events that happen the next day. Not everyone stays for those."

"Olivia, Matilda, and Paige left early," Wade said. "Peter was never there at all. Of course, Jane also left early."

"Anyone else?" I asked.

"You," Stephen said, his gaze boring into Wade.

Wade flashed a smile. "Right. That's why I didn't know who else had left because I was already gone. My family has a ton of holiday traditions."

"Well, Paige went home to be with family," Valerie said. "I remember her telling me that. They're a very close family."

"Olivia and Matilda are the big question marks," Wade said.

"Is that significant if those other events are not required?"

He shrugged, reaching an arm behind me. "It means that they weren't at Lithilea Castle at the time of the crash."

"Not sure that really matters," Stephen said.

Wade raised his hands. "Maybe not, but I'm supplying all the information I have."

"Thanks," Stephen said. "See you later."

Wade looked a little startled by Stephen's shortness. "Just trying to help."

"We're good."

"I get it, Sanor," Wade said, standing. "See you later, Julia."

He waved to me, then to Valerie and Vaughn who seemed paralyzed by indecision, and then walked off.

Immediately, I turned to Stephen. "What was that?"

"Why does he always have to do that? he said.

"Do what?"

"Be so close to you, arm around you, all that."

"You're mad that he put his arm behind me?"

"He shouldn't be anywhere near any of us. I don't trust him."

I laughed wryly. "Really? I wasn't picking that up."

"I wouldn't trust Wade as far as I could throw him. You can't let him be involved with the tiniest little thing."

"That seems like an exaggeration," I said. Sure, Wade definitely had a less-than-serious attitude, and he was a little shifty at times, but nothing I had seen of Wade made me think that I couldn't trust him. But I also didn't know anything about Stephen that would suggest that he would lie.

"Trust me, it isn't," he said.

"He's right," Valerie said softly.

"Okay, fine, maybe so, but that doesn't mean that he's wrong about the people who left the state dinner or anything else he's told us."

"I didn't say he's a pathological liar," Stephen said. "I'm just saying he can't ever be trusted."

"I get it," I said, and we all just kind of went back to doing whatever, discussing homework or planning for future events. The tension didn't go away. I wanted to believe Stephen—really, I did. I just also wanted to believe that the guy who'd sat on the floor of the museum with me while I cried and who was the only person who seemed to understand what it was like to be here when you weren't supposed to be and no one wanted you here was who he said he was. Wade understood a side of me that no one else did, and maybe that outweighed past sins.

The only thing that I knew for sure was that I was not going to let anyone else make up my mind for me. I was going to find things out for myself.

Chapter Thirteen

November 4 —

You know what I've never been good at? I can never tell if a guy likes me. Is that unusual? Rose thinks I should always know because she says guys always like me, but do they really? I mean, sure, they might like talking to me or studying with me, but does that really mean that they like me as anything more than a friend? I don't think I can tell the difference between normal friendliness and flirting.

I totally shouldn't be focused on that right now. I should be studying and focusing on training to be the duchess, but it's hard to ignore when I have feelings for someone and I can't tell if he has feelings for me, too. I just wish I knew. Even if I found out that he didn't like me, it would hurt, but at least then I would know for sure and could stop wondering.

Why can't stuff like this be as easy to study as political science or law?

***

The next day, I chose to sit outside under the trees at the edge of the walking trails once my classes were over. It wasn't as hot as it usually was, and many students had taken advantage of the opportunity to walk the trails. Many people had passed me in the hour that I'd been sitting there, but no one spoke to me. No one ever did. I used to like that, the way that everyone ignored me, because I didn't particularly like most of these people or want to exchange fake, saccharin chit-chat.

Now, I was starting to wonder if I still wanted that. I definitely still didn't want to fake niceties, but maybe I was doing myself a disservice by isolating so intensely. If no one would even speak to me or acknowledge me, how would I ever represent Graycott well? How would I barter deals or gain allies when needed?

How would I find out who had killed my family?

The problem was that I didn't know how to fix it now. Either through my own actions or theirs, I was alienated from pretty much everyone here. There probably wasn't a way to come back from this.

I glanced up as Paige walked by. We made eye contact, but we both snapped our eyes away from each other as quickly as we possibly could. If I was going to try to make amends, Paige certainly wasn't the person I should start with. I would have had better luck with Valerie or Vaughn or even Rose.

In my efforts to avoid eye contact with Paige, I stared so intensely at my class notes that I didn't even notice Stephen until I saw the toes of his boots nearly touching my own shoes. Stephen always wore boots. They were heavy work boots, the kind I expected to see on someone who did manual labor for a living. I kind of liked them. Most of the other guys wore pretentious dress shoes that were always getting dirty from the desert sand, and it just seemed so pointless just for the sake of maintaining an image. I liked that Stephen did his own thing.

I looked up at him, but I struggled to meet his eyes because of the glare of the sun from behind him. Still, there was no mistaking the slight tilt of his head when he smiled.

"Hey," he said. "Hiding out?"

I slammed my notebook closed. "Always."

Laughing, he sat down on the bench next to me. "You don't have to, you know. Hide, I mean."

I shrugged and said, "I'd rather hide," though I wasn't sure I really meant it.

"That doesn't include me, does it? I mean, you weren't just trying to hide from me and I totally wrecked it, right?"

I made eye contact with him, spotting those gold glints in his eyes again that only appeared in the sunlight. I couldn't help but think of Tristan's insistence about Stephen's feelings for me again. I almost wished Tristan had never said anything because I'd been psychoanalyzing Stephen's every word and action since then. When Tristan had first suggested that Stephen had feelings for me, I didn't think it really mattered. I wasn't here for romance. Stephen was a good friend, and I was fine with that being the end of it. But lately, I couldn't ignore the fluttery feeling I got every time I saw those golden flecks in his eyes or the way I wanted to smile whenever he smiled.

And I couldn't ignore the way he had looked at me in the courtyard the other day.

"Of course not," I finally said, realizing that I'd let too much time pass before answering because I was admiring him. "I'm never hiding from you."

His smile widened, but he looked down at his hands which fidgeted in his lap. He looked—bashful? It was the most concrete evidence I'd seen yet that Tristan's words held any water. I didn't know why I doubted Tristan—Stephen was his best friend—but for some reason, I assumed he had to be wrong. Maybe I just wasn't used to guys looking at me—or rather looking away from me—the way Stephen did. Jane always got those kinds of reactions.

"So listen," Stephen started, "I was talking to Nicole the other day, and she said that the train was supposed to go from Lithilea Castle to the school here, then to Dalmerlin, Falkirk, and then Graycott."

"Right."

"But it didn't. It never stopped at Lithilea Prep."

"What does that mean?"

"The schedule of the train changed last minute. Nicole knows because Rose texted her to say she got dropped off in Falkirk a little early because they didn't stop. I verified it in the records I showed you yesterday."

"I'm not sure if that's significant. Don't train schedules change all the time?"

He shook his head. "Not typically for trains that are carrying provincial leaders. Those are tight schedules."

I thought about it, and I couldn't remember Jane or my dad ever telling me their train was off-schedule. I used to hear about it from friends back in Graycott, but not from my family. Maybe they were more rigid with those schedules.

I said, "But arriving early doesn't really hurt schedules, does it? So does it matter?"

He shrugged one shoulder. "Maybe, maybe not. But I promised to tell you anything I found out."

"I appreciate it. Okay, so the train went from Lithilea Castle to—"

"—To Dalmerlin to Falkirk. Where was the train when—"

"Falkirk mountains," I said, not wanting Stephen to finish that sentence. "It was close to the Graycott border. That's why Rose wasn't involved in the wreck—she'd already been dropped off in Falkirk."

Suddenly a thought hit me, and I didn't know where it came from or why it hadn't hit me before. I didn't like the thought, but this whole process was pretty unsavory, so I had lost some of my sensitivity at this point.

"Wait," I added, "why weren't you on the train? Shouldn't there have been an Idlewick stop in there somewhere?"

"Normally yes, but my family spent another week with the Yores after the state dinner. Since there was no one to drop off in Idlewick, the train skipped that stop. It went straight from Dalmerlin to Falkirk. Tristan was actually late meeting us at the Yores' house."

I still hadn't gotten used to Stephen referring to the royal family so casually. I may have gotten closer to Tristan in recent weeks, but he was the only member of his family I felt comfortable thinking of as a friend. It was still so weird to me that Stephen's family was so close with the royal family, that he even referred to Lithilea Castle as the Yores' house. There was such an easy, comfortable friendship between them which was bizarre for me to picture. It was especially hard to picture during the times that Tristan seemed so severe when Stephen always seemed so warm.

"You know, I think about that sometimes," he said.

"What?"

"That if we hadn't stayed with the Yores, we would have been on that train."

"Well, not really. You still would've been dropped off before the explosion."

"Yeah. I guess it just weirds me out to think about. Rose said the same thing."

"She did?"

He nodded, but he furrowed an eyebrow in confusion. "Didn't she tell you that?"

"Rose and I don't really talk. She was Jane's friend, not mine."

"She could be both, you know."

I had to suppress a laugh because it was such an inappropriate time to laugh. "Jane and I were very different. There was almost nothing we agreed on, and that included friends. We did not have the same friends in Graycott either."

"You've never mentioned anyone from Graycott."

I shrugged. "There isn't anyone to mention."

"Friends?"

"I still talk to some of them, but the accident changed everything. They all came to the funeral, and they text or write me from time to time, but it's usually to check on me. We don't have normal friend conversations anymore."

"And your uncle?"

I looked down at the dirt under my shoes. "I don't really talk to him either."

"That feels like a loaded sentence," he said, and though I could tell his undertone was kind, I didn't need to unload everything about Joe to Stephen.

"Let's just say it's a complicated family dynamic."

"How so?" he asked.

Before I could answer, Wade walked by on the trail and chimed in with, "Not everyone's family is sunshine and rainbows, Sanor."

I noticed Stephen tighten his grip on his legs as he forced himself to smile, though it looked more like a grimace. "I didn't say it was."

"I mean," Wade continued, oblivious to Stephen's annoyance, "it would certainly make all of our jobs easier, wouldn't it? If we all had healthy, normal families, I mean."

"No family is perfect," Stephen said.

I added, "No one said they were."

"I just think Julia and I have some life experience that you can't understand, Stephen."

Stephen visibly shifted, and I could tell he was getting heated. "I'm pretty certain I have a lot more in common with Julia than you do."

"Oh, is this the whole 'we're not elite provinces' complaint again? That's always your defense."

Stephen stood up suddenly, and I was surprised to see that he was actually a bit taller than Wade. Wade seemed to have more of a presence about him that I always thought he was taller. "Look, Dalmerlin, it's not easy being looked down on all the time by the rest of you."

"Well, we're not all best friends with the future king, now are we?"

"As if that's earned me any favors."

"Look, man, I'm not trying to pick a fight with you," Wade said, his hands held up in the air in surrender. "Just making conversation."

"Oh, please," Stephen said, practically shouting. "You're always trying to get under someone's skin."

"Natural talent, honest."

"Okay, okay," I said, positioning myself in between them. "I don't know what has gotten into either of you, but you're going to have to cut it out."

Stephen clenched and unclenched his fists and jaw a few times, but he refrained from saying anything else. Wade remained calm, at least on appearances.

Wade said, "Julia, I actually came over here to tell you that I heard that the train ended up changing routes."

"We already know," Stephen snapped. Then, softer: "I just found that out and told Julia."

Wade smiled at Stephen, but I couldn't tell if it was actually friendly or not. "Sounds like we're all on the same page, then. I have to get to an appointment. Just thought I'd pass on the information. Julia, I'll see you later."

We both watched Wade walk away, but Stephen sat back down on the bench and started fiddling with his bag, seemingly looking for something, though I suspected that he was just trying to look busy.

"What was that?" I said. "What kind of weird peacocking competition did I just witness?"

"What do you mean?" he snapped again.

I gestured to where they had just been standing. "That whole thing. What is your problem?"

"What is *my* problem? Wade is the one with the problem."

"He was just making conversation."

"Wade is never just 'making conversation.'"

"Look, I know he can be kind of a jerk sometimes—"

"All the time," Stephen muttered.

"—but he's just trying to help."

"Oh, I bet he is. He just wants to get on your good side."

I folded my arms. "What is that supposed to mean?"

Stephen stood. "He's into you, Julia. Can't you see that?"

"What does that matter if he is?"

Stephen took a step back and looked at me like I had just uttered something terribly shocking. Was it so shocking? I wasn't trying to date Wade or anything, but who cared if he had a thing for me? He struck me as the type that had a revolving door of "things" anyway. I was probably just the latest obsession. It would pass.

"Julia, I don't trust him," Stephen said. "I never have."

"I know. You've made it clear."

"I just don't think it's a good idea to get so close to him or involve him in all of this. You don't know anything about him."

"I know a lot more than you think. We have a lot in common that you can't possibly understand."

"You and Wade have *nothing* in common."

"You don't get to say that! I've spent so much time here just being ostracized and judged at every turn. I don't belong here, and everyone has made it perfectly clear. How is Wade any different? We're both the black sheep that nobody wants to associate with."

"Wade is completely different. A few people being cruel to you because they're terrible people is not the same as Wade alienating everyone here because he's determined to be a loner and because he obviously hates everyone here."

"It's not really like that, you know. Maybe if you ever tried actually having a conversation with him instead of attacking him, you'd be able to hear his side of things."

Stephen scoffed. "And you believe him?"

"Why shouldn't I?"

"He's manipulating you. Don't you get that? You're just automatically going to believe everything he says?"

I stepped back, my arms folded. "Oh yeah, that's the problem. I am just clueless and totally without my own thinking ability."

"You know that's not what I meant."

"It seems that everyone here just hates him, just wants to hate him. Just like me."

Stephen rolled his eyes. "Everyone here does not hate you, Julia. Don't be such a martyr."

"Me? What about you?"

"What about me?"

"You act like you're so disadvantaged here, but Wade is right. You're literally best friends with Tristan, and whether you want to admit it or not, people do treat you differently because of it."

"Oh yeah, it's definitely an advantage to have people be fake around me just because Tristan is watching and then completely ignore me when he leaves."

"It's more than Wade or I get. Nobody cares about us because we're not in your position."

"It's ridiculous that you even think that changes the way people feel about me. I told you from the start that I don't care what anyone thinks of me, and neither should you."

"Except Wade. Apparently I'm supposed to care what he thinks of me."

He pinched the bridge of his nose. "Because you don't know what you're dealing with when it comes to him."

"Oh, and you've known him longer than I have, so you're the expert, huh?"

"Exactly! I have known him longer, and that's why I'm telling you to trust me that he shouldn't be anywhere near all of this or you."

"I don't really think that's any of your business."

He looked hurt, and I didn't like seeing that expression on his face, but I couldn't help what I had said—it had needed to be said.

"Well, I thought that you cared what I thought as your friend."

"As my friend?" I said, a laugh skirting the edges of the words. "You've made it pretty clear that you're the one who's into me. What are you, jealous of Wade? Jealous of the fact he understands something about me that you'll never understand?"

Stephen's face flushed bright red, but he no longer looked angry. He stared at me for so long that I found myself unable to stop the flood of words with baseless thoughts.

"Everyone here just pities me or judges me or condescends to me, and Wade is the only person who hasn't done that. Even you have done it. I thought you and I had a real friendship, but it was all just you trying to get with me. That's obvious by the way you squared up against Wade."

"I *did* think you and I had a real friendship!" he shouted. "At least that's what I wanted. I was only trying to protect you, but since you've decided my feelings are an inconvenience, I guess I'll stop trying."

"I don't need saving, Stephen, from Wade or anyone else. And if you think that's the way to win me over, you are sorely mistaken."

He flinched, only slightly, and I saw his fists unfurl. He looked down at the dirt and nodded slowly before grabbing his bag and slinging it on his shoulder.

"Well, then I'm sorry to have upset you. Rest assured I won't bother you again."

Without waiting for a response, he turned and walked off, faster than I had ever seen him walk. Some part of me wanted to call out to him, to make him stop, but why? What would I say? And did I even want him to turn around?

He hadn't denied anything I'd said. He had even acknowledged that he did have feelings for me. Tristan was right.

I didn't know why I was surprised. He'd made it clear multiple times, including the other day. I really couldn't have ignored his feelings for me. But did I reciprocate those feelings now? Had I at any point? And did it matter now if they were probably lost forever?

I was left feeling so conflicted. I was so angry, but the pit in my stomach told me that Stephen's words had broken something inside of me.

Chapter Fourteen

*A*ugust 5 —

Class today was awful. They made us write wills. I'm too young to write a will! That's something old people do, not people with their whole lives ahead of them. What's worse is it's a legal will, not even practice! How weird is that? How am I supposed to know what I want my will to say at eighteen years old? I don't even really have anything to "will" away.

I left everything to Julia because I didn't know what else to do. They kept saying "Later, you'll probably want to update these to bequeath your possessions to your spouse or children." Then why don't we do it then? This whole thing seems ridiculous.

I told Julia about it, and we had a good laugh over it. At least someone understood how absurd the whole thing is. She told me I shouldn't have left everything to her because she'd just throw it all out anyway. It made sense. We're so different, so why would she even want any of my stuff?

***

Feeling defeated and frankly pretty annoyed, I went back to my room to rest, but as I passed through the entryway, I noticed a pile of boxes sitting in the living room. I remembered that Joe had sent a few boxes for me which I'd had delivered to my suite, so I went to explore their contents. I shoved the letter from Joe that had arrived with the boxes aside. An attempt to lift one of the boxes proved that it was heavier than its size betrayed, so I sat on the floor next to it and opened it.

Most of it was my stuff: some books, a few journals Jane had given me that I never used, sheet music, and miscellaneous odds and ends. There were a few things that were my parents', but it looked like he had left most of that at my house, and I was grateful for it. I still hadn't gotten up the will to move anything in that house. I had left it all exactly as they had left it. I wasn't sure how long I would keep it that way.

There was a smaller box labeled "Jane Clarke," so I popped open the lid and was immediately hit with the urge to cry. It was the stuff Jane had had with her on the trip before the accident. When I asked Joe for the items Jane had left me in her will, I hadn't expected these things to be part of it. Most things had been claimed by the investigation or shipped back to Joe, but I guess they had decided they didn't need these things. It made sense. Most of it was her books from school. I flipped through a few of the notebooks and silently thanked Jane. Even postmortem she was helping me study. I spotted a few canvases and carefully set them aside. I even found a pocket knife which struck me as so odd. Jane wasn't exactly the pocket knife-carrying type. Still, I tucked it in my own bag. It might be useful at some point. She had an absurd number of spiral bound notebooks in her backpack, and I couldn't possibly go through them all, but one of them stood out, and I knew that it was her diary from the past year.

As the younger sister, I used to try to read her diary all the time. I would sneak peeks when she wasn't around. She only caught me a few times, but I must have done it hundreds of times. After a while, I stopped because I got older and understood the importance of privacy, but I also felt like there wasn't much she didn't tell me, so I really didn't feel the need anymore. Even now, it still felt wrong to read it, though I knew she wouldn't catch me and that she probably wouldn't have cared anyway. Still, the curiosity was relentless, so I flipped it to the date a few days before the accident and read.

November 27—

Dinner with King Tybalt was everything I could have imagined. Dining at Lithilea Castle was like a fairytale. Prince Tristan had described it to me, but I never could've pictured everything that I saw. It was glistening and beautiful.

I couldn't help but laugh that she still used formal titles when referring to Tristan in her diary, as if anyone would ever read it. Though I had to remind myself that *I* was reading it right now.

I only wish that Tristan could have joined everyone for dinner. Talia, too. It would have been so much more fun. I didn't think I would miss Tristan that much over such a short break from school, but somehow being around his parents and his childhood home, however magnificent a castle it was, made me feel like he was missing somehow.

Seriously, Jane?

He has promised me that we can finally sit down and talk about everything when I get back to school. I don't know what he'll say, and I'm so afraid that he'll say no, but at this point, I just have to know how he feels about—

I shut the journal and practically threw it across the room. I felt like I had just walked in on someone naked, the invasion of privacy was so extreme. Jane liked Tristan? Why hadn't she ever told me? I scoured my brain, trying to recall some memory, any memory of her implying that she had feelings for Tristan, but I couldn't, and Tristan certainly hadn't mentioned it. Did he not reciprocate? It was possible. They never got their conversation. Still, images of Tristan smiling when I reminded him of Jane, of his troubled face when he offered me condolences, of his personal involvement in the investigation of her murder, clouded my brain. It was possible he felt the same way. It was more than possible.

I wanted to keep reading, but it weirded me out to keep reading her private thoughts about Tristan, so I didn't. I couldn't even bring myself to touch the diary again, so I left it where it had fallen when I tossed it. No one would disturb this room, anyway. It would be there again if I needed it.

And I would need it. I *needed* Jane, desperately, and she wasn't here. She always saw things more clearly than I ever had. If only I could have explained everything that had happened with Wade and Stephen. Maybe she would help me make sense of it all.

Perhaps the one consolation of that awkward discovery was Jane's handwriting, her voice, her pink pen. It was familiar, and I liked "hearing" her talk again.

Chapter Fifteen

November 26 —

Tristan and I had another fight. He accused me of picking a fight, and deep down, I think I know that that's true, but I couldn't help it. Lately it seems like he's been dodging me anytime I try to have a serious conversation. I don't even know what we are to each other. Friends? Something more? Is it absolutely ridiculous to think we could be more than friends?

It's expected that Tristan will marry someone with a much higher ranking than me. He dated Olivia last year. Not for very long, of course. He isn't really supposed to date someone in the direct line for a duchy, but she is the type of person he'll likely marry. It won't be someone like me, someone from a province as low as Graycott.

I think I know that in my heart of hearts. I know he can't marry me. He can't even date me, really. But can I really ignore the feelings I have for him? Can I ignore the feelings I'm pretty sure he has for me?

I'm going to be the Duchess of Graycott one day. I should be focused on that rather than wondering whether or not a boy likes me. But Tristan isn't just any boy, and this isn't a normal situation.

So is it so wrong that I insisted that I need to know what's going on between us? It's only fair, to both of us, really. I don't think I could live with myself if we didn't get this all out in the open and know exactly where we stand with each other.

***

I woke up to silence, and normally I would have welcomed it, but I didn't today. I checked the Ledger app as I did every morning, but it was quiet. No messages from Stephen, Tristan, or Wade, no new posts about anything happening in class, nothing but a message from Rose that I ignored as I always did.

In an effort to disrupt the silence, I sat at the piano and played nothing in particular, just letting my fingers run across the keys in whatever pattern they wanted. It didn't bring me the same satisfaction it normally did.

It was the weekend, and I didn't have anywhere to be, so I was trying to decide what to do when I heard a knock on my door. I wasn't sure who I wanted to see. Did I want to see Stephen, or was my anger toward him still too volatile? Did I want to see Tristan, or would I just be annoyed by his attempts to stand in my way of the investigation? Did I want to see Wade, or would I be confronted with the Wade that sometimes used diminutives with me instead of the Wade who understood me? I wasn't sure anyone else would be welcome.

I certainly hadn't expected to see Cecily when I opened the door. She looked distressed, and she was clutching an envelope to her chest. I swung my arm out to my side in a gesture for Cecily to come in, and she did hesitatingly.

"Julia, I'm sorry to disrupt your weekend," she said.

"You're not disrupting anything," I said, and Cecily seemed cheered by that, but I didn't have the heart to tell her that it was less about her and more about my total isolation at the moment.

We both sat in the living room on opposite sofas. She still clutched the envelope and seemed to be searching for where to start.

"Did something happen?" I asked.

She fidgeted. "Sort of. There's been an update in the investigation. I'm sure you'll receive a letter soon if you haven't already, but I felt like I should come over and talk to you in person."

"If it's about the change in the train's stops, I already know."

"It's not that." She unfolded the envelope but didn't actually read from it. "It looks like they figured out how the explosives were set off."

"Okay."

"The explosives were attached to the connection between two different cars. They were set to separate those cars from the rest of the train. They weren't attached to the train car your family was in."

I stared at her for a moment, expecting her to continue, but she didn't. "What does that mean?"

"It looks like they weren't intended to explode on your family's car. Meaning it wasn't an intentional assassination."

I felt the blood rush into my ears, and I couldn't decide if I felt hot or cold. "That doesn't make any sense."

"The suspicion right now is that there was an attempt to cause a scene or cause damage but not necessarily to hurt anyone."

I jumped up. "How can explosives being attached to a train not be intended for harm? That doesn't make any sense."

Cecily sighed, but she didn't look frustrated. Instead she had pity in her eyes, and it made me hate her. "There was one explosive on the connection between your family's car and the car in front of it. There was another explosive on the car in front. There was nothing on your family's car."

"Okay, so maybe they got it wrong. Maybe they didn't know what they were doing."

Cecily shook her head slowly. "The team says that the way the explosives were attached displayed, how did they phrase it—" she opened the letter and read directly from it, "—'displayed a detailed and thorough knowledge not only of train construction and operations but of events pertaining to train travel.'"

"What is that supposed to mean?"

Cecily stood and faced me. "It means that the bomber knew exactly what they were doing, and they were not targeting your family. They likely just wanted to get a reaction, make some kind of political statement. But they had extensive knowledge of train functions, so it wasn't a random bomber."

"But there hasn't been a statement. No one has claimed the attack, no one said anything. How can it not be personal?"

"I don't know, Julia, but sometimes we don't ever know the answers to these questions."

"That's ridiculous," I said, folding my arms. "That's the whole point of the investigative team. They're supposed to find the answers."

"They're not giving up, but this looks like it wasn't as targeted as they initially thought."

"So what, my family died for some failed political stunt. For *nothing*? They're just dead because someone felt like blowing up a train, and nobody even cares why?"

Cecily grabbed a tissue and handed it to me, and I realized I was crying. "I'm so sorry, Julia. I wish I could say something else. You deserve better. Your family deserved better."

I dropped to the sofa and sobbed, loud and ugly, into the tissue covering my face. Cecily sat beside me and put an arm around my shoulders, and for once, I didn't push her away. I cried until my chest hurt and my eyes and throat went dry. I didn't know how long I had been sitting there crying as it felt like hours and mere seconds simultaneously. Cecily said nothing, and I was grateful for that. She was right: there wasn't anything she could say.

When I was sure my voice would come out somewhat normally, I said, "So, is that it? They're closing the investigation?"

"No, they're still trying to figure out who did it and why. This isn't the end of the search." I nodded but didn't answer, so Cecily added, "They're going to figure out who did this, Julia."

I nodded again. What could I say? There wasn't anything to say or that I wanted to say. I didn't want to talk to anyone.

"You should go," I finally said.

"Are you sure? I don't have to be anywhere. I can stay here if you like."

I shook my head. "I'm fine. Thank you for coming here to tell me."

Cecily eyed me as if she wasn't sure she should leave me, but I guessed that she knew better than to argue with me at this point, so she stood. "Okay, but I'm staying in town for a few days. If you need me, I'm just a short drive away."

"Okay, thank you."

Cecily left with a small wave and a forced smile.

The investigation wasn't over, but somehow, it felt like it was. It felt like I was back where I had started: no one cared that my family was dead. No one wanted to bring their killer to justice. I had kind of convinced myself that I was the only one who cared about the accident, but deep down, I think I felt like that wasn't true, that Lithilea as a whole cared. I had been wrong. My family wasn't even important enough to assassinate, and that felt like a weird thing to be offended by.

Who could I even talk to about this? Tristan likely already knew, but when would he tell me, if he would tell me at all? Stephen wouldn't talk to me right now if I wanted him to.

I needed to hear Jane's voice again. Hadn't I asked Joe for her stuff for this exact reason? I felt lost, and I didn't know that I really trusted anyone. Stephen and Tristan were keeping me at a distance, Wade was inconsistent at best as a friend, I wasn't much more than a pity friend to Rose, and everyone else hated me. Jane was dead, but she was all I had left.

I picked up her diary from where I had thrown it the other day. I had assumed she was admitting to feelings about Tristan, but what if I was wrong? What if I was right?

It still gave me a weird shiver to invade her privacy, but if it meant finding out anything useful, *anything* that would help me catch her killer, I was going to do it. I scanned her perfectly scripted writing until I saw the sentence where I had quit reading.

He has promised me that we can finally sit down and talk about everything when I get back to school. I don't know what he'll say, and I'm so afraid that he'll say no, but at this point, I just have to know how he feels about me. It really felt like we were getting somewhere, but lately he's been kind of distant.

Unconsciously, a snort escaped my nose. Tristan's penchant for becoming distant apparently was not unique to me.

I know we had a fight, but people fight. We're all in such high-pressure situations every day. How could tensions not run a little high sometimes? I hope he'll finally be honest with me even if he's angry with me. I know Tristan can have quite the temper sometimes, but I think he cares enough about me to be honest—as long as I wasn't the reason he didn't come to dinner. I never found out why he missed it, and the family seemed to act like it was a last-minute decision. If I was the reason that he skipped dinner, then I probably can't hope for a good outcome to our conversation. Still, it's better to know than live with the wondering.

I slammed the diary shut. This was more complicated than I thought, and I felt my face getting hot. Not only did Jane have feelings for Tristan, but it sounded like he was stringing her along and treating her terribly. Jane mentioned a temper, and I'd certainly seen glimpses of it. A temper like that could only run unchecked for so long.

An unsettling thought was ricocheting around in my brain, causing pinpoint pains every time it rattled my thoughts. Tristan skipped the state dinner, a pretty unusual thing for the future king to do. Nobody seemed to know why. He dodged Jane for days despite her desperately trying to talk to him. Three days later, my sister was dead.

I could hear my heartbeat throbbing inside my head, and I was aware of a constricting feeling in my throat. I didn't want to acknowledge the thoughts I was having, but how could I not?

I spoke the words out loud only because I needed to hear them to feel like they were real: "Did Tristan kill my sister?"

***

I didn't even remember the walk up the stairs to the third floor, and before I knew it, I was standing outside of the Yore suite knocking, politely at first, then more aggressively. My head was still pounding, and I needed answers. Now.

Tristan answered and looked at me stone-faced, twitching one eyebrow up in confusion. "Julia, is everything all right?"

I shook my head. "Is anyone else here? Your sister?"

He shook his head, so I barged past him into the suite. The Yores' suite was massive, and it took up basically the entire third floor. Each of them had their own suite, but the two suites connected in the center.

"Hey," Tristan shouted, slamming the door behind him. "What do you think you're doing?"

Somewhere in the back of my brain, I was aware that I was breaking every royal code I knew and probably some that I didn't know, but I didn't care, not one bit. I wasn't Jane who was too afraid to ask Tristan to explain himself. I was there to demand answers, and I was going to get them whether he wanted to give them or not.

I stood in the center of the living room and spun around to face him. "Why didn't you attend your father's state dinner?"

"Excuse me?"

"The dinner, the state dinner." I was aware that I was on the verge of shouting, but I had lost control of my voice. "The dinner that your entire family attended except for you."

Tristan folded his arms and looked at me with a fire in his eyes I hadn't seen before. I couldn't help but step back a bit in fear. Was it foolish to come here alone? Maybe. But would he have given me real answers if I weren't alone?

"That's none of your business, Julia."

"Actually, I think it is. You didn't go to the state dinner, and you shut out my sister for weeks before that."

His expression shifted, just for a moment, and I saw the mask he so often wore drop ever so briefly until he became aware of it and returned to his stony expression. "What do you mean I shut her out?"

I waved the diary in front of his face. "Jane wrote about you in her diary. She wrote all about how she had feelings for you and—"

"Julia, stop, you don't know what you're talking about."

"—how you fought with her and ignored her. She knew you were angry. She was afraid you were still angry with her."

"What does this have to do with the state dinner? Did you really come here to yell at me because you read something random?"

My voice rose to a shout. "Random? This is my sister! The last words she wrote before she was *murdered*. Don't you get it? This is all I have."

He pinched the bridge of his nose. "That's not what I meant—"

"Tristan, did you rig the train accident?"

As soon as the words were out, the air seemed to have been sucked out of the room. That was the exact accusation I came here intending to make, but somehow the words shocked even me as they were uttered. Because all of this was shocking.

Tristan, for his part, looked like I had punched him in the face, and his face was as red as if I had. "*That's* what you think? Did you actually just accuse the crown prince of Lithilea of mass murder?"

He walked toward me slowly, and the adrenaline with which I had stormed his suite seemed to evaporate rapidly into fear. I'd done this without thinking. I had burst into an unfamiliar suite, probably the most secure suite in the building, without planning or thinking ahead at all. What if he tried to kill me? It could certainly be covered up. No one would know. No one would even care about me.

"You-you changed your plans suddenly," I continued, backing away even though he had stopped advancing toward me. "No one knew why. Everyone else was at the state dinner. Jane hadn't heard from you, and then all of the sudden she's hoping she'll see you so you can talk."

I bumped into a desk behind me and was forced to stop. Tristan still stood a distance from me, but I was no less scared of the look in his eyes.

Tristan snapped, "We *were* going to talk. I wanted to explain."

"Explain what? That it was ridiculous of someone from a province as insignificant as Graycott to think the prince could ever love her?"

"How dare you?" he growled, and I found myself wishing I could back up, but I couldn't stop now. The words wouldn't stop tumbling from my mouth.

"She had genuine feelings for you, maybe even loved you, and you just toyed with her feelings until what? They became inconvenient? *She* became inconvenient? You could easily get rid of someone. And you've stopped me every step of the way that I've tried to look into the accident."

"I was *trying* to protect you."

"Why bother? Am I not just another loose end?"

"I don't know what has gotten into you, but you don't have any idea what you're saying."

"Then answer my question."

Tristan turned away from me. "I don't have to answer anything—"

"Did you rig the accident?"

"No!"

"How do I know? How can I possibly trust that you wouldn't kill my parents? My sister?"

Tristan whipped around. "Because I loved her!"

My ears were left ringing from how loudly he had shouted it. He collapsed into a sitting chair near him as if the act of shouting those words had sapped him of his strength. He covered his face, and even though I typically had trouble reading his expression, the lack of any facial features made it that much harder. Some part of me wanted to go to him—to do what, I didn't know—but my feet felt cemented to the floor.

When he spoke again, I realized he was crying. "I loved Jane. With all my heart."

I didn't know what to say. What could I say? I had just accused him of murdering my family, of murdering the girl he loved.

"I didn't—"

"I was trying to keep the same thing from happening to you. It is my duty to keep you safe as your prince, but I think I owed Jane that."

"I didn't know."

Tristan nodded, but there was a coldness to it. He stood suddenly and gestured toward the door but stood far away from it. "I think that you should go."

I nodded and walked out the door, half-expecting him to say something else, but he simply closed the door gently, and I knew I had gone too far.

Chapter Sixteen

June 29 —

Julia and I had a fight. When we were kids, we almost never fought, but the older we get, it seems we fight more. I wonder if that's just normal sister behavior, to fight, to have conflict once your lives are bigger than each other.

Usually I'm the first to apologize because I hate not talking to her, but not this time. I was right, and she was wrong. She never apologizes first, and this one time I'm going to be stubborn and dig in my heels until she admits it. She thinks I'm a pushover, and maybe I am. But this time, I'm not backing down.

I hope she apologizes soon because I miss her, but I'm willing to wait her out.

***

I stayed in my suite the entire weekend. There were a number of events that it was expected of me to attend, but I couldn't bear the thought of facing Tristan or any of the others, really. I couldn't take Olivia's condescension, Rose's fake niceties, Tristan's emotionless glare, Talia's superficiality, Valerie's ignorance, or really anything else. I didn't want to see the girls who had done nothing but gossip about me, I didn't want to find out which Wade I would get, and I didn't want to be reminded that I had attacked one of the only people who had actually made an effort to care about me. If my status suffered, so be it; it likely couldn't get any worse.

I guessed I could have reached out to Rose, but what would I even say? I'd pushed her away from the moment I met her. It didn't seem like something I could turn back time on. Besides, hadn't I decided that Rose and I couldn't be friends for a reason? Just because she missed Jane and cared about her didn't mean we had any future as friends.

There was only one other person I thought about, only one I could stand the idea of seeing, and that was Stephen. We hadn't spoken in a while—not since our fight over Wade when I had brutally exploited his feelings for me to accuse him of childish jealousy—and I wasn't even sure if he would, but I had to try. Stephen had stuck by me since the day of my first class. It was at least worth a shot.

I grabbed my phone and attempted to draft a text before eventually deciding a call was easier. I listened to the ringing sound for several cycles before the truth was unavoidable: he wasn't answering.

I slammed my phone down on the bed and hoisted myself upright with a grunt. How had this happened? How had I alienated the only people who had tried? Some inner voice that I desperately wanted to suppress murmured the answer: *You always do this, Julia. Pushing people away is what you do.* I'd done it my whole life. Jane and I were so close once, and I pushed her away until the day she died. I refused to listen to my parents. Even Joe and I weren't speaking.

Except Joe *was* speaking to me. He was trying, anyway. Desperately, for weeks, he had been mailing me letters and sending me messages on Ledger, and I had ignored every single one.

I walked over to the pile of boxes on my floor from Jane that Joe had sent and the stack of letters from him that were strewn on the end table. I hadn't opened a single one, but still, I hadn't thrown them away either. As much as I tried to convince myself that I didn't want contact, the truth was that I did, which is why I had kept them all, why I hadn't deleted a single unread message on Ledger. Joe was all I had left.

I picked up the letter on top, the most recent one I'd received from Joe. I tore the envelope open before I even realized what I was doing. It was a short letter, and I wondered if they were all that short. He didn't say much other than to give some run-of-the-mill updates on Graycott. At the end of the letter was the section I was desperately hoping I would see even if I hadn't admitted that to myself:

Julia, I know how grueling school can be. It is so much pressure in the most normal of circumstances, and you're dealing with so much. If you need help, I am here. I am always here.

Tears streamed down my face in rapid succession, and I clumsily wiped them with the back of my hand. I grabbed the stack of letters and shoved them in my bag then grabbed my phone. I called Cecily before I could talk myself out of it.

"Cecily?" I said, forcing my voice to sound as normal as possible. "Can you book me a ticket on the next train to Graycott? I need to go home for a few days."

***

I'd slept most of the train ride to Graycott. I didn't have anyone to talk to beside Cecily, and frankly, I didn't feel like talking to anyone anyway. Not until I got to Graycott.

Now I found myself in the lobby of the Graycott duchy estate staring at my feet while I waited. I'd been in this room countless times before. I'd probably spent more time here as a child than I did at my own family's house. My father and Joe used to get together frequently to discuss plans for Graycott. One day, my father would've taken over for Joe, become the Duke of Graycott, and we would've moved here permanently. Then, he would've trained Jane. I would've been happy to live a reasonably prosperous life without much effort.

That was before the train accident.

The room didn't have happy associations anymore. It reverberated echoes of screaming matches between my father and Joe. Its carpet was stained with the tears Jane and I shed together and that I later shed alone. It held the words from the Lithilea security detail who gave us the news, and it bore the heavy silence from the lack of words from Joe. I could hardly remember the laughs, the smiles, and the stories that used to fill this room.

One day, when Joe was gone, this would be my house. I would have to strip it entirely and remake it into something that didn't make me think of them ever again. Or maybe I needed it to be the same. I wasn't sure anymore.

Cecily was taking longer than I expected. She had insisted on accompanying me on the trip to Graycott despite my objections. *For security,* she had said. What did it matter? She couldn't prevent a train crash. The benefit of her coming along was that, as my handler, I had the authority to insist that she speak to Joe first and prepare him for my appearance for the first time in years. She hadn't wanted to, but she couldn't say no.

Finally, she popped her head through the door. "Julia? He's ready to see you."

I rubbed my hands on my hips to dry the sweat and stood. I'd nearly talked myself out of coming multiple times, but I had to do it: I had to talk to him.

I walked in, dismissed Cecily, and sat down, making sure I kept my posture rigid, my hands still, and my face unreadable. I'd always been good at the unreadable part, but the other two were recently acquired skills. He sat on the opposite sofa and matched my posture, clearing his throat as he unbuttoned his jacket. I was shocked by how old he looked; sure, he was significantly older than my father, but he hadn't always looked like it. Now, he made the age difference look much wider than it really was. If someone didn't know us, they might mistake him for my grandfather. He cleared his throat a few more times, and I wondered if maybe he was ill, which would offer some explanation for his appearance, but I suppressed the thought.

He spoke first. "I'm very glad you came to see me, Julia. How is school?"

I fought the urge to shrug. Rigid posture. "All right."

"My time at Lithilea Prep was not a perfect experience, but it was invaluable. I hope it is the same for you."

I considered that. I had learned a lot. I had met worthwhile people. "Not a perfect experience" seemed the perfect description. I couldn't help but wonder if Jane would've described it the same way.

His detached demeanor was surprising to me. Hadn't he offered to reconcile? His excessive formality reminded me of why we hadn't spoken in all this time, but I had to push past it. If he wrote those letters, then he must have wanted me here. I had to believe that.

He continued: "Everything is all right, isn't it? Are you in trouble?"

"No. Why?"

"Not that I'm not happy to see you, but I'm wondering what prompted your sudden visit."

I took a deep breath that seemed not to want to exit my lungs. I had already come all this way. I had to finish what I had started. "I need to know what happened. I need to know why you didn't come to the funeral."

His eyes took on a sad gloss, and I was suddenly gripped with the overwhelming fear that he might start crying, and I definitely didn't know what I would do if he did. He took a few quick, shallow breaths as he stared down at his folded hands resting on his desk. Was he trying to come up with an excuse? Hadn't he had months to prepare one?

"I'm very sorry that I didn't."

"That's not what I asked."

Another shaky breath. "I'm sure you know that your father and I were not on the best of terms for many months before—and I had meant to reach out a few times, but it just never seemed possible. You probably heard all kinds of terrible things about me."

I shook my head. "Dad wasn't that kind of person."

"You're right. But I imagined that you must all hate me. We'd had a difference of opinion, but that didn't absolve the terrible things we said to each other. When I got news of the accident, I immediately picked up the phone to call you, but I was afraid that I would only upset you. I worried that maybe in some way you blamed me for their deaths."

"Did you rig the train with explosives?"

He sat up straighter at my bluntness. "No, why—"

"Then how could I blame you?"

He nodded slowly. "Of course you're right. I guess I blamed myself, so I feared that you had, too. I couldn't help but wonder if we hadn't had our falling out if maybe they wouldn't have taken that trip. Maybe we would've been working together, so the trip would've been delayed. I don't know. It might seem silly, but I entertained all those possibilities and more."

I could hardly recognize the man who sat across from me as my Uncle Joe. The Uncle Joe of my childhood was full of life, sometimes to a fault. He was loud and confident, sometimes brusk, and powerful. The man who sat before me was frail, apologetic, and cowardly. I hardly knew what to say to him. I had come prepared for him to be combative, and I was ready to fight back, but if he wouldn't throw the first punch, did that mean I was supposed to? Or should I change my tactics?

"Then why start sending letters?" I asked.

"Despite my personal fears, you are still the heir of the duchy of Graycott now, and you were thrown into it. I thought maybe you would need help."

"I didn't need your help."

"Yes, I should have known since you were always so independent—"

"No. I didn't need help. I needed family."

We locked eyes and stared for so long that I normally would've been pretty uncomfortable, but I wasn't. I thought about adding more or qualifying, but I forced myself to stay quiet. That was it. That was the entire reason I'd come. I needed a family, and for better or worse, he was it now. He needed to drop the title for a moment and remember that I was his niece.

He still didn't speak for a few moments, but when he did, his voice was so low that I might've missed it if I hadn't been staring at him. "I wasn't sure if I still was."

I huffed, then got up and insisted he follow me. At first he hesitated, but I left the room without him, forcing him to follow. I walked him out to the main room, pushed one of the couches over, and pointed at the blue carpet where there was a dark blob of a stain.

"Do you remember what that is?" I asked.

He nodded. "You spilled grape juice. What were you, nine?"

I nodded, too. "I had been waiting for Jane to finish her lessons for the day. She'd taken longer than usual, and I got impatient and careless. You saw me spill it. I panicked because I knew my parents would be furious that I'd stained the carpet. You shushed me, dragged the couch over it, and sat back down without saying a word. Later when my dad asked why you moved the couch, you said that it made more sense for the couch to be closer to the center of the room so that people would feel more comfortable. Then you insisted that he let Jane out for the rest of the day so that she and I could play together. My parents never found out."

I spun him around by the shoulders and pointed at the family portrait hanging on the wall. It had been painted when Jane and I were barely teenagers. My parents and Joe stood behind Jane and I who were seated side by side on blue velvet chairs. "And that. The photographer wanted Jane to be the only one seated since she would be the duchess one day, and I wouldn't be. You insisted that she and I were equals, just as you and Dad were equals, so we were both seated. I was pretty mad at you about it at the time because I didn't want my photo taken. My dress was itchy, and I felt silly. But you still insisted."

I turned him slightly toward the piano that sat in the corner. "And that. You hate the piano. You were never any good at playing the piano, so you hated it, but you kept that one here because I like to play. Plus, I'm actually good at it."

He nodded. "What are you getting at?"

"All of that meant so much to me. It still does. I never needed you to be some fantastic mentor or teacher, and I definitely didn't need you to avoid me because you might upset me. My parents and my sister died. One day, everything was fine, and the next day, I was an orphan. I needed my uncle to ask me to stay with him even if I would've refused. I needed you to call and check on me. I needed you to introduce me to Lithilea Prep. Not Cecily, not Prince Tristan, you. And I needed offers of family dinner nights, weekend trips home, or care packages of junk food sent to me at school, not letters about public relations and education funding. I need you."

This time he did start crying, and I was helpless to prevent the tears that started trickling down my cheek as well. I had come here to say all of that, but I hadn't planned to unload it all like that in a torrent that was likely overwhelming. Slowly, he reached out an arm toward me, and I let myself fall into it, resting my chin on top of his shoulder. He had always been on the shorter side—I'd grown taller than him many years ago—but I could confirm that he had thinned out some. It could have been grief. I certainly didn't eat for a while after the accident. But was it something more? I couldn't help but worry.

"I'm sorry," he said, muffled by my hair. "I'm so sorry."

We both tightened our embrace, and it seemed that some of the tension in my very bones started to melt.

Chapter Seventeen

November 23 —

I'm not sure that I want to go on this trip.

I've been dying to go to Lithilea Castle basically my entire life, and I'm finally getting to go. Mom, Dad, and I are having dinner with King Tybalt this week. We've been traveling all day, and I'm so excited that it's finally here. I'm finally going to get to see the castle and meet King Tybalt and actually start to feel official. Somehow, it's easy to convince myself that I'm not really the future Duchess of Graycott if I've never met King Tybalt. That will all change in just a few days.

But something feels off. I can't explain it, and when I tried to ask Dad about it, he shrugged it off. He's been doing that a lot lately. I think it's still because of his fight with Uncle Joe. Dad should be the duke by now, and I think he knows it and is annoyed that Joe hasn't stepped down. He's been in a mood for months now, and I shouldn't be surprised that he totally brushed me off, but it still hurt.

It probably doesn't help that I can't explain my feelings or offer any proof that something is wrong, but something is wrong. I wish I knew what. I just weirdly feel like I shouldn't have left school, which is silly. Even if I weren't going to the capitol, I'd still be going home later this week for a quick holiday break. What difference does it make if I leave a little earlier and take this trip I've always wanted to take? But still, I can't help but feel like everything isn't normal.

Maybe I'm just being paranoid.

***

Sleeping in the old room in which I used to spend several nights a week as a child felt at once familiar and foreign. Joe hadn't redecorated since I was practically an infant, and I felt sure that the room even still smelled the same—lavender, like the expensive detergent Joe specially ordered from Bredon—but I almost never slept in this bed without Jane. Technically, this was supposed to be Jane's room, and mine was next door, but we always stayed in the same room because we would stay up late talking and just kind of fall asleep. Jane's room was bigger than mine, so we usually hung out here, and even though I spent more time in this room than my own, I felt like I was trespassing sleeping here without Jane, like at any moment she would walk in and demand to know why I was in here without her permission, even though she never would have done that. Joe had offered me this room, and initially I had turned it down and taken my old room, but around 1 AM, I accepted that I wouldn't be able to sleep until I switched rooms. When I had first lain down in this bed and pulled the turquoise blanket up to my chin, tears had slipped down my cheek, moistening the satin pillow below, but despite the sadness it had caused me at the realization that I would never share this bed with Jane again, I had been comforted by the familiarity and fell asleep.

However, I couldn't help but notice that the room was a little dustier than normal, the curtains had creases and faded spots from the sun, and it seemed like there were fewer employees milling around the house. There had never been that many—Graycott wasn't that economically prosperous, and Joe had always kept a bare bones staff—but it still seemed quiet. The last day I was here before now was the day

Joe and I were told about the accident, and that day, this house was packed with government officials, investigators, staff, Lithilea Prep representatives, and more that I didn't recognize, so it wasn't the normal atmosphere I was used to. I supposed that I shouldn't really worry about it, but I couldn't fight the nagging feeling that something was off.

I opened my suitcase, but most of the clothes that I had packed were Lithilea Prep's "uniform," and I felt wrong wearing that here. I felt like two different people, like the Julia at Lithilea Prep wasn't the real Julia. Or maybe the Julia here wasn't the real one? I couldn't be sure.

The only clothes I had were way too casual to wear, but I didn't think I had another option. Just as I put on shorts and a long-sleeved t-shirt, someone knocked on the door.

"Hello?" I said as I answered the door.

An older woman wearing a plain black suit smiled and held out a hanging clothes bag. "Sir Joseph sent for some things from your house that he thought you might like to have for the weekend. He also had the boxes you brought with you from Lithilea Prep put in the next room over.

"Thank you," I said, taking the bag from her.

She smiled kindly. "Let me know if you need anything else, Lady Julia."

I closed the door, tossing the bag on the bed. "Lady Julia." I had gotten used to that at school, but it sounded wrong here. In Graycott, I was never "Lady Julia," I was just Julia. It was a title I was never supposed to have here. At Lithilea Prep, the *other* Julia was training to be Duchess of Graycott and would be somebody important one day. Here, the *real* Julia, the *old* Julia was just a kid who grew up in her sister's shadow, the kid who might one day be a pianist, the kid people smiled at when she did something stupid. After all this time, I still hadn't reconciled the two, and eventually, I would have to find a way to do that.

I checked the bag, and sure enough, I found some of my own clothes and changed into a pair of dark-wash skinny jeans and a purple flowy blouse that felt much more familiar, much more normal. I couldn't be sure of what was in the boxes in the other room. I hadn't fully gone through everything yet, but I definitely needed to go through them later. I'd need those answers later. Right now, I wanted to see Joe.

I headed straight for the office, but Joe's secretary stopped me in the hallway and suggested I go have breakfast. I wasn't really hungry, but I decided it was probably a good idea to eat something to avoid crashing, so I changed my course for the dining room. When I got there, I was surprised to see Joe with a rather large spread on the table in front of him.

"Julia," he said, gesturing to the seat across from him. "So glad to see you up so early."

I shrugged and sat down. "I've gotten used to the early schedule, I guess. I'm more surprised to see you here. You never eat breakfast."

"I've started recently."

I reached for a scone because its delicious scent was wafting in my direction. "Why? I thought you hated it."

"I'm getting older, Julia, and I just don't have the energy I used to have. My doctor thought breakfast might help."

I set down my fork and stared at Joe until he did the same. "Joe, are you sick?"

I hadn't really meant to be so blunt about it, but there it was, and Joe dismissed the employee who had been bringing out different items. I'd been suspicious about Joe's health since I'd been here. He seemed thinner, older, and not the same Joe who used to march around here with confidence and a presence that made everyone else stand up just a little straighter.

"No, Julia, I'm not sick."

"Are you sure? You're not lying to me?"

He shook his head. "I'm not sick. I'm just getting older, and the body just doesn't work the same way after a while. I thought I would've retired by now."

I nodded slowly. It was true. My dad probably would've taken over by now, maybe even sooner if they hadn't had their falling out. At the very least, they would have worked together, Joe would have gone part-time, something. Now he couldn't retire, not until I finished school, at least.

"I'll be done early, you know," I said. "I've signed up for extra classes over the summer to catch up."

"You don't have to do that."

"You know I don't like wasting time."

He allowed a small smile to cross his face. "Yes. Still, I don't want you to overwork yourself."

"I'll be fine."

"I know you will."

I twisted my mouth. "But will you be fine?"

He laughed, and for a moment, he sounded more like his old self as the robust laugh echoed through the dining room. "I'm not dying, Julia. Goodness, you're making me feel like I have one foot in the grave."

"I'm just worried about you." I stopped short of saying what I really felt, what I probably should have said: *You're all I have left now.*

"You don't have to worry about me. It's my job to worry about you."

It didn't feel that way, but I didn't know how to tell Uncle Joe that. I did feel I had to worry about him. Was that because he was getting older, because he was struggling to keep up? Was it because I felt some kind of family obligation? Was it because I needed to know that he would be okay? I wasn't sure, but I didn't feel like I could just ignore my feelings and concerns about him. Not anymore. Not after everything.

Hesitantly, I asked, "What happened between you and Dad?"

"What?"

"I didn't mean to say it so bluntly, but what happened?"

"It all seems so stupid now. We didn't agree on a lot in terms of how we thought Graycott should be run. We fought endlessly over it. When I didn't retire, your father was sure that it was my way of sabotaging his ideas."

"Was it?"

He shook his head. "Not consciously, at least. I just felt that I was really in the middle of some good work, and I wasn't ready to stop it. Now I wish I had. Your father would have been an excellent duke. We were just both so stubborn."

"Clarkes? Stubborn? Never."

Another booming laugh. "Now, I know you didn't come here just to quiz me about my health and my job status."

"I also yelled at you."

He smiled, but there was a sadness in his eyes. "What really made you make this trip?"

I probably should have told him something, *anything*, before I got here and hit him with the whole *someone killed our family but apparently not on purpose* thing, but I kind of chickened out and assumed that he understood. After all, he'd been sent the same letters I had about the investigation. I'd written a letter, though I'd never sent it.

It seemed wrong somehow, after years of not speaking, to send a letter with that kind of information in the mail. A phone call seemed harder. Hence the trip. But now, looking into his eyes, further darkened by sadness and hardship, I wished I had sent the letter as some kind of preamble.

"I don't know if you have been checking the mail with any kind of regularity, but—"

"You're wondering about the investigation into the accident?"

So he had kept up to date. "Why didn't you ever say anything? You sent me, like, a billion letters, but none about the investigation."

He seemed to perk up. "You read them?"

I fidgeted, twisting my fingers together. "Uh, not really, but none of them were postmarked after that one. Except for—except for your reply when I wrote you."

He smiled in that way adults always do when they know something you don't. "Mail takes longer to get through security at Lithilea Prep and to you. I was informed before you. I was hoping my letter would get to you before that one found you, but I guess not."

I had never read the letters. I had never even opened them until the train ride, and even then, I only skimmed them. I had assumed that he didn't care, that he wouldn't try to contact me. I could have had this conversation with him a long time ago.

"I'm sorry," I blurted out before I even realized what I'd said. "I should have read your letters when you sent them."

"It doesn't matter now. What matters now is the investigation."

"Have there been any updates that I may not have received?"

He shook his head. "I doubt it. The last communication I received was weeks ago."

"Which said?"

"The attack was internal, and they suspect that the bomber was not directly targeting our family."

I knew that, of course. It wasn't news, but somehow, it hurt to hear it all over again. Somehow, I had convinced myself that it wasn't true, that I had deceived myself into thinking that someone from Lithilea could be responsible, but it was true, and I couldn't deny it any longer.

"Do you have copies of my parents' travel logs?"

"Of course, but I'm not sure what you're hoping to find in those. They're very dry, and the investigative team already has copies."

"There has to be *something*. Please let me see them?"

He sighed and pushed himself up from the table. "Okay, follow me."

Joe led me to his office where I had to help him lift a large box full of paper. It was organized, at least, but it would take me some time to weed through everything in here.

"Seriously?" I said. "This is how you keep records?"

"This is how your father kept records."

"When I become the Duchess of Graycott, we're going digital."

Joe laughed, loudly again, and I laughed, too. It was probably the first authentic moment of something that felt like happiness we had shared in who knew how long. It felt like old times, and I was grateful for that.

"Well," Joe said, wiping a tear from his eye, "that's up to you someday, but until then, you're stuck with your father's old-fashioned approach. Good luck!"

"Thanks," I said as he walked out.

I was already rifling through the pages. It didn't take long to find the itinerary for the trip. I didn't really need to read it because Jane had told me about the trip. She was very excited for it. The duchy heirs had all gone to the capital to have dinner with the Yore family. King

Tybalt liked to do that every year, have dinner with the future duchy representatives. He didn't want the first day he met them to be after they took the oath. I wondered why he hadn't sought me out yet.

They had arrived at the capitol and had dinner; I knew that. The accident had happened on the way back to Graycott. The students of Lithilea Prep went straight back to school or home to their provinces for the holidays. Jane hadn't gone back to school—she had planned to spend the weekend with me and our parents. I was so excited to see her that weekend. Now I wished she'd gone back to school.

Aerilot and Bredon reps took local transportation since they were so close. Outer provinces clustered for half of the journey, then split up individually. Falkirk, Idlewick, Dalmerlin, and Graycott shared a train until they reached the border the three shared. Then they split up by province in Falkirk's train station. It was that last train that had been rigged with explosives. It was obviously a targeted attack on Graycott since no one else would have been on board that train. The investigative team could say all they wanted that they didn't think my family was targeted, but I didn't believe it. If someone had blown up a train to make some kind of terrorist statement, they would have done it somewhere more high profile. Graycott hardly ranked.

I tossed the stack of papers next to the box and sighed. This wasn't going to get me anywhere, it seemed. There must have been something I was missing.

***

I spent most of the next day searching the travel logs for anything of interest, only stopping to eat, but I failed to find anything noteworthy. It was all perfectly normal until the explosion. I couldn't find anything out of the ordinary.

It probably didn't help that I was so exhausted that I felt like my eyes were glazing over trying to read all of these pages of tiny print.

I'd stayed up most of the night flipping through Jane's notebooks and diary. I'd started out just skimming her school notebooks for anything I might find useful, attaching sticky notes to any usable page, but I'd quickly devolved into reading about her crush on Tristan, her friendship with Rose, and her private, lighthearted thoughts. It was nice. It was like talking to Jane again. Ever since they died, I'd felt like so many people had pretended to know Jane when they didn't really. I'd felt for months like I was the only person left who really understood her. There was always Joe, but it was weirdly reassuring to read that she felt that Tristan understood her. Maybe I would ask him about it when I got back. Of course, I didn't know if he would ever speak to me again after the way I had treated him. I'd managed to avoid thinking about it too much while I was in Graycott, but seeing the way Jane wrote about him only made my guilt stronger, and it ate away at me. I wanted to see Tristan the way Jane saw him, the way she described him here.

But I also had this weird sense that I was interacting with the real, private Jane again, the Jane that was hidden most of the time under the guise of "future Duchess of Graycott." I was all too acquainted with the double lifestyle now, and it was strangely comforting to find that she experienced it, too.

Realizing I had gotten off-task, I took a deep breath and dove back into the travel logs again. They were kind of funny, actually. It looked like my dad had started teaching Jane to keep travel logs, but their styles couldn't have been more different. Our father was analytical and exact, recording only what was crucial to know with no extraneous details. Jane's logs read like a travel magazine. I could picture the look of frustration that must have crossed my father's face reading these.

I read the same travel logs over and over until I was sure I could recite them from memory, but they didn't change, and I didn't know why I had expected them to. But for some reason, I couldn't stop reading and rereading, hoping for the outcome to be different.

Tuesday, November 29: Jeremiah Clarke:

Arriving in Falkirk tomorrow. Short layover through the early afternoon, then continuing on to Graycott. Awaiting extra cargo in Falkirk before continuing to Graycott.

Wow, how thrilling. For a smile, I switched to Jane's account.

Tuesday, November 29: Jane Clarke:

One more day of travel until we reach Falkirk's train station. The hills of Falkirk are so beautiful in the winter, though it is a little cold sometimes at night. It will be nice to stop in Falkirk for a while as we wait for our extra addition to the train. Then it's back to Graycott overnight.

Extra addition. Dad had called it extra cargo. Did the difference matter? Probably not, but the word "addition" stuck in my brain like a burr. Where had I seen that before?

I grabbed Jane's diary from my bag and rifled through it quickly, nearly tearing pages as I went. I scoured until I found the entry I had read last night.

I can't wait to see Tristan. It's only been a week, but I'm so excited to see him again. I've been texting him all week, but it just isn't the same. I'll see him in just two days' time. What a wonderful addition he will be to this trip.

There it was: addition. I checked the date at the top. *November 28.*

There was no extra cargo. They were talking about Tristan. Tristan was going to meet them at the Falkirk train station.

I scrambled for the reports from the investigative team. Earlier, I had overlooked a file that had the specific logs for what each train car was used for. I found it and flipped to the records.

Train car #11: Graycott Representatives: Clarke Family: Sir Jeremiah, Lady Genevieve, Lady Jane. Secured.

Cecily told me that the explosives were attached to the train car in front of my family's, so I ran my finger up the lines.

Train car #10: Extra Cargo. Secured.

Actual extra cargo wouldn't have been labeled "secured." That was a word reserved for trains that had some kind of security to protect the royal family or the dukes or duchesses. The train car in front of my family's wasn't random—it should have been Tristan on that train.

Which meant my family might not have been the intended target after all.

Chapter Eighteen

*O*ctober 31 —

Tristan and I had a bit of a disagreement today. He'd probably call it a fight, but I think it was a disagreement.

I asked him if he wanted to be king. I don't think it's a silly question, and I didn't think it would make him angry, but he got pretty upset that I asked. "Why wouldn't I want to be king?" he kept saying, but that isn't an answer. Does he want to be king?

Abdications in the duchies don't happen every day, but they have happened. Some do it for health reasons, some for marriage, some for family, and some do it simply because they just don't want to be duke or duchess. When I was a little younger and Duke Norman of Eastcliff abdicated, I sat down by myself and asked myself if I would ever do that. Would I abdicate? Do I really want this? After a lot of thought, I decided that I do. I want to be Duchess of Graycott.

So is it so absurd that I would ask Tristan the same thing? Does he ever think about it? Even if he has decided to accept being king, does he want it? I don't think it was so ridiculous. He said I shouldn't ask such things, that he had accepted his responsibility, so there was no point thinking about it. I guess that makes sense, in a way. He had accepted his responsibility, and everyone was thrilled that he would be king someday. I don't think there's a person alive in Lithilea that doesn't love Tristan.

***

I ran straight to Joe's office and burst through the door. Some part of my brain registered that the pen he was holding flew out of his hand onto the floor when I startled him, but I was focused. I wanted to be wrong, but if I was right, then I needed to confirm my suspicions quickly before someone got hurt.

"Julia, is something wrong?"

I asked his secretary to leave and tried to catch my breath. It was not a long distance to his office from my room, but I was more winded from my own thoughts. "The logs. I found something."

"What?"

I dropped my father's log and Jane's log side by side onto Joe's desk and pointed. "They both reference that the layover in Falkirk was to pick up something."

He nodded. "'Extra cargo,' your father said."

I tapped Jane's paper. "But Jane used the word 'addition.' Look at this."

I handed Joe Jane's diary, and when he realized what it was, he held it away from him as if it were on fire. "I don't think I should—"

"She called Prince Tristan an 'addition' to the trip."

His eyes clicked up to mine over his glasses. "Prince Tristan?"

"Were the Yores supposed to join them in Falkirk? Were they coming back here for business or something?"

"I didn't know anything about that. But I suppose it's possible. Your father and I—he might not have told me in advance, and they wouldn't have named any of them in the logs for security reasons."

"They'd call them something like 'cargo'?"

He nodded.

"What if—"

"Julia, I don't think we can jump to that conclusion."

"If any of the Yores were the intended target of the explosion, we have to tell them. They could still be in danger."

"How would anyone know the Yores' travel plans?"

I shrugged. "Jane knew. My parents knew. The train conductor and staff probably knew. Whichever connecting train they took would have known. He wouldn't have been at school, so probably everyone at Lithilea Prep would've known. Come on, Joe, you know this is messed up."

"It does seem a little odd, yes."

"We have to tell Tristan. Now."

***

Trains didn't used to make me nervous. Actually, I always kind of liked traveling by train. The hum of the tracks was peaceful, and I liked the long, uninterrupted solace of a lengthy train journey. Even after the accident, I didn't mind train rides, though I thought that I might. In fact, I had slept most of the way to Lithilea Prep.

But now, with the knowledge that the killer hadn't actually killed their intended target, that they were still out there after the Yore family, I was incredibly anxious. A million scenarios kept running through my head. *Did they know I figured it out? Did Tristan know? Did Jane and our parents find out before they died? Did anybody from school know? Was it a foreign attack? Domestic? Did they even know that they were killing the Graycott representatives? Did they even care?*

I'd find out the answers to some of those questions, but some I never would. I'd never know if my family was afraid when they died, if they knew what was happening. I'd never have all of the answers.

I couldn't seem to stop my brain from picturing bombs on the underside of my train car. Every little bump on the tracks made my breath hitch. And the longer that Tristan didn't respond to my texts, the more that I worried.

It wasn't really a shock that he wasn't answering me. Why would he after the way I had treated him? Still, I had hoped that some kind of royal or professional obligation would make him answer me, even to keep up appearances as the prince. I couldn't blame him for not answering the Julia that he had thought was his friend who had accused him of murder in a fit of rage. I could blame him, even just a little, for not answering Lady Julia of Graycott when she said she had urgent business to discuss with him. I hoped he would listen to me if I showed up in person. Hopefully bringing the current Duke of Graycott would give me some sway.

"You're going to rip your fingers to shreds," Joe said, nodding at my bleeding hangnails. I hadn't been able to stop the nervous tic.

"This train is taking forever."

"It's going at a normal speed. It just feels slow because you're in a hurry."

"Gee, thanks. Really needed that train physics lesson right now."

He huffed. "You've got to try to relax."

"How am I supposed to relax?"

"I don't know, but being nervous isn't going to make the train go any faster."

I rolled my eyes, but I also smiled. "You sounded like Dad just now."

He smiled then rummaged through his bag. "That reminds me. Here."

He thrust a pocketknife into my hand. "What is this for?" I asked.

"It was Jane's. Well, sort of. I gave it to her a while bag, but it came back with all of her belongings from the train. You should have it. Just in case you need it."

"Thanks, but that's not exactly conducive to the whole relaxing thing."

"Maybe not, but—" he seemed to struggle to find the right words. "But just in case."

"Have you heard from the investigative team yet?"

He shook his head. "They're likely still processing the evidence."

"It seems pretty clear to me."

"Julia—"

"I know, I know." I waved my hand dismissively. We sat in silence a few moments longer until I finally said, "I'm really glad you're here."

Joe put his arm around me and gave my shoulders a squeeze.

***

It was probably not considered polite etiquette to pound on the door of a royal, but there I was practically trying to beat the door down with my fist. It was very early in the morning, and the logical part of my brain recognized that they were probably sleeping, but the panicked part of my brain feared every worst case scenario it could dream up.

Finally, the door swung open, and Talia glared at me. "Julia, what on earth is wrong with you?"

"Where's Tristan?"

"What? What are you—"

"Is Tristan here?"

"Well, yes, he's probably in his office, why?"

"Go get him."

"Julia, what is going on?"

"We need to talk to both of you." I gestured to the door. "May I?"

Talia looked skeptical, but she stepped aside anyway, accepting Joe's brief introduction.

I had stood in this suite once before, the day I had accused Tristan of being my family's killer. I hadn't paid attention to it then, too blinded by my rage. Standing there again, I felt like I could hear Tristan's voice screaming again, declaring his love for my sister and commanding me to leave. It felt like the words still ricocheted around this room in echoes so loud I almost wondered if Joe and Talia could hear them. I felt somewhat uncomfortable standing in here again with that memory so visceral in my mind, but I had a different reason for urgency today.

The shared space was a spacious living room, office, and kind of parlor room for receiving visitors. I imagined that the more sane visitors, unlike myself, were greeted there, likely by a servant. I couldn't see all of Talia's suite, but it looked like a bigger version of mine with more defined rooms. The only difference was that everything was white. I guessed that was intentional—every other suite was decorated to match the province, so it would make sense that the Yores would have neutral suites—but I wondered how many maids it took to keep such large rooms so pristine.

Talia changed her clothes and got her brother. She'd been right: Tristan was already awake, working in his office. We sat in the joint living room waiting for Tristan to emerge from his office. When he finally did walk in, I stood immediately.

"Why haven't you answered my texts?" The wave of relief I felt seeing that he was okay and that I could put my irrational panics to rest was replaced by annoyance at a rapid rate.

"You texted?" He pulled his phone from his pocket and searched. He seemed so unaffected, but I had seen the flash in his eyes when he saw me. I knew the wounds I had inflicted were still stinging. "Oh, yes. So sorry about that. I've been very busy, and unfortunately, it hasn't allowed much time to talk."

"It was important, Tristan."

Tristan was taken aback. "Everything I do is important."

I huffed and pointed at Joe. "This is my uncle Joe."

"We've met."

"You have?"

"He's the Duke of Graycott, Julia, of course we've met."

"Sir," Joe began, "with all due respect, Julia does have something important to discuss with you."

Tristan sat, so I did, too, and I laid out the entire thing. I showed them the travel logs, the investigations, the itineraries, and while I spared Jane and Tristan the embarrassment of showing the diary, I explained the important parts. Talia interjected several times to ask questions for clarification, but Tristan said nothing the entire time.

"So, it was us?" Talia said. "They were after us?"

"Wait," I said. "Both of you were supposed to join them in Falkirk?"

She nodded. "We had business in Falkirk, Graycott, and Idlewick, but we didn't end up going because of the threat of war between Trilland and Riagala. We had to communicate with Trilland as our ally, though the war didn't end up happening after all."

Tristan added, "I left earlier, even before my father's royal dinner, to meet with some representatives from Trilland, so I was supposed to meet Talia later to join them on the trip to the southwestern provinces as planned, but the international situation was so fragile that I didn't feel it was right to leave."

Vaguely, I did remember the war. I couldn't have cared less at the time—my family had just died—but it was all over the news. Everyone was sure that war was imminent, but in the end, Trilland was able to fend off Riagala's threats without involvement from Lithilea. But at the time, it was definitely a more pressing concern than routine business in the provinces, and it was a very sudden announcement, so the Yores' travel plans would have changed in a moment.

"I forgot about that," I said.

"You thought it was just Tristan?" Talia asked.

I shrugged. "Jane only mentioned Tristan by name," I said, but when I saw Tristan wince, I wished I hadn't. Quickly, I added, "So, you didn't tell Jane that that plan changed?"

Tristan looked at me as if it was a ridiculous question, as if I had somehow offended him. "I wanted to tell her. I didn't want to leave her wondering, but it happened so last minute."

As if to soften the moment, Talia said, "We do try to keep those last minute changes quiet to avoid causing concern and, well, for safety reasons. We had intended to communicate with your family that we were no longer going to meet them in Falkirk, but everything happened so fast."

"Why didn't the train stop here?" I asked. "The records showed it was supposed to be here."

Talia answered, "Because Tristan skipped the state dinner, he actually stayed here to work. He figured it would be easier to work without distraction since everyone was at Lithilea Castle. The plan was to go back through here to pick him up and go on as scheduled, but when we decided it was better to stay, we shifted to meeting them in Falkirk. Then Tristan got held up again, so we canceled the trip entirely. Tristan went back to the castle."

Finally, Tristan said, in a low voice, "Have you communicated all of this with the authorities?"

"We have," Joe said, "but they've yet to respond."

Tristan nodded slowly. "I'll alert our parents."

"Mom'll panic," Talia said.

"They have to know. We'll have to inform the directors of Lithilea Prep as well. Extra security may be needed. For all of us."

"That's it?" Talia said. "Just 'hire more guards,' and you call it a day?"

Tristan pinched the bridge of his nose. "What would you have me do, Talia?"

"I don't know, *something*. You find out that someone tried to assassinate us, and you don't even react."

"This is me reacting. I'm handling the situation."

"Can you stop being king for a second?"

"I'm not king."

Talia huffed loudly and stood. "Shut up, will you? Do you care? Do you even care beyond your responsibilities, your duties? We could have died. Julia's family did die, and for us. It should have been us. Don't you care that people are dead right now because of us?"

"Of course I care!" Tristan shouted, standing, and though Talia was not much shorter, she cowered in the presence of her brother's wrath. "How dare you accuse me of being so unfeeling? You think I wanted any of this to happen? You think I wanted to lose the Clarkes? But it's done, and now I want to protect everyone else here. I want to protect Mom and Dad, I want to protect you, Talia, and I want to protect Julia and everyone else here. That is my *job*, and that is my *duty*. You should know that by now."

"I *do* know that. You really think I don't get that? I train for this job just like you do, you know."

"But it's not your job. It's mine."

Talia took a step back, and the look on her face made me regret Tristan's words though I hadn't spoken them.

"Okay, okay," Joe said, standing and holding his hands out between Tristan and Talia. "This is very unsettling news. Maybe we just all need to take a break and process it."

Talia said quietly, "Sir Joseph is right. I'm going for a walk."

This was the side of Tristan that occasionally scared me. It was the side of him that had made me doubt him, though I so deeply regretted it now. He was so forceful and intimidating. I imagined that he had to be to be the future king. A spineless ruler couldn't bode well for a nation. And I was glad to know I wasn't the only one capable of provoking such ire. Still, it was unsettling. I wondered if he and Talia often had fights like this.

Talia walked out, reluctant to look Tristan in the eye. I nodded my head in Tristan's direction, and luckily, Joe took the hint.

"Julia," he said, "I'm going to head back to your suite."

"I'll meet you there later," I said.

Once Tristan and I were alone, he finally let down the facade that he'd only let down with me once before, the facade that Stephen assured me came down every once in a while. He collapsed onto the sofa, undid his jacket button, and sighed, one arm draped over his eyes. I wanted to be the first to speak—I owed him so many apologies and explanations—but he beat me to it, and he didn't say what I expected.

"I didn't mean to blow up at her," he said.

"I know."

"This is a lot to take in."

"It is."

He moved his arm and looked at me. "You really figured this all out based on some random reference to cargo?"

"It wasn't just that. I figured out that you were the cargo because of the way my sister talked about you in her diary."

"Please don't read it to me," he said quickly. "I don't want to violate her privacy. Even now."

"I won't."

He nodded, and a lone tear slipped down his cheek, hanging from his jaw line as he continued to nod.

"I wanted to tell her how I felt. I was going to see her when she came back to Lithilea Prep."

"I know."

"I even thought about coming to Graycott for the holidays to clear everything up. I hated thinking she'd have to wait to know how I felt. But then—" his voice stuck in his throat, and he trailed off.

"I think she knew."

"It shouldn't have happened this way," he said. "It shouldn't have been her."

"It shouldn't have been you, either."

"But Jane was—she was—" he was unable to continue as his chest shook with sobs.

"I know," I said, moving to the same sofa as him to rub his shoulder. "I know."

Chapter Nineteen

July 10 —

Julia apologized, and we made up. Then we had another fight.

I thought maybe she would change her mind about Lithilea Prep, but stubborn thing that she is, she didn't. I probably shouldn't have tried, but whatever.

It just feels wrong to be here without her. It always has, and I don't know if I'll ever get past that. Just the other day I was talking to Paige and Peter. They're so close. Julia and I used to be like that. Is the reason we strayed because she didn't come to school, or was it destined to happen? I wish I had their relationship. They're clearly going to be close forever. It's the perfect sibling relationship. Is it wrong that I'm jealous?

***

The next day at school, everything felt heavy. I couldn't have said that I ever really enjoyed being at Lithilea Prep, but I realized then that I had enjoyed at least some part of it. I wasn't sure what, exactly, but I knew that everything was different. Something had broken, and I wasn't sure if it could be fixed.

I'd always known that Lithilea Prep was guarded to ensure not just our security but, more importantly, the Yores' security, but I'd never noticed them before. They were good at staying hidden to keep the illusion that we were somehow attending a normal school. Now they were everywhere, and they didn't bother to hide. Were there more than usual, or did it just feel that way now that they were out in the open? Did it matter?

Everyone was a little more cautious. The usual hiking on the trails had all but stopped, fewer people ate outside, and not because of the heat, and there was less laughter and joking. Everyone was just going through the motions, it seemed. Attending class, eating lunch, going home. It wasn't much more than that.

The absolute worst part, though, was the distrust. No one trusted each other anymore. Someone in Lithilea had killed, and everyone here now felt that weight. Friendships were strained, enemies were more volatile than ever, and even general acquaintances were scrutinized. That was the part I wasn't sure could be fixed again.

It had only been a day since Tristan had made the announcement, but it was already so drastically different. Even though Tristan had kept the details about his own family being targeted quiet for now, he had officially made it known that my family had been murdered instead of dying in a freak accident, and that put everyone on edge. Weirdly, it kind of felt like everyone at Lithilea Prep had only just realized that Jane was dead. It's like they could tell themselves that she was just away from school, that I was taking her place, maybe temporarily, but that she was okay. Somehow, the news that she had been murdered made her death real to everyone. I had already processed my grief, but everyone here was only just starting to grapple with it. It was a lot more uncomfortable now because people were acting strangely with me. Before, it was like most people either hated me or avoided me. Now, some people tried to smile, some started crying when they saw me, and some avoided any contact with me altogether. It was a weird feeling. I almost preferred when everyone hated me.

Desperate for some sense of normalcy, I ate lunch outside, alone. No one had offered to join me, and I was perfectly happy to be by myself for a little while. It was really too hot to sit outside comfortably, but I accepted the sweating in exchange for the fresh air and solitude. That is, until Paige sat down across from me very suddenly.

"What?" I said. Paige had finally figured out that I didn't want her around, and now here she was.

"I'm so sorry," she said, rather emphatically.

"For what?"

"Well, Jane—"

"Did you kill her?"

She sat back, and for a moment, I thought she might burst into tears. What would I do if she did? "N-no. Of course not."

"Then why are you apologizing?"

She huffed. "I don't know, Julia, I'm just trying to talk to you. That's all I've been trying to do since you got here."

"Yeah, right," I said, rolling my eyes. "All you've done is talk *about* me. Big difference."

"What are you talking about?"

I slammed shut the book I had been reading. "You know, at least Olivia is up front. She might hate my guts, but at least she's honest about it."

"Olivia is a jerk."

"And you laughed right along with her when she called me 'poor man's Jane Clarke.'"

She slouched suddenly, and she seemed to search for the right words, opening and closing her mouth several times. I started to get impatient with her, but eventually she spoke.

"I never would have done that."

"I *saw* you that day. You were right there with Olivia and her groupies. *You're* the one who asked the question in the first place."

"Yeah, I'm also the one who ripped into her after what she said. I guess you didn't hear that part, did you? *I'm* the one who told her that she was being cruel and insensitive and that she should shut up because she doesn't know what she's talking about."

I stared into Paige's eyes, noting the intensity, the fire in them. She meant what she said. I thought back to that first day at Lithilea Prep, how Paige had asked who I was, how Olivia had said those words—*poor man's Jane Clarke*—and realized that Cecily had dragged me away at that moment.

"I thought—"

"Well maybe you should pay more attention. Not that I would've done it anyway, but I've got a lot going on in my own life. I don't have time to obsess over you like Olivia does. Do you know where Peter is right now? Did you notice he wasn't in class again? He's in the hospital for the third time this semester. He's my priority, not the new girl. I felt bad hearing about what happened to Jane because I felt like I'd been ignoring you due to Peter's health, but boy, was I wrong to feel bad. This entire time you thought I was some narcissistic jerk like Olivia."

We sat in silence for several minutes. I half expected her to get up at any moment and storm off or start yelling again, but she didn't, and her frequent glances at me suggested that she thought the same of me. I thought about Peter: he had missed more classes than he'd been present for. I thought about how they always had their arms around each other. I had thought they were just oddly affectionate, but now I realized that she was supporting his weight. I thought about all the times she had tried to reach out, how I had been the one to shut her down.

I couldn't afford any more enemies, and Paige was the furthest thing from my enemy. Someone had to be the first to break the ice, so I nominated myself.

"I didn't know about Peter."

She shrugged. "We've all gone to school together for so long. Sometimes I forget that the new people don't know."

"What is—why is he sick?"

"Inoperable brain tumor," she said, so cavalier that I wanted to be sick. "Had it for a few years now. He shouldn't really be at school at all, but he begged our parents to let him go. He wanted the rest of his life to be normal even though he'll probably never be the Duke of Hadleigh."

Paige was the younger sibling, and yet she'd known for years now that she was basically the heir. It was like we were living the same life just with a different path. Neither of us was ever supposed to be the duchess of our respective provinces, but our siblings were lost, and here we were. Without that stupid misunderstanding, we might have been friends. I decided that I saw no reason why we couldn't be now.

"I didn't want to be duchess, you know," I said.

"Me neither. Peter would be so much better at it."

"Jane would have been so much better than me."

"I wish I could trade places with him."

"I wish Jane were still alive, that I could have saved her. I know I couldn't have, but it feels like I could've if I had known."

She smiled sadly. "Before I realized that I would have to be Duchess of Hadleigh now, I thought I would go to medical school."

"Really?"

She nodded. "I thought the doctors treating Peter must not be trying hard enough if they thought the tumor was inoperable. I thought

I'd somehow figure out the one way to save him. He's just such a better person, especially compared to me."

"Jane was the same way."

Neither of us spoke for a few moments, just letting the wall between us come crashing down. We were finally healing, and somehow, it felt like I was healing on my own, too.

I said, "I'm sorry I thought you were a colossal jerk."

"I'm sorry I didn't yell at Olivia in front of you."

"If it hadn't been for Olivia, I think my first few days would've been pretty different."

She snorted. "That's probably true of everyone."

"I hope we can put this behind us now?"

Finally, she smiled genuinely. "Me, too." After a moment, she asked, "So have you been able to find anything out about the murderer?"

I shook my head. "It's hard to trace anything. I'm trying, but it took long enough to figure out that it wasn't an accident."

"Don't give up. They deserve to pay for what they did."

"Oh, you can bet I won't stop until I find them."

"Good." She smirked again. "I had a feeling. You've never been one to back down from a fight. Didn't think you'd start now."

Paige and I had only just started to get to know each other, just started to communicate, and already it felt like we'd known each other forever. I was furious, both at Olivia and at myself, that so much time had been lost with Paige because of a stupid misunderstanding. We could have been such good friends from the start. I could have had someone to talk to, someone who would've understood everything—the inferiority complex compared to our siblings, the survivor's guilt, the complete lack of desire to be here—but I willfully avoided her. I had let Olivia color my opinions of people well before

I knew her or anyone else. I wouldn't make that mistake again. From now on, I would make up my own mind about everyone here.

***

As I zipped up my red plaid skirt, tucked in my white shirt, and tied off half of my hair with a red ribbon, I found that I didn't hate the way I looked in the Lithilea Prep uniform anymore. I didn't think that I liked it, but it was starting to seem normal. After all, it was just clothes.

I'd just finished doing my eyeliner when someone knocked. Joe had gone back home to Graycott, so I didn't know who I was expecting it to be, but Talia definitely wasn't on the list.

"Could I come in?" she asked, and I was struck by how meek she looked. She held the side of her arm like she felt nervous, and her face looked softer like she wasn't trying to keep everyone around her out. She looked more real, less like the artificial TV princess I'd become accustomed to seeing. Something about her seemed more humble, more honest. I'd never seen Talia like this. She looked so different from her usual public persona. I liked this Talia better.

I gestured to let her past, and she wandered in like she didn't know why she was there. Maybe she didn't.

We hadn't spoken since the other day when I told her and Tristan that the attack had been meant for them, and while that wasn't exactly unusual since we didn't really talk before that, it still felt odd. Tristan and Talia had blown up at each other when I told them, but she remained entirely unreadable. I'd watched the Yore siblings a million times on TV. They were always unreadable. That must have been a skill royals were taught to maintain some kind of presence or image. Talia was certainly the more skilled at it. But somehow, this unreadable expression differed from her usual easy smile and casual hair flip, that enigmatic glint in her eyes that captivated everyone. This was a blank look that betrayed a touch of concern only around the edges.

"I brought you something," she said, both hands behind her back.

"Oh?"

She held out her fist and opened it to a flat palm, revealing a tube of red lipstick, and I couldn't stop the laugh that squeaked out of my lips.

"You brought me lipstick?"

"What's so funny?"

"You were so serious," I said. "I was expecting something intense."

Talia suppressed a chuckle. "Look, I don't know how to do this, but I'm really good at picking lipstick shades for other people, and this color would be perfect on you."

"Not good at what?"

"Friends. Bonding." She gestured half-heartedly around her. "This."

"Well, if you're looking for advice, you're talking to the wrong person."

The blank expression cracked for just a moment, but I couldn't be sure of what I saw. She looked almost nervous, and that wasn't an expression I often saw on Talia's face. She was so good at looking like the epitome of poise and calm. She looked down at the lipstick in her hand, and it was as if it reminded her why she had come to see me.

"Come on," she said, suddenly pushing me toward the bedroom. "You've got to trust me on this lipstick."

"Oh my gosh, you're obsessed."

I sat down on the edge of my bed, and Talia pulled the chair over from the vanity and sat across from me. When she first twisted the lipstick out, I had to laugh.

"You're insane," I said. "That's practically purple."

"It's not, it's a berry. Just chill."

She gripped the side of my face rather forcefully and smeared the lipstick across my lips swiftly but carefully. It was some comfort that even if the color looked bad, the lipstick was very high quality, and I liked the way it felt: smooth instead of cakey. I shouldn't have been surprised that a princess would have good taste in lipstick quality.

I asked, "So how does one become a lipstick color aficionado?"

"Be a second born royal."

I sat back. "Pretty cynical."

She smirked. "Pretty accurate."

"Talia, what is your life like? Like, what do you do?"

"Tristan trains to be king someday. I'm supposed to know everything Tristan does, but I'm also supposed to be charming and dynamic. When we were younger, I used to joke that it was harder being me than being Tristan because I was pulling double duty. He said that being charming wasn't something you had to work at, but he's wrong."

I laughed. "So wrong. It's not a skill I've mastered."

"Honestly? Me either."

I wasn't sure I could ask the question on my mind—were Talia and I close enough to delve into this?—but I couldn't ignore it, and I decided it was worth the risk.

"Do you and Tristan often fight like that?"

To my surprise, she kind of snorted in response. "Something about Tristan not being charming made you think about that?" I laughed, too. "Don't get the wrong idea. We fight like any brother and sister would. At the end of the day, I know he'd fight for me rather than against me."

"I was just surprised at what he said, I guess."

"About me not being the heir?" She shrugged. "It's fine," she said, though something about her tone indicated that it wasn't. "He's not wrong. It's not my place."

"Can I ask kind of a weird question?"

"Sure."

"Would you want to be queen? I mean, would you even want it if you could have it?"

She was quiet for a while, and I started to wonder if I had offended her. Finally, she said, "I used to think so, yes. I used to think I would be better at it than Tristan. Later, I thought I'd be just as good. Now, I think he's just so well-suited to the job. He deserves to be king."

"But do you *want* to be queen?"

She smiled a little sadly. "Well, it doesn't really matter now, does it? I never will be."

"You know, everyone always asks me why I didn't go to Lithilea Prep this whole time. I always say that it's because I was too far down the lineage to have a chance at the title, but the truth is that I didn't think I was good enough. I didn't think I was capable of being a duchess. I'd been told my whole life that Jane was perfect for the role, and maybe she was, but it was just drilled into me that she was it and I wasn't."

She nodded slowly. "That's definitely how it feels sometimes."

"If I could change things, if Jane somehow miraculously came back, I think I'd hand the title right back to her, if I'm being honest. I'd jump at the chance to give it up. But that's not reality. I'm here now, and I think I'm pretty decent at it."

"You are."

"And I think you're a pretty decent princess—queen or not."

Another smile, but happier this time. "Thank you. I just have all of this useless knowledge, you know? I know just as much about foreign affairs, taxes, treaties, budgets, and environmental impact as Tristan, but, if I'm lucky, I'll never need it." She reached behind her and grabbed a small, handheld mirror. "Instead, I'm expected to be really good at smiling and dressing right and saying the right thing. And I am, but—I don't know. It's like I want everyone to know that I'm smart and that I work really hard, but the only way I would ever get to use that knowledge is if Tristan were gone, and I never want that to happen."

"I totally get it."

She thrust the mirror up in front of my face. "But I'm really good at color matching."

She was right: the lipstick was perfect. It was still a red, but it had a heavy purple undertone that turned it truly berry, just as she had said. I always thought red lipstick suited me, but this was the best red lipstick I'd ever worn. It was bold, but it complemented my skin tone.

"Okay, I give. You were right about the lipstick."

Chapter Twenty

June 7 —

Sometimes I wonder what I would have become if I weren't in line to be the duchess. Julia knows she wants to do something with music, but what about me? I feel like I never took the time to study any other skills that weren't directly related to politics or leadership. What if I'm really good at something else and I'll never know because it isn't considered useful?

Sometimes, when the lineage shifts, surprising people become the duke or duchess, and they trained for other positions. Some people were teachers or training to be doctors or engineers. Some had blue collar jobs and did manual labor that they were good at. Are those skills just wasted now?

I wonder if first born is really the best way to do this. Maybe we're taking people with skills that would be more useful elsewhere and plunging them into other fields they never should have occupied. What if Julia would be a better duchess than I would, but we'll never know because I was born first? It seems wrong to put people that were never meant to be in government into such politically charged and powerful roles.

***

There was a shuttle students could ride to get to the buildings that were further away like the library or the main offices. I supposed that I could have taken one today, but I didn't feel like being on a vehicle or being around people who didn't want to speak to me. Instead, despite the oppressive heat, I walked. The heaviness of the hot weather was preferable to the heaviness of silence.

On weekends, the dress code was a bit more relaxed, but I no longer wanted to be relaxed about my appearance. I was the future Duchess of Graycott. My family had been murdered accidentally. I was going to find their killer. It was time for everyone to take me seriously. To that end, I wore black jeans and a Lithilea Prep issued red polo shirt. I still wore my ankle boots because wearing heels to walk in the desert sand was wildly impractical, and even though I was only going to see Tristan today, I wore a full face of makeup and styled my hair. I looked the part now—the way Jane always did—and I was going to act the part.

I was only a few yards from the library when Stephen rounded the corner of the walkway, nearly crashing into me. We made eye contact only briefly before his eyes darted away, and he fidgeted with the books in his hands.

"Hey," I said.

He replied, "Hey," but there was a bite to his response that stung.

I pointed at the stack of books he held. "That's a lot. Did I miss an assignment or something?"

He shook his head. "Research. For a proposed bill."

I nodded. I was desperate for something else to say, but how could I even start? A very loud and persistent part of me wanted to apologize, but a louder, more stubborn part of me insisted that he had overstepped.

"I hear you went home," he said abruptly, and while the words felt civil, his tone was still edged in bitterness.

I nodded. "I'm glad I did. I talked to my uncle. We found out something about the train accident—"

"Yeah, I know. Tristan told me."

"Have you heard anything else?"

"No. I'll tell you if I do."

"I guess I'll ask Wade if he's heard anything."

His face twisted, and I almost regretted bringing him up. "Wade?"

"Yes, Wade. What is your problem?"

"Whatever, sorry I said anything. Don't blame me if you find out he doesn't really care anything about you or the investigation."

This was a worthless venture. He was so mad that he could barely talk to me. I was only getting frustrated with him. After everything, was this all he could offer me? I had thought he had really cared about me, but now he was freezing me out and shutting me down. I knew that he was hurt, but this felt too cold, especially from Stephen.

"Okay, well, I guess I'll see you later," I said, letting the frustration creep into my voice.

"See you later," he said, and he kept walking without looking back, and I didn't know why I expected him to turn around. Maybe I wanted him to.

I continued into the library study rooms where I knew I'd find Tristan. He had told me to meet him here, and I honestly hadn't spent much time in this library since I had started school at Lithilea Prep. I knew that Tristan spent a lot of time either here or in his family's suite, and now I understood why he liked it so much. It had the perfect library vibe: it was quiet but not void of sound, and it didn't look like many people used it very often. I liked the serenity. I made a mental note to make use of this space more often.

It didn't take me long to figure out which room Tristan was in. There were guards outside of it. It was so unusual to see that, and I still hadn't gotten used to it. I wondered if that would go back to normal after the bomber was caught or if this was a permanent change I'd have to get used to.

I smiled at the guards and started to introduce myself—whether that was actually necessary, I didn't know, but I was intimidated enough to do it—but Tristan saw me through the glass window and shouted out an okay to the guards who opened the door for me.

"Hello, Julia," he said, not glancing up from the massive stack of papers he held in his hands.

"Hi," I said, taking the seat across from him.

There was still a strange tension between us. We hadn't really discussed his relationship with my sister, and I had never really apologized for accusing him of her murder. I thought that we both knew how the other felt, but I didn't want to make any assumptions regarding how I had treated him. At the very least, I owed him that apology.

"Are you busy?" I said, nodding in the direction of the stack of papers.

He laughed. "Always, but it's fine. Besides, I asked you to meet me here."

"I know, but still. I don't want to interrupt."

Tristan finally looked up, and his expression softened. "You're never interrupting, Julia. I mean that."

I nodded. "We haven't really talked since—"

"There's nothing to say."

I glanced over at the guards, and even though I was pretty sure they couldn't hear us, I still feared saying these words out loud in their presence. "There is. I never should have yelled at you like that. I never should have accused you of—"

He held up his hand to stop me. "Later, when I wasn't so caught off guard and was less angry, I understood why you reacted the way that you did."

"You shouldn't. There wasn't a reason. I just overreacted."

"But you knew I was hiding something from you. It wasn't intentional."

"I know that," I said quickly.

"I just—I didn't know how to tell you or if I should or if you already knew—"

"I didn't know, which is honestly kind of surprising. Jane and I used to tell each other everything. I guess I hadn't realized how much our relationship had drifted until I realized she had kept a massive secret from me."

"She used to talk about you, you know."

I sat up straighter. "Really? What did she say?"

He laughed loudly. "What *didn't* she say? I think you were the topic she brought up most often. She used to tell me childhood stories, things she respected and admired about you, and how she missed you."

I nodded, feeling my eyes well with tears. "We used to fight all the time over my decision not to attend Lithilea Prep. My parents gave me the option, but I thought it was pointless. I think Jane just wanted me here with her, but I felt like I would have been living a lie. Now I wish I had spent that time with her. Or at least not fought with her about it."

"I wish I could take back the fight we had before—" he cut off and rubbed his hands over one another nervously. "I just wish I hadn't left it that way."

"Even though she never told me about you, I think it's pretty obvious how much she cared about you. You're all over her diary. I think she knew."

"I hope so," he said. We sat silently for a few moments before he added, "And she only fought with you because she believed in you. She thought you would have made a great duchess."

"I don't know about that."

"I do," Tristan said, locking eyes with me. "She told me so."

"She did?"

He nodded. "She usually said it in moments of insecurity, but she used to identify specific attributes about you that would make you a perfect duchess. She said you were determined and passionate and, well, stubborn," he said with a laugh. "I see what she meant now."

Neither of us said anything for a while. It felt like something had healed between us, and not because I apologized, though I needed to do that. We had both given each other the missing piece we'd lost with Jane's death. I didn't know what the future held for me as a duchess or for my professional relationship or my friendship with Tristan, but I knew that we understood each other in a way I didn't think anyone else would. I used to think that no one knew Jane the way I did. All they saw was the image Jane projected. But Tristan had seen the real Jane.

After a while, I asked, "Have you heard anything new from the investigative team?"

He shook his head. "Not since the report that the bomber must be knowledgeable about train systems. When I reported your findings, they confirmed that that aligned with other information they had found, but they still haven't been able to connect it to anyone, not even a specific province."

I glanced at the guards again. "Does all of this unsettle you?"

He looked at me, and his eyebrow raised slightly. "Why do you ask?"

"Well it's scary. If I found out that my life was on the line, I'd be concerned."

He smiled ever so slightly. "No one has asked me that, you know. Everything has been all business. What am I going to do about it, what plans are in place, how am I protecting Lithilea. No one has asked about my own feelings."

"And?"

"It is unsettling. These are the ugly realities of being the heir, but I try not to think about them. Usually, the concerns are focused externally. I never thought I'd have to worry about my own people."

"If they want you dead, they're not your people. At least, they shouldn't be."

"I appreciate you saying that. I've certainly had my conflicts with different provinces, but I never thought it would escalate to this."

"What kind of conflicts?"

He sighed. "Oh, everything, really. Sometimes our fellow future leaders develop bills that they want me to sponsor. They know that if I sponsor them that they are far more likely to pass, but I can't just put my name to anything. I've shot down a few bills over the years."

"Really?"

"In the last year alone, I've rejected bills from Aerilot, Carlisle, Dalmerlin, and Falkirk."

"Aerilot?" I snorted. "Olivia must have loved that."

He smiled, and I could tell that he was suppressing a laugh. "She didn't receive it too well, no. Really, I feel bad for Stephen. I've never rejected one of his bills, and some people think it's because I favor him, but really, he just does his research. He's very good at what he does."

The mention of Stephen made my heart sting a little, remembering our conversation moments ago. I wished it was different between us, but I didn't know if we'd be able to get over what I had said to him. I thought about the books I'd seen him holding. Tristan was right: he did his research.

"Are you okay?" Tristan asked, and I realized that my face must have betrayed my feelings.

"I'm fine," I said.

Thankfully, my phone buzzed right at that moment. I checked it to see a text from Wade. He agreed to meet up with me today. Despite Stephen's warnings, I had to talk to him. I knew he would know more than Tristan or maybe even Stephen. I replied that I'd meet him on the trails and stood up, grabbing my bag.

"I'm so sorry to run, but I have to meet someone. Can we talk more later?"

He smiled. "Of course. Let me know if you need anything."

***

I waited at the gates of Lithilea Prep for Wade. We couldn't talk on campus—there was already so much security everywhere that I couldn't imagine we'd be able to talk freely. I wasn't planning to stray too far from campus. There were some walking trails on the outskirts of the campus as well, and many of the students used them as well as the internal ones. With the latest state of security implemented by King Tybalt, I was sure that the trails were not totally void of guards. Still, I needed to be away from listening ears to talk to Wade.

I checked my phone: still no response from Stephen. I was trying to fix what I broke when it came to him, but it looked like I wasn't succeeding. Maybe he just needed more time. I could only hope.

I saw Wade approaching from a distance, and for some reason, I was surprised to see that he looked the same. I wasn't sure why I expected something different. I guess everyone was so different now that I didn't know what to think. I had been so wrong about Paige and Talia, even Rose. I hadn't known how deeply Tristan's affections for my sister ran. Stephen had been a real friend this entire time. It seemed that ever since I found out the train accident was carefully orchestrated to attack Tristan's family, not mine, I didn't know how I viewed anyone anymore. But Wade was still Wade. He'd never been anything else.

"Hey," I said, mostly because I didn't know what else to say. I hadn't seen Wade since I got back from Graycott.

"Welcome back, stranger," he said with a smile. "How was Graycott?"

"Really good. I'm glad I went. I needed to spend some time with my uncle."

Wade raised an eyebrow but didn't say anything. He knew my relationship with Joe had been strained, but I'd never gotten into the gory details. They didn't matter now.

We started to walk along the trails as Wade asked, "So, what did you want to talk about?"

"Have you heard the latest about the investigation?" I asked, and he shook his head. "The bomber wasn't targeting my family. They were actually targeting the Yore family."

Wade's eyes widened, and he kicked a few rocks along the trail. "Really? How did they figure that out?"

"The explosive wasn't attached to my family's car. It was attached to the car in front of theirs, and that's where the Yores were supposed to be."

"I didn't realize the Yores were going to be on that train. I thought they were staying at the castle."

"Well, just Tristan and Talia. They were supposed to stay, but then they had to join to visit some of the provinces, then ended up not going. It was a last minute change that they weren't on the train."

He nodded slowly, and I was shocked by how solemn he looked. I'd never seen Wade look so serious except for when he talked about his own family drama. This was the rare side of Wade that most never saw: the vulnerable side.

"So they never intended to hurt your family."

"I guess not. That's why the security has been so intense lately. Whoever set off the explosion is probably still after the Yore family."

"Security?"

I stopped walking and looked at him until he stopped. "Yeah, they're everywhere. Haven't you seen them?"

"I guess I didn't notice."

We kept walking. I wondered how he hadn't noticed. Is that what it was like to be from an elite province? You just didn't notice danger? Or had I only noticed because I knew what was happening? Maybe the guards had been more subtle than I realized. Or maybe Wade was just clueless.

"How does that change things for you?" he asked after a while.

"What do you mean?"

"I mean, does that change how you view the investigation?"

I shrugged. "Not really. Even if my family wasn't the target, they're still dead, and now my friends are on the line. I still want to know who did it."

"How will you find them?"

"I have no idea."

He sighed. "This is such a mess."

I couldn't help but laugh. "Tell me about it. As if school isn't hard enough without all of this happening."

"You'll find your stride eventually. It just takes time."

"How long was it before you felt like you hit yours?"

Wade thought for a long time. "Honestly? Longer than you probably want to know."

"That's not reassuring."

"It's just a process. I think a lot of the students here wonder if they're cut out to rule a duchy. It's just such a weird concept to think about as a teenager." Neither of us spoke for a moment. Then Wade added, "What did you want to be? Before the accident, I mean. You thought you'd never be a duchess, so what did you picture for your future?"

"Concert pianist," I said without hesitation. "Or something in music."

"I didn't know that," he said with a smile.

I nodded. "I've played the piano since I was tiny. I love it. It's the only thing that always makes sense to me. But that's gone."

"Doesn't mean you can't still play."

"What about you?"

"What about me?"

"What did you want to be? You weren't always going to be a duke."

"But I've known for a lot longer than you have," he said.

"Still, you must have thought about it. Come on, if you weren't the future Duke of Dalmerlin, what would you do?"

He twisted the corner of his mouth. "I don't know. Probably something with my hands. Desk jobs aren't for me."

I laughed. "Ironic."

He laughed, too. "I know, right? But I've always liked working with my hands, building something or fixing something. I think I get that from my dad."

"Yeah? What does he do?"

"Well, these days, mostly just support my mom as the current duchess. He's good at that. But before my uncle died, when he didn't think he was marrying the future duchess, he was a mechanic."

"And he quit? Couldn't he have continued being a mechanic since he's not the duke?"

Wade shrugged. "Yeah, I guess, but he didn't want to be distracted from my mom and her responsibilities. He traveled a lot for work, and he wanted to be home more. He was a train mechanic, so he used to follow the trains on their treks to maintain them."

My blood froze in my veins, and I suddenly stopped walking. Wade's dad was a train mechanic. He would have extensive knowledge of how the trains worked and their travel logs.

No. It *couldn't* be. I had to be wrong.

Wade turned to look at me and raised an eyebrow. "You okay?"

I nodded a little too fast. "Yeah, fine. Sorry, I, uh, got a rock in my shoe."

Wade nodded and kept walking, so I forced my legs to move. I could have been wrong. I could have been completely and totally wrong. How many train mechanics must there have been in Lithilea? Besides, why would Wade's family have wanted to hurt the Yore family? I had no reason to think anything.

"So," I said, trying to maintain normal conversation, "your dad was a train mechanic? That's cool."

"Yeah, I guess so. I've always thought I was a lot like my dad, so I always pictured myself alongside him on the trains. Never thought I'd be here."

This was perfectly normal. This was why Wade and I had connected. There was nothing odd about anything Wade was saying. He never really had fit in here, so it made sense he was more comfortable around machinery instead of politics. My pulse started to slow, and I felt a little more at ease. This was just a weird coincidence.

"Okay, so what is your plan for Dalmerlin?" I asked.

He laughed. "What do you mean?"

"Prince Tristan told me once that I needed to figure out what my plan for Graycott was. I needed to decide what angle I would approach to help fix Graycott's problems. What do you want to do for Dalmerlin?"

"Honestly?" he asked, and I nodded. "I just don't think Dalmerlin is as well-respected as everyone thinks. Sure, it's an elite province, but what does that matter in the grand scheme of things? Dalmerlin is kind of stuck in the middle. It's not Aerilot or Bredon, but it's not Idlewick either." I winced at the put-down of Idlewick. "I just feel like nobody thinks very much of Dalmerlin or my family."

"I don't think that's true."

He shot me a glare before he softened his expression. "You haven't been here very long. You haven't seen it."

"Stephen always says it doesn't matter what the others here think about us."

"Yeah, I'm not so sure Stephen would say that to me. I think he only meant that for you."

"I don't think so. Besides, Tristan's opinion is what actually matters, isn't it? I mean, he's who you will report to."

"That's not reassuring. Prince Tristan hates my family."

That icy feeling crept back into my neck. "I'm sure that's not true."

"He's had it out for me for a long time. He likes to say he's all friendly and wants us to be one big happy family, but he doesn't mean it. I'm low on the list of people Tristan respects."

The thought was nagging at me, and I couldn't ignore the chills I was getting on my arms despite the heat outside. I glanced around and noticed that I didn't see any guards. Surely they were there, right? They were just hidden? How far down this trail had we walked, away from the campus?

I slipped my phone from my back pocket and texted Stephen: *With Wade. You were right. I think he did it.*

As soon as I sent the message, I questioned everything about it. So what if Wade was mad at Tristan? It didn't necessarily mean anything.

Besides, it was a pointless text to send; Stephen wouldn't answer any-way.

"Everything okay?" Wade said suddenly, nodding in the direction of my phone.

"Yeah, yeah, everything's fine. Just a text from Rose, that's all."

Wade maintained eye contact with me for a few seconds too long, then said, "Didn't realize you were friends. Like texting friends."

"We're not, really," I tried to say casually. "She keeps trying to be friends because of Jane, but she can't take a hint."

I threw in a laugh at the end, but it sounded so fake, and I worried about how Wade would react. If I was wrong, if he wasn't responsible, at best, I would have seemed really weird and suspicious, like I didn't care about what he was telling me. At worst—well, I didn't want to think about that.

"It's so hard, isn't it?" he asked.

"What?"

"Being fake. It's so hard to be fake with all of these people."

"Yeah, I guess so."

"I feel like I'm always faking it for everyone. Looking all nice so that people accept me."

"You don't have to," I said. "You could just be yourself."

"That's ridiculous. Nobody really wants someone like me to be myself."

"How do you know if you never try?" I asked, hoping to maintain some kind of normalcy in this conversation, but Wade's tone and eyes were becoming increasingly intimidating, and I wasn't sure how to keep him calm, to avoid letting him know my thoughts.

"Believe me, I've tried. It doesn't work out too well."

He turned away from me, seeming to fidget with something in his pocket. I flipped my phone over in my hand and pulled up Tristan's name. I started to type out a warning message while I spoke.

"It worked with me, didn't it? You and I became friends."

"I'm not so sure," he said.

I think Wade—was all I got out in a text to Tristan before the side of my head cracked, and I hit the ground, blacking out quickly.

Chapter Twenty-One

*O*ctober 20—

There are so many things I have to think about in terms of becoming the duchess of Graycott that I never imagined I'd have to think about. I guess I always pictured the work: the meetings, the writing of bills, the national events. I didn't think about the more practical things like safety.

Dad and Uncle Joe tell me that I have to think about my own safety and have plans in place, but I'm not sure I agree. Lithilea isn't at war, and Graycott wouldn't exactly be at the top of anyone's list to attack anyway. Why would anyone try to harm me?

I think Uncle Joe believes that I'm not taking this seriously enough. Yesterday, he gave me a pocket knife. What am I supposed to do with a pocket knife? I didn't tell him, but I just tossed it into one of my boxes at school. If security is really so important, then I'll have guards or some kind of security detail. When am I ever going to have to face someone in hand-to-hand combat, and what good would a pocket knife do for me?

***

I felt my heartbeat in my head before I even opened my eyes which felt too heavy to function. My pulse pounded in the exact spot on my head where I'd felt the crack. It was so strong that I was convinced I must have been bleeding, but I was still surprised to see streaks of blood running down my arm. When I shifted, my head pounded more aggressively, but I noticed that my arms were restricted behind my back. Panic set in as I realized they were zip-tied.

I tried to look around, moving my head very slowly, and I didn't recognize where I was. It looked kind of like a small warehouse, but I didn't know of anywhere near Lithilea Prep that looked like this. There was some machinery in here—though I wasn't sure what kind—and it produced a dull roar. Other than the machinery, a few cardboard boxes, and the chair I was sitting on, I didn't see anything else. Or anyone else. I spotted two doors: one wooden door on the other side of the room and one garage-style door that was not very far in front of me. It wasn't totally closed, but it was only cracked slightly at the bottom, and I wouldn't have fit through if I tried.

I closed my eyes and took a few deep breaths. *Think, Julia, think.* I didn't see Wade. It was possible that he wasn't there. I looked down at my feet. They weren't zip-tied. I could run. But I wouldn't get very far with my hands tied, and I didn't even know where I was. If I ran, and Wade caught me, I wasn't sure what he would do. I had to be smart about this.

I wiped the side of my head on my shoulder and saw that blood and sweat soaked my sleeve. I was a little dizzy, and I wasn't sure if it was from the heat, the blood loss, the blow to the head, or the fear. Likely, it was a combination.

Suddenly, my phone rang, and I realized it was across the room sitting on top of some cardboard boxes. I hoped, prayed that it was Stephen, but what good would it do me if it was? I couldn't answer, and he didn't know where I was. Besides, Stephen hadn't answered any of my texts. Why would he answer now? He would get to say "I told you so" about Wade. That is, if he ever saw me again.

My phone kept ringing. Someone was calling multiple times. I thought about getting up and trying to grab it, but before I could move, I saw the garage door move up and a black silhouette hoisted it up. I could tell by the way he moved that it was Wade. He picked up the phone, checked the screen, then tossed it into the gears of the machine near him, and the machine ground and squealed as it crushed my phone. I tried to ignore how my heart rate quickened and my throat felt tight.

"Oh," he said suddenly, looking a little surprised to see me. "You're awake."

"Wade, what are you doing?"

He set a small box on top of the box where my phone had been and opened it. He seemed to be looking for something, and it wasn't a very large box, but he also didn't seem to be in a hurry to find whatever he was looking for. I noticed that he had left the garage door half open.

"Wade," I said more forcefully when he didn't answer.

"Please, Julia," he said, "be quiet for a moment." I was surprised by how quiet his voice sounded. I hardly heard him over the stuttering of the machinery.

"But Wade—"

"Stop it!" he shouted, and the room felt strangely quiet despite the machinery's roar. "Don't make this harder than it has to be."

He sounded—upset? How could I describe it?—unsure of what he was doing. He was still rummaging in the box, and I was sure that I heard the click of a bullet in the chamber of a gun. My head throbbed, but I forced myself not to look afraid, not to shake or cry in front of him.

"Please talk to me," I said, though I wasn't sure why. What did I want him to say? Maybe I just wanted to delay him.

"There's nothing to talk about."

"Please. I've always stood by you. I've always heard you out. Don't you owe it to me to explain what you're doing?"

He slammed his fist down on the box, and I was glad that he wasn't facing me so that he didn't see me jump. "You don't understand!"

"Then explain it to me."

He went still, and he seemed to contemplate that. I saw him tuck the pistol into the back of the waistband of his pants. The motion jogged a memory. Before I left my suite this morning, I had tucked the pocketknife Joe had given me in the side of my boot, tucked under the cuff of my jeans this morning. I felt uneasy with all of the extra security, and I wanted to feel like I could handle myself if someone came after me. I shifted my foot and could have cried when I realized that it was still there. I tucked my foot under the chair and tried to lift it high enough to reach my hands. It was hard, and the angle of the chair didn't help. I just had to hope that Wade didn't turn around and see me. I finally caught the edge of the knife and tucked it up into my fists. It definitely wasn't hidden, but as long as Wade didn't walk behind me, he probably wouldn't notice. I'd done it just in time, too, because just as I moved my foot back, he turned around.

"It wasn't supposed to be like this, you know."

"Like what?"

He gestured to me. "This. You weren't supposed to get hurt. Neither was your sister, your family."

"Then what happened?"

"It was only supposed to be the Yores. No one else was supposed to get hurt. We checked the train schedules. It was only supposed to be the Yores."

"But my family's schedule isn't the one that changed. The Yores' did."

"We checked the schedule!"

"Who's we?"

His expression softened just a little. "My dad and I didn't want anyone else to get hurt. We're not the bad guys here. We chose the holidays because everyone else would already be home. Only the Yores would be traveling."

I moved the knife painfully slowly against the zip tie, careful not to move my arms so much that he would notice. I had no idea how long it would take to cut through at this rate. I didn't even know how sharp the knife was. "Why the Yores?"

He started pacing. "Why not? They hate Dalmerlin, my family. They've done nothing but cause us problems."

"What kind of problems?" I asked, and when he scoffed, I added, "I don't know this history. I wasn't at Lithilea Prep."

That seemed to appease him, and he stopped pacing. "They've never approved any bill my mother or I have proposed. Dalmerlin is suffering, and they don't care. They're struggling, and they need the reforms we're proposing, but they just keep shooting them down. They don't even ask us or visit Dalmerlin to see what's going on. They just assume we're wrong. They've never liked us, they've never liked my parents, especially my dad."

"Why especially your dad?"

"Oh, he doesn't fit the mold. None of us do, but my mom gets a pass. At least she was born in the line of succession. You know how that is, Julia. When you're the outsider who was never supposed to sit in the duchy office, you're not exactly popular."

"But you were born in the line of succession."

He laughed, and it sent a chill down my spine. "A lot of good that did me. I thought maybe Tristan would be different from his father. I thought he would actually care like he pretends to. I was sorely mistaken. He is his father's son, but, unfortunately for him, so am I."

I felt the zip tie give a little, and I knew I was making progress, but I had to freeze at his words. He was staring right at me, and I couldn't risk that he would see my arms moving. Besides, I felt paralyzed by the look of wild anger in his eyes.

"Weren't you afraid that someone would find out you killed the Yores had you succeeded?"

"No one was supposed to find out. But then you wouldn't stop looking into it."

"I had to," I said quietly. I didn't know how he would react, but it was all I could say because it was true.

To my surprise, he said, "I know," and it sounded almost like he was near tears. "I know you couldn't. It's your family. I don't blame you for that. I never wanted to hurt anyone else. Especially your family. Especially Jane. She was the only person who was ever kind to me here before you came."

I accidentally poked my hand with the knife and flinched, but luckily, Wade either didn't notice or assumed I had flinched in reaction to what he had said. I felt wetness on my finger and knew I was bleeding.

He continued: "I tried to distract you. I thought maybe I could get you to drop the investigation or steer you in a different direction. I even thought maybe I could win your trust and show you what kind of a person Tristan really is. But none of it worked. He conned you just like he has conned everyone else here."

Slowly, I started moving the knife again, keeping my arms taut. When the tie finally snapped, I would have to be careful not to let him know, so I held the edge of it against my wrist with my finger. "You did win my trust, Wade. I feel like you were one of the only people who really understood me."

He nodded slowly. "I thought the same thing. But I can't—I can't—"

"You can't what?"

He inhaled sharply, and it almost sounded like he had choked back a sob. "I can't just go back to the way it was. We can't go on being friends. Not now, now that you know everything. You're a loose end. My dad says there can't be loose ends."

At the same time that I felt the zip tie snap, Wade grabbed the gun from his waistband. I turned the knife in my hand so that the blade now pointed out, but I didn't know what to do. He would definitely be able to shoot before I'd be able to get an arm up.

"Wade, please," I said. "I don't think you mean that. I don't think you want to hurt me."

"Of course I don't want to hurt you!" Tears streamed down his face, but somehow, he looked even more fierce with his skin red and blotchy and his eyes watering. "Don't you get it? I never wanted to hurt you. I never wanted to hurt anyone but Tristan and his monstrous family. But now you know what we did, and you'll tell Tristan. You'll tell everyone. I can't let you walk out of here. I just can't."

"I won't," I said, and I wondered if it sounded convincing. "I know you didn't want to hurt Jane. No one could ever want to hurt Jane."

"No," he said softly.

"I should have realized that sooner. And I know you don't want to hurt me. Your problem isn't with me. Why should I make it my problem?"

He looked at me with a quizzical expression, but he seemed to want me to continue, so I did. I didn't even know what I was saying anymore, but as long as I kept talking and he remained relatively calm, I would have a chance to think.

"Besides, who would even believe me? You and me, we're the black sheep of this place. No one ever listens to me. Why would they start now? I'm already hated enough here as it is. There's no reason for me to commit social suicide by claiming something no one would believe."

He raised the gun slightly, and I held my breath. "They would believe that I would do something. They all hate me."

"But I wouldn't say that. It's too big of a risk to me. I'll tell Tristan to drop the investigation."

"He won't listen."

"I'll make him listen."

"He won't. He never does."

The grinding sound from the machinery shifted, and I heard a strange bell sound coming from outside, though it was muffled by the grinding. Suddenly, I knew where we were: we were in the control room for the train station.

If it was the Lithilea Prep train station, we weren't far from the school itself. We weren't close, but we weren't too far to run. I didn't know this area well, but I knew how to follow train tracks to the school. I wouldn't even have to get all the way to the school, just close enough to encounter King Tybalt's security detail.

"Wade, listen," I said. "Like you said, Tristan trusts me. I can convince him that the whole investigation is pointless, that it's time for me and everyone else to move on. That finding out who set off the explosion wouldn't bring my family back. He'll do it. He's tired of me obsessing over this. He'll think he finally got through to me. I won't even have to convince him."

"But you'll know. You'll always know."

"I wanted to catch whoever had decided my family wasn't worth living. That's not what happened here. I'm not angry anymore." The words hurt to say, but of course, I had to say them. I was still angry. In fact, I was livid. But my fear overrode any sense of anger I was feeling. I knew that I didn't mean anything I was saying and that none of it was true. I just had to make Wade believe that it was true.

"But my dad—"

"Don't tell him I know. He doesn't have to know. He doesn't have to be afraid of me."

He seemed to think that over, and I silently hoped against hope that he would go for it, even for a moment, so that I could get the upper hand. He still held the gun halfway up, and I needed him to drop his guard, drop his arm, and then I would be able to move.

I held my breath as he started to shift his weight back and forth. Just as it seemed that he was going to answer, a train sounded in the distance. Wade whipped his head around to listen to the train, and in an instant, I decided I wouldn't get a better opportunity. I dropped the zip tie, swung my arm up, and cut the side of Wade's face. He screamed and lost his balance, dropping the gun. Blood gushed down his face. I was glad to see that I must have nicked a vein or something because he was bleeding out of proportion with how hard I had hit him. I stuck out a foot and tripped him, and as soon as he fell, I ran, ducking under the open garage door.

I stumbled as I ran along the tracks, finding that I was much dizzier than I realized. The tracks were shaking, and I knew the train was fast approaching, but I didn't know which way I was going without following the tracks. Some strange part of my brain thought about the irony that a train now represented safety when it was the very vessel that had claimed the lives of my family. I felt like I was running in a funhouse the way my vision kept twisting and spinning around me.

The sun was setting, and the glare coming through the trees wasn't helping. I heard Wade shouting in the distance, and I realized too late that I should have grabbed the gun on my way out. He probably had it now.

I followed the tracks around a bend, and I was vaguely aware that Wade's voice was getting louder which meant he was getting closer. I wasn't sure I could outrun him in my current state. I looked around quickly, trying to get any sense of where I was, and I realized I was near a side road. This was the road that led to the train station. I'd noticed how close the road ran to the tracks when I was with Cecily. At the time, it had bothered me. Now, I was so happy I could cry.

I took off through the trees toward the road. I could only hope that either Wade would think I was still following the tracks or that I would be able to flag someone down on the road before he caught up to me.

As the train got quieter behind me, I could hear a car on the road, and I wondered if I was hallucinating. I kept running until I saw headlights and started waving my arms. It was hard to see past the headlights—especially since the light hurt my eyes—but I saw enough to see the royal flags on the front bumper. This was royal security.

The car slowed, and I stopped running, putting my hands on my knees. I could hear footsteps behind me, but I hoped I was close enough to the car that it wouldn't matter if Wade caught up to me. When the door opened and Tristan stepped out, I finally did cry as I ran into his arms.

"Julia," he said, panic in his voice. "Are you okay? Where is he?"

Suddenly, I realized that Tristan wasn't safe and tried to push him back. "He's coming. You have to—"

"Shh, it's fine," he said, pointing to the guards getting out of the car all around us. Another two cars were already pulling up next to Tristan's car. Guards were swarming the area within seconds. I saw Wade, then saw him try to run, but it was pointless. He'd been surrounded and was in cuffs before I even fully processed what was happening.

"Julia," Tristan said, a bit louder this time. "Are you okay? You're bleeding."

I looked down and saw that Tristan's shirt had smatters of blood right where I had rested my head when I ran into him.

"I'm so sorry," I said frantically. "I ruined your shirt."

"I don't care about my shirt."

"But it's—"

"Julia." He held me by the shoulders and looked me right in the eyes. "Are you okay?" I nodded slowly, then quickly, then felt tears stinging my eyes again. "Are you hurt? I mean, I know you're hurt, but do we need to take you to the hospital? I've got medics on the way, but if you don't think you can wait—"

"I'm okay. I'm okay, I promise."

Tristan nodded and stepped back. "I was so afraid I wasn't going to get here in time."

"How did you know?"

"The investigative team got a lead that it was the husband of the Duchess of Dalmerlin. When they found out that he had previously been a train mechanic, they immediately sent out a police squad to Dalmerlin and to Lithilea Prep, but they couldn't find Wade. Then Stephen called me."

"He did?" I had thought Stephen was still ignoring me. In the control room, I had hoped that my phone was ringing because he was calling, but a very sad part of me feared I was wrong.

"He said you texted him that you thought it was Wade. How did you know?"

"I met up with him after I talked to you, and we were just talking. He said something about his dad working on trains, but I didn't know if it was a coincidence. When he started talking about how he was convinced that your family hated his, I was pretty sure."

Tristan ran a hand up and down the back of his neck and sighed. "I can't believe you were with him."

"I know. Stephen told me not to trust him, but I had to know—"

"No, Julia. I can't believe you were with him because I can't believe that I almost lost you, too. As soon as I received word from the investigative team and Stephen, I was terrified that I would be too late, that I would lose you like I lost—like I lost Jane."

His voice shook, cracking over my sister's name. I'd spent so much time lately thinking that no one loved my sister like I had, maybe not even Uncle Joe, but I was so wrong. Uncle Joe loved Jane. Tristan loved Jane.

Softly but confidently this time, I said, "I'm okay."

It seemed as if he wanted something more—another hug, perhaps, or more consolation—but I wasn't sure what to do, and I had the impression that even he wasn't sure what it was he sought. We just stood there for a few moments in a silence that was not uncomfortable. I wondered if I should say something, but it finally felt like everything that needed to be said between us had been said. We were both okay.

At the sound of footsteps, I turned to see police officers leading Wade to a patrol car in handcuffs. He was quiet. It was weird to see Wade like that. He had always been so effervescent as a person, always making his presence known. I could hardly recognize the chaotic, impulsive person who had stood before me only moments ago waving a gun at me. Somehow, this solemn person I now saw was even less recognizable.

He didn't make an attempt to speak to me, and I was glad. I wondered if he knew that most of what I had said to him in that control room was a lie. Did it matter? Did I still care what Wade thought about me?

As they put him in a squad car, another royal security car pulled up behind Tristan's car. I didn't think much of it—chances were cars were going to keep showing up for a while—but I was elated when I saw Stephen step out of the back seat.

Tristan looked over his shoulder, and when he saw Stephen, he smiled at me and stepped aside. I was sure he would give me a hard time about it later, but I didn't care. I ran straight for Stephen and threw my arms around his neck. I was so happy to see him that I didn't even think about where we stood. Did Stephen want me to hug him? Sure, he had let Tristan know where I was, but not wanting me to be murdered was a far cry from caring about me.

I tried to step back, but I was glad to find that Stephen's arms tightened their grip around my back. I couldn't stop the smile that spread across my face at the realization that he didn't want to let me go. When he finally did let go, it was only enough for me to lean back and look at him face-to-face.

"Julia," he said, "I'm so sorry. I never should have let you walk away earlier. I was too busy being mad at you to think straight. I never trusted Wade, and I should have trusted my gut and stopped you or gone with you or—"

"You couldn't have stopped me. I was going to go no matter what."

"But I'm so stupid. You're bleeding. You could have died." He gently touched the side of my face. "Look at this bruise."

"It's fine."

"I was just being stubborn."

I couldn't help but laugh. "Oh please, I'm the stubborn one here."

He laughed, too. "I never would have been able to forgive myself if something had happened to you."

"But I'm fine, thanks to you."

"I was looking through our notes for the transportation renovation bill, and I noticed Wade's father's name on a lot of the reports. I didn't realize he was a railroad engineer."

I choked out a laugh. "Neither did I."

"And then you sent that message, and of course I missed it. I kept calling you, but you didn't answer, so I panicked."

"Wade crushed my phone."

I regretted saying that immediately because of the look of absolute devastation on Stephen's face. I hadn't meant to make him feel worse.

"I hope I didn't cause trouble for you."

"Absolutely not. Stephen, you saved me."

He wrapped his arms around me again, and I pressed my face into his shirt. For the first time in months—really for the first time since I found out about the train accident—I relaxed.

Chapter Twenty-Two

February 12—

Dear diary (I guess?)

Jane always used to tell me that I should keep a diary. I always thought she was weird for doing it, and truth be told, I definitely made fun of her for it. I never understood the point of keeping a diary, but things change after you experience something like I did. Tristan insisted that I see a therapist after everything that happened, and he was actually the one to suggest keeping a journal. Apparently Jane had the last laugh on that one.

Even though I thought Jane was silly for keeping one, I never would have read it without her permission. But after she died, I took solace in being able to "hear" from her again. I've also found her diary very helpful: it helped me study for my classes, get to know Tristan better, and trust my instincts. It even helped me catch her murderer.

I decided it's at least worth a shot. Who knows? Maybe I'll find out I really like this. Maybe I'll hate it and burn my entries. Either way, maybe I'll feel closer to Jane again.

So I don't really know how to do this, but I guess I'll take a stab at it. It's been a wild few days. Wade got arrested, and so did his father. It was so weird seeing him get arrested. I really thought I had found a kindred spirit in Wade. I'm so disappointed that I was so wrong. I wonder what made Wade the way he is. Could he have been different if some factor of his life had been different? I guess I'll never know. I'm told that he's asked for me, that he wants to explain. For now, I don't think I want to see him. Maybe one day I'll feel differently, but for now, I think I need as much space from him as possible. It's hard now not to think of him hitting my head and the gun in his hand.

Joe called me immediately after Wade's arrest in a frenzy, but, of course, I didn't answer since Wade destroyed my phone. Finally, he called Tristan and begged to talk to me. The look on Tristan's face when Joe called him was pretty funny, but I felt bad that he had gotten so worried. It took a lot of work to convince him that he didn't need to come out to the school, that I was okay. I think he only relented because I told him that Tristan and Stephen were with me. It was going to take some time for us to adjust to our new relationship and for us to trust that each other was safe, but I'm so glad to have him in my life again. Honestly, I'm a little mad about the time we had lost, but I couldn't change that now.

I'm kind of dreading classes starting back up tomorrow. Everyone will know by then what happened with Wade and with me. I don't really want to deal with it, but the sooner the better, I guess. I'm just glad to finally put this behind me. I feel like I haven't truly been able to mourn Jane's and my parents' deaths ever since I found out it wasn't an accident. I've been so consumed with finding some kind of closure, and now that I have it, it's like I've exhaled for the first time in weeks. It's a weird kind of tension and fear mixed with peace that I'm feeling now.

In the name of recovery—and to avoid everyone—I spent most of the weekend by myself working on the transportation bill. I'm pretty proud of it, actually. I think it's going to be good. I hope Tristan approves. After everything that's happened, I hope that he thinks well of me and sees me as an asset to Lithilea.

The time I didn't spend alone I spent with Stephen. We had to work through some of the ugly things we said to each other. We'd blown up at each other in anger, but we had such strong feelings for each other that they became explosive. I'd trusted people above him that weren't trustworthy and used his feelings against him. He doubted my independence and tried to assert greater wisdom. We had to heal. We still do. It'll take time, but I do know that Stephen is the person I most want to be around. Stephen was kind to me when I most needed it and never let me doubt my worth. He did his best to help me, and now I guess I'm optimistic about what our relationship looks like now.

I'm not really sure how to end one of these things. Jane always just kind of stopped writing, but I'm not sure that's my style. I think that's what I'm trying to learn now. Jane would have made a fantastic duchess of Graycott, but it would have been for different reasons than the reasons that will make me a potentially fantastic duchess of Graycott. If I try to be what Jane was, I'm only going to fail. We were so different. But if I try to do what I do best, it'll be so much better. Graycott isn't getting the duchess they thought they were getting, but my hope is that I'll be a duchess they're still glad to have.

So maybe I won't end these things the way she did. Maybe I'll write a more concrete ending, tie a bow, and write "the end." Maybe I'll give myself the ending Jane never got to have.

—Julia

***

I clipped Jane's rose gold chain bracelet on my wrist and ran my finger across the red marks I still had from the zip ties. The weekend had passed, and they didn't look as angry anymore, but I wondered if they were still noticeable to people who weren't me, who weren't keenly aware of their presence and the irritation they caused when my sleeves ran across them. Even though it was beastly hot outside, I considered wearing a cardigan or a jacket of some kind to cover them, but when I looked in the mirror and saw the bruised gash on my forehead, I decided it was futile. I could hide my wrists, but there was no hiding the cut on my face.

Tristan had written a press release explaining the situation with Wade and his father, and it had already been distributed to all of Lithilea, including Lithilea Prep. Everyone already knew I had been attacked, but Tristan had spared me and everyone else the gory details. I was sure to draw some attention when everyone saw me.

What else was new?

I grabbed my bag and the stack of notebooks next to it and headed to class. Today's first class was "Succession," one of the first classes I had attended when I started at Lithilea Prep. It was the first class in which I had really stood out. Everyone was painfully aware of my presence as we discussed the succession of lineage in the event of untimely deaths. In class that day, I had wondered if I would ever feel normal, if I would ever fit in with everyone here.

I still wasn't sure if I did.

I looked in the mirror one more time and seriously considered grabbing my concealer or calling Talia in a desperate attempt to capitalize on her extensive makeup knowledge, but I forced myself to walk toward the door. I wouldn't be able to cover the scab or the butterfly bandage. I just had to face it.

When I opened my door, I was startled to see Rose. She smiled as cheerfully as ever, but her smile flickered just for a moment when she saw me. I had to give her credit for developing a better poker face in recent days.

"Julia. I stopped by to see if you wanted to walk to class together."

In my early days here, I would have immediately declined Rose's offer. I hadn't wanted to be anywhere near her. We hadn't seemed compatible as friends, and everything about her was a reminder of Jane, and I hadn't wanted to hurt every time I saw her. Now, Rose was still a reminder of Jane—that hadn't changed. But now I welcomed the reminders.

"Sure," I said with a smile. "I'd love to."

Rose smiled, and Rachel walked out of her suite right then, and we started toward Yore Hall. I was glad when we stepped outside that I had foregone a jacket. I would have roasted. Still, I was painfully aware of everyone's eyes on me as we walked. I had never been more grateful for Rose and Rachel's chatter to distract me.

When we got closer to Yore Hall, I spotted Paige, Valerie, and Vaughn sitting at a table together. I waved, and they came to join us on the walk.

"Oh my goodness," Paige said when she got close enough. "Julia, are you okay?"

I nodded. "I'm fine. It doesn't hurt much anymore."

"Really?" she asked with a hint of skepticism that made me smile. "It looks pretty gnarly."

Valerie tilted her chin up and smiled at me. "It just makes her that much cooler. It's like a battle scar."

I laughed. "Yeah, okay."

"You didn't get a concussion, did you?" Paige asked.

"No. The doctor said I was really lucky."

"In more ways than one," Vaughn said, and it still surprised me whenever he spoke because he was so quiet. I had to wonder what kind of duke he would be. "You could have been seriously injured."

"She *was* seriously injured," Valerie said.

I held my hands up between them. "Guys, it's okay. Seriously, I'm fine."

Paige spoke quietly. "Can I—I don't mean to make it weird or pry or anything, but—"

"Go ahead."

"Was it scary? I mean, did you know—"

"I figured out it was Wade right before he hit me." Talking about it was weird. I hadn't really had to explain it like this. Tristan and Stephen could tell what had happened, so I really didn't have to tell them. I had to give a lot of reports to the police and the investigative team, but those felt so official and emotionless. Nobody had asked if I had been scared. "It was scary. I thought I knew Wade really well, but I didn't know him at all. I didn't know what he was capable of."

"And they arrested his parents?" Rose asked.

I nodded. "Well, his dad. They think his mother was unaware. They're still investigating that."

"I can't imagine finding out that your spouse and child were responsible for something like that," Vaughn said. "She must be a wreck."

I said, "I think she's taken a leave of absence from her position as duchess."

"Probably for the best," Valerie said. "I wonder what will happen to Dalmerlin's line of succession."

"I don't know," I said with a shrug.

If someone had told me weeks ago that I would be having a normal conversation with Rose, Rachel, Paige, Valerie, and Vaughn and that I considered them friends, I would have laughed in their face. But here I was considering them to be some of the most important people in my life. I had judged them all too quickly. I had thought Rose and Rachel were trying too hard and doing me a favor because of their friendship with Jane, but they were actually some of the kindest people here. Rose was the first person who showed me any kindness when

I thought there was none to be found. Valerie and Vaughn seemed to have nothing in common with me, and I'd considered them to be too elite or haughty, but they were people who saw injustice and wanted desperately to combat it. I knew we'd have disagreements in the future, but they were honest. And Paige: I had judged her so harshly, and she me, but we had let others color our perceptions of each other. I had learned how dangerous it could be to trust first impressions. With Paige, it had nearly cost me a friendship. With Wade, it had nearly cost me my life. Paige, in fact, had turned out to be one of the most authentic and passionate people that I knew.

Tristan had told me when I first got to Lithilea Prep that the relationships built at the school were what would carry me through life as a duchess. I hadn't really given that serious thought at the time, but it made sense now. Joe and I were close again, but he was in Graycott and busy. I knew I could trust Cecily, but she had other duties as well. One day, the people at this school—the very people with whom I was now walking to class—would be the people with whom I would have the most contact professionally. They had become a really important support system, a system I had only recently accepted that I needed. I had been so wrong to try to handle all of this on my own. That wasn't a mistake that I wanted to make again.

"Paige," I asked, "How is Peter?"

She forced a smile. "He's all right. He actually wanted to come to class today, but he had a migraine, so I encouraged him to rest. He said to tell you that he's glad you're all right and that you got justice for your family."

My eyes stung a little bit, so I furiously blinked back the tears trying to force their way out. That was what I had wanted: justice. I wanted to know that whoever had killed my parents and Jane—who hadn't even meant to kill them—would be brought to justice for their crime.

I was glad I had that. But more than that, I was glad to know that everyone else I now cared about was safe. Tristan and Talia were no longer in danger. The oppressive security on the school grounds had lessened again to a sense of normalcy. I didn't have to relive the train crash anymore.

We made it to Yore Hall and walked into that classroom that had given me so much anxiety weeks ago. It was a big room, and I felt intimidated by everyone. I knew that someone had killed my family, and I doubted everyone. I felt so deeply inadequate for this job. But the room wasn't scary anymore. I still wondered sometimes if I would be as good at this or better than Jane. I guessed I would never know, but I knew now that I was capable.

I waved to Nicole as I passed directly to Tristan's seat and plopped a clipped stack of papers on the desk in front of him. Talia, who was sitting next to him, smiled. He looked up at me with a raised eyebrow.

"What is this?"

"The completed bill. Stephen and I finished it. It includes progressive compliance plans for provinces who need the time to secure the financing. It also includes regulations that can be used for standards. It will still need more data from engineers, but it's a start on what needs to be addressed. It even includes some ideas for where the provinces can acquire the money that won't involve raising taxes or anything else that will strain the leaner provinces. I asked Nicole to take a look at it as well, and she felt it was reasonable."

"Impressive," Talia said.

"When did you find the time to do this?" Tristan asked.

"Stephen and I worked on it together last week when you suggested it, but I worked on it this weekend to finish it."

He stood and buttoned his jacket. With a lowered voice, he said, "Julia, this could have waited. I didn't expect you to finish it this weekend. Not after—"

"I needed the distraction, and this was a good one. Now it's done for the next 'Domestic Relations' class."

"Still—"

"I needed to know that our railroad system would be safe again. This is a big step in that direction."

Finally, without reservation or judgment, Tristan smiled. "Well, it's very impressive. I'm glad you found something you were passionate about. Graycott is lucky to have you."

I couldn't stop the smile on my face. "Thank you."

He leaned his head a bit to look at the cut on my face. "It looks like it's healing well."

I nodded. "It is. I go back to the doctor later this week for him to check on it."

"Would you like me to go with you?"

I still wasn't sure where I stood in terms of royal protocol, but I lifted my hand to his shoulder and smiled. "I can handle it. I'm okay. Everything's okay."

He smiled and sat back down, returning to his work. I imagined that it would take Tristan time to let go of his protectiveness toward me, but at least he had the peace he had also been seeking. He had the reassurance that Jane hadn't died angry with him or without loving him. I knew he was still struggling to get over her death, but at least he knew he had caught her killer.

Olivia walked by right then, and she seemed ready to hurl some insult at me, likely for touching Tristan's shoulder, but something in her expression changed when I turned to face her. I couldn't be sure if it was the cut on my face or the way I squared my shoulders when I faced her, but just this once, she backed down, saying nothing to me as she took her seat near Tristan.

I hadn't expected Olivia to be any different than who she had always shown herself to be, but I was glad to see that even Olivia had a line she wouldn't cross. At least I knew that one day we would be able to work together. Olivia was a mean girl, but one day she would be the Duchess of Aerilot and I would be the Duchess of Graycott, and I knew that she would fight for her province fiercely. I could, at least, respect that about her even if I would never like her.

Professor Tenneton walked in and shouted, "We'll start in five minutes, everyone."

I walked back to my seat, and I smiled when I saw Stephen at my desk. He leaned on one palm that was face down on the table, and I liked seeing him there, knowing that he was waiting for me. We still had so much to talk about—I didn't know what a relationship between us could look like, and I didn't know what happened when two first-in-line heirs dated, or even where we stood after everything that happened—but I knew I wanted to talk to him more. I knew I liked it when he held my hand the entire drive home after Wade's arrest. I knew that I regretted the words I had screamed at him, the one who truly cared, in defense of someone who never cared about me at all.

And I knew that despite everyone's eyes being on me right now that I was hoping Stephen would kiss me.

"Hey," he said when I got close enough. "Did you give Tristan the bill?"

I nodded. "He seemed impressed."

"Of course he did."

"He's always impressed by you."

Stephen laughed. "Definitely not. But he has always been impressed by you. Everyone is, including me."

Had Stephen said that weeks ago, I would have laughed in his face or called him insane. I didn't feel impressive back then. I felt wildly insufficient, inadequate, and ill-suited to take the place rightfully reserved for Jane. *Poor man's Jane Clarke.* But I no longer felt that way. I was good at this. I had so much catching up to do, but it suddenly felt possible. I had something to offer here, and I was going to do what I could to make it count.

Stephen took my hands in his, slowly running a finger over the marks on my wrists. "Does it still hurt?" he asked.

I shook my head. "That feels good, actually."

He tried and failed to suppress the smile that took over his face. "I'm glad. How about this?"

And with that, he leaned in and kissed me softly. It was a quiet kiss, the kind that you just kind of sink into. It's not wildly passionate or intense, but it's pleasant and enjoyable—and safe.

I hadn't felt safe and loved in so long, and I couldn't believe how much that had changed in the last few days. I had friends, Uncle Joe and I were talking again, and I was succeeding. For so long I believed all of this was impossible. I had been so wrong. This was more than possible. This certainly wasn't the way I had wanted my life to turn out—without Jane or my parents—but I was learning to let go of the inferiority complex that plagued me. I was learning to trust my own instincts and intellect and drive. I was learning to trust myself in all things.

When we separated, I was aware that pretty much everyone in the room was watching. It was a quick moment, but still, it had attracted everyone's attention. I didn't mind anymore. I had embraced the fact that I was always going to attract this kind of attention. I was always going to stand out, but now, it was a positive thing. I would do what I could to stand out in a way that bettered Graycott and Lithilea as a whole.

"All right, everyone," Professor Tenneton said. "Let's take a seat and get started." Everyone trickled back to their seats. Stephen gave my hand a quick squeeze before he left, and I smiled at the warmth it gave me. "Today we're talking about the particulars of the actual succession process when an heir becomes the new duke or duchess. There are specific protocols that must be followed, but many current dukes and duchesses have said that there was a lot of mystery around what exactly happens and how they should adjust to that new role. My goal today is to demystify that for you all. Hopefully this will equip you for your own day of succession someday."

That was a day I no longer looked toward in fear. One day, I would succeed Uncle Joe and become the Duchess of Graycott, and even though I was painfully aware of the empty seat next to me, somehow I knew that Jane would have been proud of me.

* * *

Acknowledgments

This was the hardest book I've written to date because it was ambitious and took on so many different forms over the years I worked on it. This book started as a weird dream I had in 2020. I chalked it up to the general weirdness of the COVID-19 lockdowns, though I did joke that if I could ever make that scene into a story, I might have a book. I'm so grateful to all of the people who helped me actually turn this concept into a full-fledged story.

Thank you to Kayla Tirrell for listening to me ramble about all of my plot indecisions and talking through my ideas. You helped me fix so many problems in this story, and I really couldn't have done it without you. Thank you to Morgan Brownlee for always encouraging my work and encouraging me to take a risk with a new kind of story. Thank you to Laina Strickland for being an early reader of a very rough draft. Your feedback was so helpful, but your encouragement was even more helpful.

Thank you to my professors and classmates at Emerson College for helping me develop this idea when it was nothing more than a single scene and a roughly written first chapter. This story became what it was because of the feedback I received in my classes at Emerson. I didn't see the potential in this idea back then, but I am so glad that all of you did.

Thank you to Lorissa Padilla of Lorissa Padilla Designs for designing an incredible cover based on Morgan Brownlee's concept. The more I stare at this cover, the more I absolutely love it. You perfectly captured the aesthetic of this story, and I'm so glad that it is the first impression people will have of this story.

Thank you to MockingbirdArtist for designing an incredible map of Lithilea. I love a good map in a book, and you created a stunning one.

Thank you to friends and family who continue to support my writing in all of its forms. It means so much to me to see you buy my books, attend my events, and share my posts on social media.

Thank you to my sister Ashley for encouraging me to pursue new genres and new things. Thank you to my parents for your unwavering support of every crazy idea I have and every new thing I want to try. I am so grateful for the support to do whatever I want to do.

About the author

When she's not writing about high school students, she's teaching them AP and DE English. Kristen Grafton is a Florida native with an MFA in Popular Fiction & Publishing and an MA in English Rhetoric. She was a triple major in college. She has an unhealthy obsession with her cats and Taylor Swift. She is also the author of *Thank You for Applying*.

To learn more about Kristen Grafton, follow her on Twitter/X @KristenMGrafton, Instagram @kmgrafton1, and visit www.kristen mgrafton.com.

www.ingramcontent.com/pod-product-compliance
Lightning Source LLC
Chambersburg PA
CBHW020144310726
48970CB00006B/2003